THE ADVERSARY

THE ADVERSARY

A novel

~

MICHAEL CRUMMEY

Alfred A. Knopf Canada

PUBLISHED BY ALFRED A. KNOPF CANADA

Copyright © 2023 Michael Crummey Ink, Inc.

www.penguinrandomhouse.ca

Knopf Canada and colophon are registered trademarks.

Library and Archives Canada Cataloguing in Publication

Title: The adversary : a novel / Michael Crummey.
Names: Crummey, Michael, 1965- author.
Identifiers: Canadiana (print) 20230161278 | Canadiana (ebook)
20230161286 | ISBN 9780385685443 (hardcover) | ISBN 9780385685450 (EPUB)
Classification: LCC PS8555.R84 A72 2023 | DDC C813/.54—dc23

*This book is a work of fiction. Names, characters, places and incidents are
products of the author's imagination or are used fictitiously. Any resemblance
to actual events or locales or persons, living or dead, is entirely coincidental.*

Text design: Emma Dolan
Jacket design: Emma Dolan
Jacket image: Flying Raven: ex libris, from *The Raven (Le Corbeau)*,
(1875) print in high resolution by Édouard Manet. Original from
The Art Institute of Chicago. Digitally enhanced by rawpixel.

Printed in Canada

10 9 8 7 6 5 4 3 2 1

Penguin
Random House
KNOPF CANADA

For Mike Basha

Although a black hole does not emit light, matter falling toward it collects in a hot, glowing accretion disk that astronomers can detect.

SVS.GSFC.NASA.GOV

But they lie in wait for their own blood,
they ambush their own lives.

PROVERBS

THE DRIVEN SNOW. A WINTER WEDDING.

There was a killing sickness on the shore that winter and the only services at the church were funerals. The Beadle stood at the bare wooden table that served as an altar in his shapeless cloak and black skullcap, offering a reading and a prayer over the departed. There was no sermon and no hymns were sung. The few people well enough to mourn the dead carried them to their rest, rasping shallow graves in the frozen earth.

The sanctuary was almost empty on the day of the wedding as well and there was the same forsaken air about the occasion as the sparsely attended funerals. The bride was a girl of fourteen, her hands manacled in a fur muff on her lap. Everyone in the church but her father was a rank stranger and even her father the young-ster barely knew.

He was a merchant from Jersey, twenty years in Newfoundland but for spending every second winter with his wife and daughters in the old country. He'd arrived home in September as planned but stayed just long enough to attend to immediate business before shipping out again. And against her mother's useless protests, he packed his oldest daughter along for the journey. She had never been to sea and they sailed into storm as soon as they left the Channel, the vessel shipping green water as each wave overwhelmed the bow. She didn't leave her cabin for sickness and for fear of being swept overboard the entire voyage.

The groom was late for the ceremony and Misters Matterface and Heater were dispatched to find him. The girl had laid eyes on her intended only once, when he came to her father's house with the Beadle the day after her arrival. The three men fell into a protracted discussion while she sat in the parlour, rocking slightly in her chair as if she was still at sea. She spoke little English and gleaned almost nothing from the conversation, though there was a businesslike sullenness to the back and forth, as if the men were negotiating the cost of a schooner or a hogshead of curing salt.

Before leaving they stepped into the parlour and her father introduced one of the men as her fiancé. The second he introduced as the Beadle who would sanctify their marriage directly, but she couldn't shift her eyes from the sight of the one she was spoken for. He was a fright for a child to look upon as a prospective husband, bacon-faced, with a small full mouth that gave him the air of a greedy infant. He looked her up and down in her seat as if vetting a questionable purchase before turning to say something she didn't understand to her father. The Beadle inclined slightly toward her, a bow of apology it seemed, and he took the man's arm to lead him out.

Almost three months she'd been kept to herself then, until the illness burnt itself to embers and those who survived the scourge agreed the wedding could proceed. A fire rattled in the church stove but the windows were rimed with frost and the few wedding guests sat in a wooden silence. The girl stared at the expensive beaver muff as she waited, raising the fur to her face now and then to wipe at the clear line of snot on her upper lip. She could not feel her feet for the cold.

The door to the church opened behind them and everyone turned expectantly. The man who entered stopped to glance about the hall, surprised no doubt by the groom's absence. He removed his woollen hat, his dark hair clipped severely at the back and sides and combed to one side. It took the bride a moment to realize a girl had come in behind him, a servant wearing a grey bonnet and a length of rough calico about her shoulders as a shawl. It was almost impossible to tell with servants, but she thought they might be near the same age, herself and this girl.

The newcomers sat together at the back of the room and the young man shrugged out of his overcoat, revealing a fashionable dragon-green jacket over a striped waistcoat with two watch fobs. He nodded at a handful of those present and eventually caught the bride's eye and held it. She felt oddly naked in the light of that stranger's gaze. There was something comfortless but knowing in it. And before her father nudged her attention away, she surprised herself by wishing it was him she was about to marry.

The groom arrived finally in the company of Matterface and Heater, not so much hungover as still in his altitudes. He walked between the two men like a prisoner being led to a cell under guard. He took his place at the wooden altar table, ferret-eyed and stinking, and his escorts stepped to one side as the father of the bride delivered the girl to stand next him. He didn't look at her or his future father-in-law, nodding at the Beadle to indicate he should get on with things.

"We are gathered here today," the Beadle said, "to witness the joining together of this man, Abe Strapp, and this woman, Anna Morels, in the bonds of holy matrimony. Who gives this woman to be married?"

The Jerseyman nodded his head. "I do," he said.

He remained at the bride's side though his official duties were completed. He whispered a translation of the Beadle's words to his daughter as the bare ceremony progressed, though the buzzing of panic in her ears made it difficult to follow. She fixed on the Beadle as he spoke, on his lenten-jawed face, on his peculiarly equipped mouth—a full set of ivories on the left, the gums on the opposite side boasting not a single tooth. The division so even it seemed impossible it could be accidental and not part of some unfortunate design.

"If anyone present," the Beadle said. He paused there and sighed. "Know of any reason why these two should not be joined in matrimony. Let them speak now or forever hold their peace."

The groom's eyes were closed and he seemed half-asleep on his feet until he startled at the sound of a woman's voice behind them. The girl turned to follow his look to the back of the hall and was surprised herself to see the man in the green jacket and striped waistcoat on his feet.

"That bloody witch," Strapp said.

The Beadle placed his hand on the groom's arm. "You have an objection to this marriage, Widow Caines?"

The girl stared at the figure of the man she'd wished to marry moments before—the narrow shoulders, the hips. The face that looked almost the face of an adolescent boy but for the eyes which were certain, unflinching. And the high clear voice of a woman.

"The banns of this union have not been published according to custom," the Widow Caines said.

"And what do you care for Christly custom?" Strapp called back to her.

"Mr. Strapp," the Beadle said.

The girl's father left her side and took a seat in the front pew. She didn't know if she was meant to follow him or not and she stood where she was. Watching the strange creature in green.

The Beadle said, "The late affliction has disrupted much of our custom, Widow Caines. We have not held regular service since the death of your husband."

"Of course," the woman said. "I would have raised my objection weeks ago otherwise." She turned to motion the servant girl to her feet. "This is Imogen Purchase. She has been in my employ these last two seasons."

"What has she to do with these proceedings?" the Beadle asked.

"Miss Purchase is willing to swear that at the end of September last, Mr. Strapp encountered her while she was alone at Looking Glass Pond. And that Mr. Strapp did, without her invitation or permission, force himself upon her."

Strapp pointed at the servant girl. "I never laid eyes on this maid in all me born days," he said.

"He has laid more than eyes upon her," the Widow said. "If he fails to recognize her, it is because he was much disguised with liquor at the time."

"You miserable Jack whore," Strapp said.

The child bride watched the back and forth as if it was a Punch and Judy performance, trying to guess at what was unfolding by facial expressions and gestures, by tone of voice. She was praying for the unflappable dragon-green woman to stand her ground.

The Beadle looked squarely at Strapp. "Did you force yourself upon this girl?"

"Look at her," Strapp said vehemently, stumbling slightly with the effort. "She bolts the door to her notch with a boiled carrot."

"So you do know her?" the Widow said.

"I knows her *kind*," he said. "She's as common as a barber's chair."

"Miss Purchase will attest to this matter under oath."

"And I will swear the plain opposite," Strapp insisted.

The Widow reached into an inside pocket. "I have a sworn statement from Dallen Lambe, a man in the employ of my late husband nigh on fifteen years. It states he came upon Mr. Strapp and Miss Purchase in the midst of this encounter and did his utmost to protect Miss Purchase, though he was too late to prevent a ravishment."

The Beadle said, "Why is Dallen Lambe not here to give this testimony in person?"

"He was struck low with the sickness and is still not well enough to leave his bed."

"And what of it?" Strapp demanded. "How does any of this concern my marriage?"

"It concerns your marriage if Mr. Morels withdraws his consent," the Widow Caines said.

"She is lying," Strapp said. He turned to the Jerseyman. "She is against our interests aligning and has concocted a story to capsize the ship."

"More to the point as regards Mr. Strapp's marriage," the Widow said. She raised her voice to regain the attention of the room but returned to the same register of calm once she had it. "Miss Purchase is almost four months gone with child."

Strapp turned around in a furious circle. "God's reeving nails," he said. "She is trying to see me cheated of my inheritance."

The Widow said, "Miss Purchase is a girl of little experience in the ways of the world. She has been known by no other man save Mr. Strapp."

"Certainly, Jesus," Strapp said. He shook his head in cold amazement. "She's as pure as the driven snow."

"Mary Oram has examined the girl and confirms her condition," the Widow said.

There was a long pause in the proceedings then, as if no one present seemed sure what the next steps might be, the young bride least of all.

"Mr. Morels?" the Beadle asked finally.

The Jerseyman got to his feet and reached for the girl's arm. He looked left nor right, but led her down the aisle of the little church and out into the bitter cold of the morning.

Cornelius Strapp, father of the groom and the largest merchant on the shore, had been dead almost a year.

He'd left his native Bristol at seventeen and worked several years as a ship's chandler and cooper. He paid off in St. John's and with his savings ran a small credit office, offering loans to sailors and itinerant whores and sturdy beggars for the purchase of rum and wine, and with the proceeds of five years' lending he moved to the farthest reaches of the island's northeast coast. He built a salmon weir on a river so profligate his servants took seventy-five tierces a day. After two seasons he overtook a foundering cod plantation and, several years on, bought out a merchant operation in Mockbeggar. For more than three decades he engaged and outfitted fishermen who arrived on the shore in increasing numbers every year. Half the livyers on the coast were indebted to him. Only Elias Caines and the Jerseyman, who ran a business in Nonsuch on the far side of Tinkershare Head, boasted anything remotely near the holdings of C. Strapp & Son Co. Ltd.

Cornelius seemed equipped with a sixth sense that revealed every detail's mercantile possibilities. But there was no miserliness in the man, no particular meanness. He helped fund construction of the Church of England and built the tiny school on a corner of his property and he paid the teacher's salary out of his own pocket. He was appointed Justice of the Peace by the island's governor before his marriage, an office he held until his death.

Abe Strapp was the merchant's only son and he lived all his days in the expectation his father's empire would come to him. He had enough innate cunning to recognize the advantage his birthright afforded and to use it as a cudgel to bully his lessers. But he'd never felt the need to expend himself in making his own way in the world. He was like a mirror image of Cornelius, people said, with all that was admirable in the father's nature reversed.

He had a spark in his throat he could not douse and spent most of his time in one of Mockbeggar's alehouses, standing drinks and losing money at cards while arguing whether the Red Indians were a lost tribe of Israel or exaggerating his exploits among the few young women on the shore. The only thing that roused him at all was the chance to go shooting in the country, though even Matterface and Heater were leery of his company on the hunt. Twice he'd shot a good hunting dog while making an attempt at a deer.

His general dissipation and ineptitude led some to refer to young Abe as *Not-Able*. I see Master Not-Able slept at the alehouse last night. Was it Not-Able Strapp nailed these boards so crooked? His taste for drink led to a widely repeated rumour that even when he cornered a girl he was Not Able to raise a horn sufficient to complete the deed.

His father was unaccustomed to circumstances that resisted his influence and he swung wildly and uselessly in his strategies to correct the wayward youngster. He beat him black and blue with a billet of firewood. He changed the mercantile firm's legal name to C. Strapp *& Son*, thinking the weight of impending responsibilities might call him to his senses. Nothing made a difference.

It was the Beadle who suggested the appointment of overseers to ensure Abe didn't find his way into trouble that couldn't be ignored. No one other would have dared interfere in so personal a matter. The Beadle began working with Cornelius before Strapp married and stood loyal in his service for decades after his wife left the world. As headman, he kept track of all goods and curing salt and twine distributed on the company books and it was his hand that set this debt against the cured cod and salmon the fishermen offered as payment. People said Abraham Clinch's word was as good as Strapp's own and Strapp himself would not have argued it. He thought enough of the Beadle to name his only son after the man and to have Clinch presented as the motherless child's god-father at the christening. Which made Clinch feel Abe's myriad shortcomings were somehow a personal failure on his part. He singled out Matterface and Heater for the role of chaperones and presented them to his employer.

"They aren't idiots, I hope," Cornelius said.

The Beadle vouched for their character and the elder Strapp waved his hand dismissively. "They aren't to lay a hand on him," he said. "If a beating is required, they're to come to you."

For a time the two men managed to blunt Abe's most destructive instincts. But in the course of carrying out their duties, they fell into drinking and gambling alongside their charge. Protecting him soon enough meant baiting and insulting anyone Abe took a disliking to, and settling scores on Abe's behalf. They followed servant girls out to Looking Glass Pond and harassed them as they did their washing. They chased them around the flakes on pretence of helping lay out the waterhorse, trying to lure them into the shadows below the spruce platforms to get a hand up their skirts before some salt-faced harridan flushed their hiding place.

The Beadle tried to separate the trio eventually, relieving Matterface and Heater of their positions. But they found each other regardless, falling in together by choice. Cornelius realized by then he lacked the stamina or know-how to alter the studied course of that river and seemed resigned to let it flow as it wished.

In the last years of his life, he was periodically bedridden with a wasting illness that left him each time more arthritic and weakened. The Beadle had years ago come into possession of *Blake's Practice of Physic*, which taught him to treat lacerations and stomach issues and all manner of swellings and sprains and infection. Several times he'd been called upon to amputate hands and feet blackened by frostbite or gangrene, employing a carpenter's saw to sever a limb at the joint, and some of those patients survived their treatment. But whatever afflicted Cornelius Strapp was beyond his knowledge and skill.

For the first time, staring into the near abyss of his own death, Strapp was completely preoccupied by the baffling fact of his son—his pernicious appetites, his vanity, his incurious scorn. Abe was hopelessly stunted somehow, he careened through his days like a boy playing at being a man.

"He that begetteth a fool," Strapp said, "doeth it to his sorrow, and the father of a fool hath no joy."

The Beadle shifted forward at the bedside. "The wise servant," he countered, "shall have rule over a son that causeth shame."

Strapp smiled half-heartedly. "I am open to suggestions."

"The Jerseyman—Morels. He has a marriageable daughter across the pond, does he not?"

"Years I've been after Abe to take a wife," Strapp said. "It would be ballast to the keel to marry, to father children. But he hasn't shown the slightest inclination in that direction."

The Beadle sat looking at his lap. "Forgive me this impertinence," he said.

"I'm dying, Mr. Clinch. Impertinence is the least of my concern."

"You could make it a condition that he marry before he is granted ownership of your concerns."

"Alter my will, you mean?"

The Beadle nodded.

"Have you spoken to Morels?"

"Only in the most general way. But he is a practical man. He can see the advantages of such a union. And it would be a help to Abe to have the Jerseyman as a partner, rather than a rival."

Strapp turned to his headman and watched him a long moment. "Do you regret it yourself, Abraham?" he asked. "Not marrying?"

"I never felt that calling, Master Strapp."

The sick man studied the Beadle a while longer. He sighed and closed his eyes. "Abe has never felt it likewise. Though I expect his reasons are different than your own."

"At this point, I would suggest his reasons are less intractable. He may refuse to marry for a time, but he will not spurn his inheritance forever."

"And what becomes of the business in the meantime?"

"In the meantime, the firm could be left in trust to a legal caretaker."

"You have someone in mind for this."

"I am best equipped for it. If you see fit."

Strapp shook his head. "My son will not like that arrangement."

"Then he will marry out of spite if nothing else."

Strapp gazed up at the ceiling with the rictus grimace that was all he could manage for laughter, his Adam's apple jigging freakishly in the cadaverous neck. "Vindictiveness is the only spur that has ever moved him," he said.

Cornelius Strapp died two days after that conversation, without ever leaving the bed where he signed the altered will or speaking to his son again. It fell to the Beadle as executor to present the man's final wishes when the document was read at the firm's offices.

Abe had been waiting years to see his father on six men's shoulders and he was not happy to have Cornelius reaching back in death to make a butcher's dog of him, forcing his son to lie by the beef without touching it. He sent the room up, accusing the Beadle of employing quirks and quillets to confound his lawful claim, of using some Jesuitical witchcraft on the mind of a sick man to steal Strapp's business from its rightful inheritor. A handful of servants were called upon to remove Abe from the premises when he began tipping chairs and throwing paperweights while he threatened to kill the headman dead.

The two men didn't exchange a word for weeks afterwards. When the Beadle finally approached him to discuss the terms of his inheritance, Abe announced he had as much need for a wife as a dog of a side-pocket, and there was not a single woman on the shore besides that he would stoop to marry.

The Beadle smiled his oddly bifurcated smile. "The opposite might also be the case, Mr. Strapp. But there is more to the world than this shore." He could see that Abe hadn't the slightest notion what he meant. "I understand that Mr. Morels has a daughter of marrying age in Europe."

"The Jerseyman clogs around in wooden shoes. What would I want with a girl raised by the likes of that arse?"

"O simple ones, learn prudence," the Beadle said. "O fools, learn sense."

Abe shook his head.

"Morels has no sons, Mr. Strapp. You would stand to inherit his operation as husband to his eldest daughter. And I expect that Elias and Mrs. Caines would find the alliance distasteful in the extreme. It might make their livelihoods a little less certain to find themselves in a pen with one large ram, rather than two sheep."

"I could take over their operation, you're saying."

"Given due attention and the right circumstances, yes. The entire shore could be yours eventually."

It was the only point at which their interests had ever obviously aligned. The Beadle returned to it at every opportunity and still it took the winter and most of the summer for Abe to come around to what he considered the headman's design. Once he'd made the turn, he was characteristically, childishly impatient, insisting Morels sail back to Mockbeggar with his daughter in the fall rather than waiting to return in the spring as he'd planned.

"A late fall crossing will not be a pleasant experience for the bride," the Beadle said.

Abe cupped the breech of his trousers. "She won't recall a moment at sea after a romp aboard this vessel," he said.

"I trust," the Beadle said, "you will spare Mr. Morels such expressions of enthusiasm."

"Let the cock pimp marry his daughter to a monk if he be so easily offended," Abe said. And he shook his package a second time.

Abe Strapp watched the Jerseyman and his daughter leave the church as if the world he had pinned all his hopes upon was walking out the door with them. He could not for the life of himself recall if he'd bedded the servant girl as the Widow claimed. As like as not, he had. One was much the same as another.

"Miss Purchase will be suing for recognition of the child," the Widow called out from the back of the church. "And for financial support."

The Beadle stared down at his feet, his lips pursing and relaxing, as if he was trying to work up enough saliva to spit. Not quite able to credit how completely the Widow had sabotaged the ceremony and all that was meant to follow from it. The water around them awash with the wreckage of the day and he was casting about for some bit of flotsam large enough to stay afloat.

It was the first time in his life Abe Strapp sensed the slightest tremor of uncertainty in the man and he felt a larval stir in his gut, an oily impulse to fuck something until it was dead. He jabbed a finger at the Beadle's chest. "This is your doing," he said.

"There is one other option to consider," the Widow said. She walked halfway up the aisle.

"And what is that exactly?"

"We are present and prepared for a wedding, are we not?"

Clinch looked to the Widow where she stood, offering her half-smile. Ruthless and calm. He said, "Don't listen to her, Master Strapp."

She said, "The will doesn't specify *who* you marry, does it? Say your I do's now and you walk home as sole proprietor of C. Strapp & Son Company Limited."

"You will lose any chance at Morel's operation."

"Christ's ears," Abe shouted. "The Jerseyman idn't about to let me touch his sow child now, is he. And what odds does it make who lies under me of a night?"

The servant girl was horrified at first and refused the proposal outright. "You never said nothing about marrying that one," she whispered.

"That man," the Widow said, pointing to where Abe Strapp had laid his drunken bones flat out on a pew, "is about to become the wealthiest merchant on the coast."

Imogen Purchase looked to the front of the church and back.

"You will never have to work on the flakes again," the Widow said. "Or carry a load of wash to Looking Glass Pond. Your child will have all it needs or wants."

From where he stood at the altar, the Beadle could see the girl's recalcitrance slowly bleeding from her expression, her posture. When they turned toward him, the Widow Caines nodded.

So Mockbeggar's first wedding of the new year was consecrated. Matterface and Heater stood for the groom who gave his yes and amen to the vows and the Widow Caines offered herself as witness for Imogen Purchase.

"I now pronounce you," the Beadle said to the nearly empty sanctuary.

~

After they left the church, the Jerseyman and his daughter rode down through Mockbeggar. The girl fighting a wash of vertigo unlike anything she'd felt since her first days off the ship in the fall. They were seated in an open sleigh, but the cold didn't touch her. In shock to have been spared an execution at the eleventh hour.

There wasn't a soul moving in the little village, the rocks and hills showing black through the snow, so it seemed she was passing through a world without colour, without life. She was overcome by a feeling of disgust for the place. There was nowhere a stretch of level ground, the fishing rooms and warehouses and outbuildings and houses propped on higgledy stilts, looking like wooden insects perched on hillsides and out over the beach rocks and the harbour shallows. It made the entire accretion seem inadvertent and temporary, one decent storm from being swept into the ocean. And she imagined a biblical wave descending on the shore and hauling every stick of it into the deep.

Her father turned the horse and sleigh toward the country above Caines's gardens as far as Looking Glass Pond and then along the Scrape over Tinkershare Head into Nonsuch. The further they travelled from the church, the colder the girl's initial feeling of relief became. They didn't speak a word on the trip home and she went straight to her room while the Jerseyman unhitched the sleigh and put up the horse in the stable.

She sat on the edge of her bed with her hands in the fur muff, angrier than she considered it was in her to be. To have been tied and placed on that altar, her own father holding the blade to her neck. It occurred to her then she had no idea what it meant that the ceremony was halted. That it didn't necessarily follow her engagement to Abe Strapp had ended. Or that she wouldn't be forced to marry some other stranger and live out her days on this gaunt, ascetic coastline.

She went downstairs where she found her father sitting near the fireplace. He was toasting an apple on the grate as was his habit each day at noon, turning the fruit periodically to heat the juice through the flesh. He didn't look at her at first, staring into the fire. The room dense with the smell of the roasting apple, sweet and slightly vinegary. He took it off the grate onto a plate, cutting it in two and turning to offer half to his daughter.

"It's the last one of the winter," he said.

She didn't know what he meant.

"The barrel is empty," he said. "There won't be another until next fall."

She hadn't shed a tear through the entire ordeal, not in all the days of puking at sea, not after laying eyes on the leering face of her intended, not once during the months of quarantine when she was cut off from everyone and everything she loved. But the sight of the steaming, wizened apple undid her.

"Promise me," she said between sobs. "Promise me I will go home to my mother and my sisters."

Her father seemed almost as stunned by the day's events and his role in them as his daughter. He nodded helplessly. "This spring," he said. "I promise you."

In the days that followed she occupied herself with carding wool and knitting and writing forlorn letters to her mother and sisters about the fallen world in which she'd found herself, where women wore the dress of men and her father behaved in the timid manner of a girl. None of the missives would be sent before she sailed herself in the spring, but there was a comfort in speaking to her mother and sisters directly. Even after the sickness overtook her she forced herself to write a letter every day for as long as she could manage. Each one like a knot in a string that tied her to the place she came from, the people that sustained her, and she held on with all her waning strength.

In the worst of the delirium she asked repeatedly for a pen and paper though her wide eyes stared blindly at the ceiling, seeing nothing. Her father sat day and night at the sickbed and often observed her making motions with her right hand, as if she were writing words in the air above her.

Anna Morels was the last person on the shore to perish in that season's plague, on St. Valentine's Day. The Beadle asked her father about arrangements for the funeral but he wouldn't hear of burying the child in Newfoundland. He had his daughter laid out in her wedding dress and placed her in a puncheon tub that was filled with rum before the cask was sealed. He found the letters she'd written and he read them at the fireplace where he'd toasted the year's last apple. He placed each on the coals as he finished it, the pages and the oddments of his daughter they carried flaring briefly before settling to smoke and ash.

The girl's body in its strange wooden sarcophagus was loaded aboard the first ship bound for Europe in May of that year, during the season's final driving snowfall, and she was shipped home to be with her mother and sisters as she was promised. Which was the only real act of kindness her father ever bestowed upon the child.

Elias Caines died in late October but the reading of his last will and testament was delayed by the ongoing pestilential outbreak that killed him. It wasn't until three days after Abe Strapp's wedding that Aubrey Picco brought together the Widow Caines and Myles Taverner, second cousin to Elias, his long-time accountant and only blood relative in the new world, to hear the dead man's final wishes.

Elias Caines was a Plymouth Quaker and very nearly a life-long bachelor. His late marriage was a surprise to everyone on the shore. The Widow was at least thirty years his junior. She was raised in the Church of England but abandoned that faith to attend Quaker meetings a year before the wedding. The Quakers held strange notions on the place of women in the world, allowing them to speak as the spirit moved, the same as men—a practice no one doubted appealed to the Widow. But her conversion seemed a studied decision after the marriage.

The wedding took place during one of the Quakers' queer, silent meetings in the office Elias made available for them. The entire Society of Friends was present—the firm's headman, Aubrey Picco, and his wife and the youngest of their grown children, Myles Taverner and his family, along with a handful of servants who had converted to the Quaker faith. There were no vows or rings or flowers. The bride and groom stood from their chairs to affirm their desire to be married and all the Friends who had their letters signed a document to witness the couple's pledge.

The old man was likely desperate to produce an heir to his property and business, people guessed. Though the general view held his wife was deficient in some obscure feminine quality that made her an unlikely candidate for motherhood, and she was already a bit long of tooth to lay those hopes upon. Whatever the cause, there was no issue from the marriage before Elias died of the sickness in his sixtieth year.

In every other way, their marriage was a true Quaker union that, like their church, had no head or ruler. Mrs. Caines brought a schooner with a burden of one hundred and fifty tons named *Success* and two hundred pounds sterling as her wedding dowry. She had a fine hand for letters and a head for numbers besides, an aptitude which in the eyes of some was suspect. She immediately made herself a fixture at Caines Mercantile, inserting herself into matters with a certainty that Myles Taverner chafed against. She lacked a proper sense of caution, he warned Elias. In every circumstance Mrs. Caines advocated for the riskiest option, arguing for more debt to underwrite expansion, looking for markets beyond the established buyers in Europe and the West Indies. It was arrogance at best, Myles told him, and recklessness at worst.

Elias smiled at his cousin. "When has she steered us wrong?"

"The question is," Taverner said, "when *will* she steer us wrong?"

"I will take your caution under advisement," Elias said.

But the old man fell further under her sway with each passing season, turning to her for advice on transactions and investments and strategies and making no final decision before his wife weighed in.

His funeral was held in the Church of England to accommodate the crowd wanting to pay their respects. Elias was evenhanded and generous even in years when the business struggled. He'd lend his arse and shit through his ribs, people said dismissively, as if he was a guileless cake. But no one questioned the sincerity of his motivations and he was often called upon to mediate disputes between planters and their servants, between rival fishermen. The pews were full and livyers stood outside the open doors as well. There were no hymns and no reading of scripture, there was no officiant. The Quakers sat adorned in their plain clothes, the men wearing their hats even inside the sanctuary. At intervals someone would stand to offer a few words about Friend Elias and even some members of the Church of England were moved to speak.

The Widow Caines sat near the casket at the front of the church, not in her everyday dress or in mourning black, but wearing a dragon-green jacket and striped waistcoat and men's breeches and her husband's brimmed hat. She had ordered the suit of clothes from Poole as a wedding present for Elias. He wore it only once and never outside their house. It was the latest in English society, she told him when he expressed his misgivings.

He looked down at himself. "Two watch chains?" he said.

"It's the pink of fashion," his wife offered.

The man had worn the same suit of ditto for almost twenty years, a jacket and waistcoat and breeches all of a grey russet. He looked shyly at his new wife. He'd always been a small man and he'd settled further into that slight frame over time. They stood eye to eye and were near to the other in size. A marriage of equals. She was wearing a plain cotton dress with a simple ruff of lace at the sleeves that had once been her mother's.

"I'd be happier in your dress than in this fit-out," he said.

It was as close as he could come to an admonition. She put the suit away and it never saw the light of day before she wore it to the funeral.

It was a bizarre sign of grief, some said. More saw it as an indication that what they'd long suspected was true—something essential to a woman's station was lacking in her. She'd usurped Elias Caines's waning manhood and put on a man's uniform to make it plain to the world.

The bewilderment and revulsion her appearance stirred up might have become something darker if the pandemic hadn't overtaken everyone's concern. Several mourners hacked their way through Elias's funeral and within days two dozen others were down with the fever. Three men died within a fortnight and the Beadle announced a pause in regular Sunday services. Everyone retreated to their houses and tilts, going outside only to collect water or firewood or to use the outhouse.

Hardly a soul laid eyes on the Widow Caines during the plague months. Those who did reported she was dressed always in her bizarre widow's weeds and Elias's hat. And she was never again seen in public wearing anything other than the dragon-green coat and a pair of leather breeches.

She arrived for the reading of the will in her husband's heaviest winter jacket. Underneath she was attired as had become her custom. She hung the jacket on a rack near the door and sat beside her husband's cousin, the sealed document on Aubrey Picco's desk before them. They were in the same office in which Elias and the Widow had married. It was a bitterly cold day, a northeast wind setting its shoulder to the building, making the rafters creak. A servant had laid a fire in the room an hour before the meeting and it had taken some of the frost from the air, but their breath still steamed about their heads in the chill.

The Widow took out a clay pipe and a silver box of tobacco. She tamped the bowl full and went to the fireplace, touching a lit shovie to the pipe.

When she took her seat, Aubrey Picco said, "Our friend Elias has named me executor of his last will and testament and charged me with ensuring his properties and monies are distributed in every detail according to his wishes. I trust you are both sensible of my role in this matter?"

"I am aware," Taverner said.

The Widow nodded.

"This testament was notarized two years past by Cornelius Strapp in his position as magistrate for the district."

Taverner shifted in his seat. "I witnessed Elias's will five years ago."

"This document is clearly the more recent."

"He reported nothing about the change to me."

The Widow said, "Even those closest to us have inner chambers to which we are not privy."

Taverner looked her up and down in her chair and turned back to Picco. "She has taken to this preposterous dress which is vain and worldly and unnatural," he said.

"We have no proscription as to a person's dress, Myles."

"I am wearing neither lace nor flounces nor lappets," the Widow said. "I wear no rings or bracelets. My necklace is meant only to carry keys."

"This is an issue to be dealt with at Meeting," Aubrey said. "It is irrelevant to the task at hand."

The Widow said, "I am sure that my husband's will looks after all as they deserve."

Aubrey raised the envelope to make it plain to the people across the desk. "This is the magistrate's seal," he said and both nodded. He lifted the wax with a knife and opened the testament. He fitted his eyeglasses onto his face. "I, Elias Picco," he read, "of Mockbeggar, on the island of Newfoundland, ever mindful of the uncertainty of life."

Elias Caines's will directed discrete sums to the erection of a meeting house to host services for the Society of Friends and also to each of Myles Taverner's three children when they came of age. In the absence of any direct male heir, Elias left all his worldly possessions, the house and warehouses and gardens in Mockbeggar, the fishing posts and the buildings thereon along the coast, *Success* and five other schooners, the Caines Mercantile operation and all its assets, as well as sundry cows, pigs, ducks, chickens and other livestock as might be about the properties at the time of his death, to his wife.

"It is signed, Your true friend, Elias Caines."

Taverner turned his head sharply toward the window. "Half the firm was to come to me. You have heard him say as much, Friend Aubrey."

The headman raised his hands helplessly. "There is no evidence of such in this document."

"A woman has no legal claim to the ownership of property."

Aubrey said, "There is much under the law that the Society of Friends does not recognize or support, as you know. Even by the laws of the British court, in the absence of a male heir a widow may enjoy her husband's wealth until such a time as she is under the legal provenance of another man. Until the Widow Caines remarries, or until she passes, even the Privy Council would find the company is hers to do with as she sees fit." Aubrey raised the testament to show it across the desk. "This is Elias Caines's signature," he said. He pointed to the name of the Justice of the Peace. "And this is Cornelius Strapp's hand. I recognize it, as do you I'm sure."

"I have worked by Elias's side since I was twenty-one," the cousin said. "I helped him build this concern."

"I don't call facing the threat of receivership building a concern. If not for the dowry I brought into the firm—"

"Elias would never demand a dowry as down payment on a marriage."

"He did not refuse it either, Friend Myles."

"Please," Aubrey Picco said. He lifted his hands in a pacifying manner. "Friends," he said. "We are bound by the provisions as laid out in his will."

Taverner stared at the Widow until she turned her head toward him. "If your father were alive to see this," he said.

"It is an injury to all," she said, "that he is no longer with us."

After Elias's cousin left the office, the Widow Caines and Aubrey Picco sat in silence. The bare rafters straining against the wind like the timbers of a vessel at sea. It was as if they were sitting in the stillness of a Sunday meeting, waiting for the spirit to move one of them to speak. And failing that, satisfied to let the silence speak for them. Aubrey got up from the desk and stood at the window that looked out over the harbour. A score of ships at anchor. Two schooners hauled into winter dry-dock below their offices.

He said, "I am surprised Elias didn't tell me he'd gone to the magistrate to make these changes."

"It was my suggestion," the Widow said. "To be certain no legal challenge could be brought against it."

Aubrey nodded at the comfortless world of ocean and granite, at the day's relentless winter weather.

The Widow rose and collected her jacket from the coat rack. "Myles has no head for business," she said. "He is barely fit for totting figures. Had the will not been altered, we would all be the poorer for it."

There was a broken line of sea ice pinnacled on the near shoreline by wind and tide and looking like the outer wall of an Arctic fortress, glowing against the bay's dark water. A voice like the voice of the spirit spoke to Aubrey then. *The fortress walls are useless*, it said. *The Adversary is already within.*

"I am hoping that you will stay on as headman," the Widow said.

"Was that Friend Elias's wish?"

"I wouldn't have asked otherwise."

He nodded again. But he didn't turn his head from the window.

By March month, a thronging herd of ice overtook the coastline on its annual migration from the Labrador Sea, the pack miles wide and grinding its monumental weight against the shore. The harbour blocked with pans rising and falling on the tide-swell like a flock of sheep rubbing tight in a paddock.

Imogen Purchase endured a difficult pregnancy up to this point. It was a torture to walk or to stand still any length of time on her swollen legs and feet. She was nauseous each morning and the smell of cooking meat or chamber lye made her urge. Her days were a misery. But the near-constant illness at least managed to shield her from the attentions of her husband.

On their wedding day the groom passed out as soon as they returned to the Big House. The hunting dogs set the place on end when they arrived, barking and jumping and racing up and down the stairs as Matterface and Heater deposited Abe in his bed. They took the dogs away with them, saying something about allowing the newlyweds their privacy. There was no one else in the building. The two servants who had lived and worked at the Big House gave their notice after Cornelius died and the hunting dogs took up residence. Imogen sat and waited in the parlour, considering the unlikely circumstance she found herself in.

There was a mirror above the sitting room fireplace that ran the width of the mantel. Imogen had never seen one larger than her hand before. She'd worked in the Caines house as a maid but the Quaker allowed no looking glasses and she spent a good portion of her wedding day watching herself. She moved her right hand and the reflected figure moved her left. She raised her left and watched the right hand lifted up. She studied the glass, trying to catch some flaw in the likeness there. It seemed a kind of devil's trick that the world existed in it to every detail, but aligned exactly opposite to how God intended.

Hours later she heard her husband shouting for Matterface and Heater from the bedroom. The day was slipping into a winter twilight and the house was nearly dark. Abe Strapp came downstairs muttering to himself and stopped short when he saw her in the moving light of the fire. She stood to present herself, as a servant would.

"Who are you?" he asked.

"Imogen Purchase," she said, and then corrected herself. "Imogen Strapp."

He made a motion with his hand, indicating she should go on.

"We two is married," she said. "By the Beadle's hand. At the church this morning."

Even in the near dark she could see the sequence of events play over his face as they came back to him. He shook his head. "That bloody witch," he said.

"It wouldn't ever my intention," Imogen said. "It was the Widow pushed it upon me. And yourself consented to it. The Beadle set us down in his book, so."

"Can you cook?" Strapp asked her.

"Cook?"

"Yes, *cook*. Jesus help me. I've been standing bitch in the kitchen for months and my guts are cursing my teeth."

"I knows how to cook. Sir," she said.

Strapp disappeared after the supper meal was cleared away and Imogen made up the bed in the servants' quarters behind the kitchen. She shut the door against the dogs and stripped to her underclothes in the cold darkness. Sometime during the night she woke to a stranger climbing in beside her.

"Mrs. Strapp," a voice said. "Can you cook a bird?"

His icy hands were already up under her shift. He'd been drinking and the curdled stink of alcohol on his breath made her stomach turn. She covered her mouth to stifle the vomit and a helpless noise accompanied the urging, a sound and involuntary motion her husband mistook for something else altogether.

She turned away from the smell of him and he shoved into her from behind.

"You had the look of a dirty bunter," he said.

When he came to her room the next night she wasn't able to wrestle her body into submission, vomiting over herself and onto her husband and the bedclothes. Abe Strapp bellowed like a gut-shot animal, heaving himself upright and hauling off his nightshirt as if it was on fire. The dogs barking and jumping at the closed door. He cursed the girl and swung at her drunkenly, Imogen burrowing under the sullied blankets to muffle the blows raining down on her. She lay there a long time after he left, completely still but for her heart hammering in her chest. Strapp's dogs circled the bed and climbed up to walk over her, lapping at the sick.

The Beadle came by the house the next afternoon. "I was wanting to speak with Mr. Strapp," he said. He inclined his head. "With your husband."

"He's out with Misters Matterface and Heater," she said.

He noticed a dark swelling around her left eye and paused. She was an orphan sold into indentured servitude by a parish church in the English West Country. She had the look of a stray dog on a city street who'd been kicked often enough to be shy of passersby. It galled him to see the girl installed in circumstances for which she was manifestly, irredeemably unfit. He gestured toward her. "These clothes," he said. "They are not suited for a woman of your social position. We will have to see about finding something more proper."

Imogen smiled at the thought, in spite of herself. "It won't do to get anything new just now," she said. "I'll be the size of a puncheon the once."

"Of course," the Beadle said. "After the baby comes then."

The girl nodded, her face red with a mortified sort of pleasure.

Three more days passed before Abe Strapp came to her bed again. "Mr. Strapp, sir," she said as he shifted on top of her. "I feels the sick coming."

He left the room in a rage so sudden and incoherent it made the girl afraid for her life. She barred the door with a dresser and sat awake all night listening. But he didn't come back to the room and hadn't made a nocturnal visit since. Which made the pall of sickness on her days well worth the suffering.

She didn't announce the fact, but her nausea ended abruptly at the beginning of March, with the same suddenness that the pack ice appeared in the harbour. There were mirrors in several rooms in the house and she sometimes stood before them soberly. Imagining how she would look in the new clothes she'd been promised, the dresses and petticoats and stockings and shoes befitting her station. Exactly the opposite, though it seemed, from what God intended.

On the seventeenth day of March each year, the Irish servants in Mockbeggar and Nonsuch forswore all work, holing up in their tilts and drinking stingo or knock-me-down or rank potato liquor to mark the feast day of Saint Patrick, men and women and not a few children besides getting blind drunk and descending into communal singing and arguments and fist fights and brawling. The season's foul weather usually confined the anarchic turmoil to the homes of the celebrants but St. Paddy's that spring dawned almost pleasant, the sky clear. The wind off the ice in the harbour had a winter edge to it, but nothing fierce enough to keep the drunken Catholics inside. The absence of a magistrate on the shore added to the day's sense of unbridled release.

The festivities began before light and by noon the Irish were trawling the paths of Mockbeggar, half a hundred in a loose pack, tipping over outhouses and chasing sheep and hens, the lot of them singing and bawling their heads off. Most of the English in Mockbeggar barred their doors and their window shutters, waiting for the storm to pass. But for some it was too much to resist, and half a hundred more came out of their houses and tilts to join the furious campaign underway.

It was Strapp's first Paddy's Day as legal owner of his father's mercantile operation and his first as a married man. Neither situation had offered him the satisfactions he expected. He complained publicly about his bracket-faced wife who connived her way into his house and wouldn't so much as spread her legs to pay her keep. And that grievance inevitably led to the Beadle whose smug self-importance and naked scheming lay at the heart of all that was disagreeable in his life. "I'd be better off without the likes of that shitten shepherd," he announced in his cups.

Shortly after his marriage in January, Strapp had surprised Clinch at the firm's offices. It was the first time he'd shown his face in the business premises he'd inherited. He bantered mind-lessly as he wandered about the room, men at their desks studi-ously ignoring him for fear of being singled out. He went to his father's office and picked through papers and ledgers before opening each drawer in turn.

"Are you looking for something in particular, Mr. Strapp?" Clinch asked from the doorway.

"I can't put my hand on his magistrate's seal." Abe straightened from his search and stood with his hands at his hips. He said,

"A portion of all fines levied in the course of a Justice's duties is kept by officers of the court, isn't that so?"

"As payment for his time and efforts, yes."

"The coast has been without a Justice of the Peace since my father's death."

The Beadle stared at the ridiculous figure, the look of surprise on his face edging toward laughter before he reined it in. "That is true," he said.

"It might serve you," Abe said, "to put in a word on my behalf with the governor in St. John's."

The Beadle nodded slowly. "There is a certain amount of experience and education required for such an appointment."

"There is a certain amount of chop and change required for such an appointment," Abe countered. "I trust you are an old hand at that."

The Beadle inclined his head. "I will make inquiries on your behalf."

"Thanks to your meddling," Abe said, "I am married to a filthy dishclout who is bad shag into the bargain. If you wish to retain your position, you will do more than make inquiries."

Ever since, Abe claimed Clinch's influence on the governor in this matter was all that stopped him dismissing the man and driving him out of Mockbeggar altogether. Though his patience was wearing thin as they approached what passed for spring on the shore.

Abe Strapp had always celebrated St. Patrick's Day with the same licentious fervour as the Catholics. Only Christmas offered anything close to it for sheer drunken abandon. But the intensity of the Irish feast day had a tinge of bloodlust about it, a recklessness that only people with nothing to lose could rise to, and he and Matterface and Heater each year made their way from one squalid uproar to the next, throwing in with a native passion. But this season Abe brought an air of malicious affability to the celebrations that even Matterface and Heater were wary of.

The grog shops and alehouses were open all day long, though most of the Irish were too impoverished to drink liquor they hadn't brewed themselves. In a nod to his father's beginnings, Abe Strapp offered credit to men unable to pay up-front for their spree. The loans were offered at six in the hundred though most who made their mark were too drunk to know the outrageous terms. Some had no memory of borrowing at all, though they signed away a goodly portion of the coming season's wages to the cause.

Shortly after midday a brawl erupted on the waterfront among two of the many factions that the Irish swore allegiance to. Strapp and his hangers-on rushed to take in the spectacle as the riot travelled up from the harbour like a roiling nest of snakes, starting and stopping and veering to one side, before moving suddenly in the opposite direction. There were no camps an eye could distinguish in the melee. Occasionally Abe sent Matterface or Heater in to straighten out someone for beating on a smaller opponent or an overmatched woman or for some other underhanded tactic. It was the first bit of fun he'd had since he married.

Before long the combatants had exhausted themselves and the spite quickly went out of the affair, the fighters drifting apart in concert like dancers when the music stops. And there was a general lull in the aftermath. Most of the Protestants had had enough of the celebration and disappeared back into their houses. The Irish were nursing their injuries or settling down in the straw laid on the grog-shop floors, lying bung-upwards to sleep.

Abe was poisoned by the hush, as if the short-lived scrap had only been a taunt. "This won't do," he said. "Once a year does St. Patrick grace us with his day." Heater had nodded off at the table and Strapp raised his boot to kick him awake. "A disgrace to spend these sacred hours asleep. People," he shouted as he got to his feet. He went about the room, rooting at the figures snoring in the straw. "To honour the good saint," he said. "On your stumps you lazy bastards."

He stood in the centre of the room with his arms wide. "I propose a race," he said. "The first annual St. Patrick's Day Race. Is there a Fenian here with legs for it?"

"What kind of race?" a voice called from the straw.

The door of the alehouse stood open and Strapp caught sight of the pack ice glinting white below. "Across the harbour," he said. "From Strapp's warehouse to the dry-dock on Caines's side."

There was no enthusiasm for the idea. Several people roused by Strapp's boot were back on their hands and knees, crawling toward the warm impression in the straw they'd just abandoned.

"A free drink for every runner," Abe said. "A free drink of Caribbean rum to every runner at the start and a drink at the end."

Heads came up around the room.

"And sixpence for the first to make the crossing."

He made the rounds of the other alehouses with the same proposal, collecting more participants at every stop. Those too old or lame or drunk to consider joining the race rimmed the harbour as far as Caines's warehouse to watch.

Matterface walked along the lineup at the edge of Strapp's wharf, parcelling out a shot of rum to each contestant. The pack chafed tight to the finger piers and the beach rocks and the pinnacle ice on the shore and it stretched out the harbour mouth to open ocean. The men spent a portion of their days slaughtering and sculping seals miles out on the Labrador ice every spring. The race seemed a lark.

Abe Strapp stood on the wharf's apron with a pistol. "Ready," he called. At the shot, two dozen men and boys scrambled down to the ice like they were going over the side of a sealing vessel, mad to be first into a patch of swiles. They were everyone as drunk as David's sow and still managed to pick their way ahead at an astonishing clip, kicking up wreaths of seawater as they fanned across the harbour. People shouting their lungs out from the shoreline.

No one was certain they saw the boy go under among the muddle of moving bodies.

"Did that one fall?" Heater said. "Matterface, did you see someone go down?"

The youngster had slipped between ice pans into the frigid water and the ice immediately closed over him again. A general, drunken panic took hold and every sensible thing people could think to do took three times as long to organize and carry out. The racers who made the shore cast around for gaffs or poles and headed back toward the spot where the boy was last seen. Abe was staring out at the ice when Heater called to him, he and Matterface hauling a punt toward the waterline. Matterface climbed in to pole the boat ahead while Heater pushed along from the port gunwale, going through to his waist on times and hauling himself up to more solid pans to push again.

"Come on then," Matterface shouted.

Two other men made their way out to help heave the punt along. Abe stuffed the pistol into his trousers and ran down to join them, the icy water filling his boots as he started off the shore and he never quite collected his balance before getting within reach of the stern, coming down face-first onto the gunwale and every stitch he had on was suddenly soaked through.

Someone grabbed him by the jacket and dragged him aboard. He lay satched and stunned in the bilge, the punt rolling and shifting like a vessel on the open sea, his ears ringing from the blow to his face. Something hard was digging into his legs and stomach. He tried to sit up but couldn't manage the complicated series of movements required to make it happen. Someone else stretched out on the bottom of the punt beside him and he tried to shift away from the stinging cold radiating from the figure.

More shouting, more rocking. Hands lifting his companion up out of the boat and eventually someone, Heater he thought, taking his arm to help him find his feet and step out over the gunwale onto the beach. Seawater raining from the sleeves and the hem of his coat.

"We'll have to get you into some dry things," Heater said. He reached into Strapp's waistband. He said, "That's quite the horn you have there, Master Strapp."

Abe slapped his hand away from the pistol. Collecting his senses just enough to feel a wave of embarrassment come over him. His right eye was starting to swell closed. He looked up toward the warehouse where the boy was being laid over a puncheon and men rocked the barrel forward and back. "Is the youngster drownded?"

"He's alive yet," Heater said. "But he's not half nor quarter well."

"He've gone and ruined a perfectly good day," Strapp said.

The Beadle was sent for, in hopes he would be able to offer some physic to help the boy. Matterface and Heater tried to talk

Abe into having Clinch look at his face where it was busted open over the cheekbone when he was done with the youngster.

"It's all bad enough," Abe said, "without that granny clicking his tongue at me like I'd pissed me bed." When they suggested Mary Oram, he made the sign of the cross. "Deliver us from evil," he said.

He'd started shaking with the cold and wet and they herded him to his house where they got him into dry clothes while Imogen Purchase hid herself away in the servants' quarters. Both Matterface and Heater were nearly as wet through and they borrowed trousers and shirts before hauling on their wet boots and coats. They headed back to the nearest grog shop then, but it was clear the bloom was off the day's festivities. Only a handful of people at the tables, two or three figures passed out in the straw along the walls.

Abe carried on drinking in a sullen way, talking through his many grievances with the day, and with the larger forces at work in the world to keep him from the heights he felt himself heir to. The loan agent reported the day's transactions as it grew dark and Strapp spent a while arguing the take would have been double that amount if not for the near drowning. He shifted to a discussion of how clever he'd been to think of offering credit for drink then, talking up the innovation as if it had never been undertaken in the history of the British Empire.

All this time, Strapp worked away at the pistol he'd taken for an unexpected swim in the harbour's salt. Matterface and Heater had tried to convince him to leave the useless firearm at the Big House but Strapp wouldn't hear of it. He'd brought a cloth package of felt and linen rags and a ramrod, along with oil and a metal file, and he wiped out the barrel and scoured at the flint as if returning the pistol to working order might repair his injured pride.

When he was done, Strapp loaded the pistol with powder and ball and wadded the barrel and then set it on the table in front of him. Finishing that job seemed only to set him more on edge. He ragged awhile on the bitch of a girl who had moved body and bones into his house and pretended to be his wife while puking her guts up whenever he laid a hand upon her.

He started up from his chair suddenly, announcing it was time to pump ship, and he stood over one of the men passed out in the straw and pissed on the unconscious figure. There were murmurs of protest from the other drinkers in the room and Strapp turned his head to tell them they were welcome to go swive themselves.

"If I was you, Master Strapp," one of the drinkers called back, "I'd be home and taking me sweet young wife to bed, puke or no."

"I could put you to bed with a shovel," he said as he tied his trousers. "How would that suit you?"

The talker turned to his companions. "As I understand it," he said, "Master Strapp is hunting rabbits with a dead ferret after a few swallows and is Not Able to bed man nor woman."

Heater went over the table then, giving the mouthy drinker a beating to save him being shot dead by Abe Strapp. Everyone else fled the room and Matterface let the shellacking go on a few minutes before wading in to save the man being permanently disabled at the hands of his partner.

They ushered Strapp toward the door and he put his hands to the frame to stop them.

"My pistol," he said.

"I have it," Matterface told him.

"Give it here."

"There's nothing you needs a pistol for between here and your house, Mr. Strapp."

"On my mother's life," he said.

Matterface relented, handing over the firearm apologetically, as if he was simply wanting to spare the man the bother of carrying it.

They led him to the lower path along the harbour-side, hoping to walk off a little of Strapp's obstreperousness before he was left alone with a helpless young girl and half a dozen boisterous hunting dogs and a loaded pistol. As they turned up away from the water towards the Strapp property the last weak light of the day silhouetted a figure coming toward them on the path.

"Who is it goes there?" Strapp called out.

"Master Strapp?" the figure answered. "Is that you?"

"Who is it there?"

"I'm sorry to report, sir, young Seamus Fleet has passed."

"Who?" Strapp demanded. "Seamus who?"

Matterface leaned in to tell him it was the youngster who had fallen through the ice.

Heater crossed himself and Abe slapped at the stupid gesture before turning back to the stranger. The whole day had gone to shit and he was sick to death of it. "You," he said, "what is your name?"

"Lambe, sir," the man said. "Dallen Lambe. The Beadle sent me up to give you the news."

"Lambe," Strapp said. The name niggled at him though he couldn't locate exactly why and he was forced to turn to a more generic complaint while he worked through it. "And you were at my house?"

"Just now, sir, yes."

"And you saw my wife, did you?"

"I spoke with the lady," he said. "Yes."

"The *lady*," Strapp said. "You *spoke* with her, did you?" It came clear to him in that moment. "Dallen Lambe?" he said. "The same Dallen Lambe signed a declaration for the Widow Caines? About a ravishment of the lady at my house?"

Lambe was inching off the path, trying to find a way around the men blocking his way, and Strapp raised the pistol.

"Jesus, Mary and Joseph," Heater whispered.

Matterface tried to step between them, but Abe held him at bay with his free hand. "The Widow Caines had you sign a declaration against me," he shouted.

"Mrs. Caines asked me to make my mark on a paper," Lambe said. "I didn't know the first thing about what it said. As God is my witness."

Everything that had gone wrong in his life stood six feet away in the gloam and that fact gave strength and focus to Abe's drunken anger. "You Irish dog," he said.

SOLEMN. A DIRTY PUZZLE. A BASTARD.

The funeral was held at the Church of England and the pews were crowded with English and Irish alike. There was no Catholic sanctuary on the shore and it was a rare occasion that an itinerant priest stole into the harbour to minister to the popish fishermen, hearing confession and offering the sacraments in kitchens and fishing rooms. Most of the Irish refused the churching offered by the Beadle and made do with the intermittent attentions of their own faith. But Dallen and his family attended regular services. "The clothes have a queer cut about them," he used to say, "but they keep the wind at bay."

In the days after the killing, several men took young Solemn Lambe aside to advise him against doing anything rash to avenge Dallen's death. Abe Strapp was best left to God's judgement, they said. Solemn was not quite twelve and the notion of God's judgement was too hypothetical to offer comfort. You won't be helping anyone if you winds up dead like your father, people insisted.

As if they wanted to make the boy complicit in their own infuriating helplessness.

Solemn had been working as his father's kedger since he was just able to walk, following the man around to hold his tools or keeping the puncheon tub filled with water on the stagehead. Three seasons he'd been cutting tail with Dallen's crew, carrying a little hatchet for the purpose, the notched tails identifying his cod among the catch and that total totted up at season's end as Solemn's wage. He was just about old enough to take on a full share in the boat now. And his luck at the fish was all his mother and sister would have to keep them from going hungry of a winter.

Mrs. Lambe was so grief-stricken she didn't recognize any of her visitors or the mourners at the church. Solemn in his turn did not recognize this woman, who was his mother in appearance but in no other detail. His sister, Bride, had to lead Mrs. Lambe by the hand from her bed to her chair and she fed her mouthfuls of potato and fish that her mother swallowed without interest. She seemed to have forgotten her own children's names. The two youngsters, people said, were as good as orphaned.

Before the service began the Widow Caines took a seat in the front pew beside the grieving family. She sat close enough to Solemn Lambe he could have touched the arm of her dragon-green coat. He had to force himself not to turn his head to take in the spectacle, out of respect for his father. But he could feel the singular pull of her, like a tide drawing a boat taut on its anchor-line, before she disappeared in the waterfall of grief that was praying and singing over his father's body and leading the procession to the cemetery for the Catholic dead in a clearing at the end of Oram's Drung. Winching the man into the boggy earth among graves marked by bare wooden crosses or black, unlettered plinths of shale carted from the coastline and set upright at the head of the lost.

He didn't think of her again until she appeared before him as they led their mother from the graveyard. Mrs. Lambe looked blindly through her as she offered her condolences and the Widow Caines turned her attention to him. "I'm sorry for your loss, Solemn Lambe," she said.

He nodded but couldn't speak for the lump in his throat and for the shock of standing so close to the Widow in the brimmed black hat of her Quaker husband, in her fashionable jacket and striped waistcoat with its two watch chains. He'd never been within twenty feet of her before that day or looked directly at her face. She was not beautiful. But there was something more striking about the woman than beauty. She was fine, he thought. He'd never seen clothes as dear, clothes that seemed custom-made to fit the body they dressed. He'd heard the stories about her habit in the months after her husband passed, and he'd seen her now and then walking about her property in the new uniform, or making her way to the mercantile offices. From a distance it had the look of costume, a brazen make-believe dress-up. But within arm's length of her he could see there was nothing sham about the figure she cut. She was contained, in a way Solemn envied. It looked as if the Widow occupied exactly the space she was made for.

That graveyard inspection lasted only seconds and Solemn spent days turning his impressions over before they approached the condition of thought. In the moment he was vaguely ashamed to be appraising her so closely with his father just set in the ground. To be considering her in a way he suspected was at odds with general opinion.

"You will be taking your father's place on the crew this year," she said.

It didn't sound to Solemn like a question and he simply nodded.

"Come see me at the house tomorrow evening," she said.

He nodded a second time and led his mother past the Widow toward home, relieved to be out from under her gaze, to return to the ruinous grief a son ought to feel when he's just buried his murdered father.

The day after the funeral a blizzard blew through Mockbeggar, with blinding snow adrift on a northeast wind that barred every soul inside for the duration. Doorways lay buried above their latches and for most of two days the animals went unfed. The wind drove smoke back down the wooden chimneys of the fishermen's one-room tilts and people alternated between sitting in the interminable cold and choking on the fire's swirling exhaust.

Solemn's mother lay in her bed for most of that time. He boiled water and heated food when the fire was lit and lay beside his mother and sister to keep warm when it was not. Once the storm passed, he and Bride spent a full day digging out, clearing paths to the root cellar and privy and down to the fishing room on the water. At no moment in all that time did Solemn forget his encounter with the Widow Caines or her summons. But he hoped the woman might have let it slip her mind since.

He was outside collecting a turn of splits for the wood box when he saw the Widow walking from Caines's offices with her headman. She carried on toward her house but Aubrey Picco broke off and made his way down toward the tilt where he stood waiting.

"Solemn," the headman said.

"Mr. Picco."

"Aubrey," the Quaker insisted. "You were meant to call at the Caines house."

"It's been a hard stretch to get free, Mr. Picco, sir." And he corrected himself. "Aubrey, sir."

The headman smiled at the boy. "Now would be a good time."

"All right."

"I'll take you up, shall I?"

Solemn tried not to let the relief show on his face. "If you idn't too busy, sir."

There was a riddle fence around the Widow's property, its tips just showing above the drifts. There was a gate shovelled clear that the youngster had never stepped through. Aubrey led him along the side of the house to the servants' entrance and they stamped the snow off their boots inside the porch door.

"Wait here," Aubrey Picco said before disappearing into the rooms beyond.

There was a full water barrel in the porch where he stood. Half a puncheon tub with the last eggs from the fall coddled in straw. Solemn shivered the length of himself and he bore down to stifle the butterflies adrift in his gut. Then he heard Aubrey calling him inside.

A fire was burning in the kitchen as he passed through it. Brick chimney. Wide plank floors, the grain scrubbed clean with water and sand. A handwoven mat laid along the hallway. There was another fire in the parlour where the sound of voices led him. The headman was standing near the fireplace, the Widow sitting opposite on a long stuffed bench with a high back that he shortly learned was called a chesterfield. She was smoking a clay pipe.

Solemn reached up to take off his hat and he flinched as something skimmed above his head. Something else shot past his ear, buckling the air, and the boy let out a little bark, collapsing in the doorway with his hands over his head.

"Get up, get up," Aubrey Picco said. He leaned down to lift the youngster by his arms.

"It's all right, Aubrey," the Widow said. She was smiling, or nearly. "It's a shock if you aren't used to them."

He heard them then, two grey jays making their wiry racket as if they were calling out in the woods. He watched them rifle about the room, flicking from mantel to side table to the glass of a lamp. There was a cage in one corner made of willow, the door standing open.

"I caught them with bird lime last spring," the Widow said, "on the back step." She held out her hand and one of the birds swooped down to perch there. "I kept them in the cage most of the summer, but they have the run of the house now." She set her pipe down on a side table to stroke the bird's head with an index finger.

Solemn had never seen anything as fantastical and strange as the Widow Caines seated on her brocaded furniture, wearing her green jacket and sporting a tamed bird like a living ring. Seeing the woman up close a second time made some of what he'd been told about the world seem too absurd to be true.

He said, "You're Mr. Strapp's sister?"

"Solemn," Aubrey Picco said to warn him off, but the Widow raised her hand.

"This isn't news to you, surely."

"It just don't seem likely."

"I will take that as a compliment, if you don't mind."

Like everyone on the shore, Solemn had grown up with stories about his betters. Abe Strapp's virulent stupidity, his brawling appetites. The Widow bringing *Success* into the marriage with Elias Caines as her dowry from Cornelius Strapp. The split between father and daughter so complete she didn't attend the man's funeral. They were like characters from scripture, ubiquitous and intimate and untouchable.

"'Solemn,'" the Widow said. "That's an unusual name."

"Twas me sister," he said.

"What was your sister, Solemn?"

"She couldn't quite fit me whole name in her mouth, I guess. When she was just learning to speak, so."

"And what is your whole name?"

"Solomon," he said. He hadn't heard the word in so long it seemed an alien thing. "She could only manage the first of it. And after so long everyone took it up the same."

The Widow nodded and offered her half-smile again. "Solemn Lambe."

It suited the boy to a T, which is why his sister's childish corruption displaced his given name. A little man from the time he could walk. Serious, deliberate. A bit of a thinker, his father said, meaning it as a mild rebuke.

The Widow said, "Aubrey tells me you're a good hand, Solemn."

"I don't mind work."

"We've lost our best servants to the sickness. I need someone to work about the house. To fill the water barrel and keep the wood boxes full and tend the animals."

One of the jays flew from the windowsill into the cage and it drew his attention away from her. He felt much like those birds in the moment, lighting one place and then another, not able to settle long enough to take anything in properly. He was being offered the opportunity to work on the Widow's property, to walk the outer hallways of her exotic existence. And all he could think to say was, "I expect I'll be going out after the fish come the summer."

"You and your family have suffered a loss," the Widow said. "A position here will be helpful in the months ahead."

"Starting tomorrow, you will report each morning before light," Aubrey told him. "When the fishing season is upon us we can revisit the arrangement."

"Does that suit you, Solemn?"

"I expect so," the youngster said. He was too trammelled up in the head even to offer a thank you.

"You can go now," the headman said.

"Yessir," he said. "Aubrey, sir."

As he passed through the kitchen to the servants' entrance, he encountered Imogen Purchase. Her belly about the size of a puncheon tub. Solemn hadn't seen her since her surprise marriage when she moved into the Big House with Abe Strapp. She straightened from the fireplace to stand with both hands at the small of her back.

"Imogen," he said.

He had no idea why she was in the Widow's kitchen. In the dark, insular days after his father was killed he'd missed the fact she'd abandoned her husband and returned to the Widow's service. Leaving the Big House before Mary Oram arrived to lay out Dallen's body and walking across Mockbeggar in the pitch. Crawling into her bed in the servants' room at the Caines house which had been sitting empty since her marriage and refusing to leave ever after.

"What is it the Missus wants with you?" the pregnant girl asked.

"She've given me a position here at the house, I guess it is."

"Don't let that one get her hooks into you," she said.

He stood with that declaration a moment. "She seems fit enough."

Imogen said, "That woman would eat her own youngsters." She turned back to the pot over the fire, as if to keep herself from saying more. A moment later she said, "I'm sorry about your father, Solemn."

He heard Aubrey Picco leaving the parlour and Solemn flit into the porch and out the door, running all the way back to the family's hovel above the harbour. His head was too full to face his mother and sister and he waited outside in the cold until the light went duckish and the day was nearly gone to dark.

The next morning and every morning after, Solemn Lambe made his way to the Caines house, arriving before light and staying till evening each day but Sunday when he left after the Widow returned from the Quaker service. He ate his meals in the kitchen with pregnant Imogen Purchase and part of Solemn was waiting each time for the girl to say something more about her cryptic warning during his first visit. But she seemed to have lost interest in his welfare or had said as much on the subject as she was willing.

Solemn couldn't bring himself to mention the girl's presence to his mother, afraid the news would cripple the woman's already crippled heart. She had taken a visceral dislike to the Widow's servant after Imogen married Abe Strapp, arguing her character with his father. "That dirty puzzle," she said. "She'd spread her legs for any whore pipe could be coaxed into the light of day." If Dallen Lambe offered even a half-hearted defence of how

Imogen found herself spliced to the richest man on the coast, his wife stood over him in a rage that filled Solemn with inexplicable embarrassment. As if his father was the one being shamed.

A dirty puzzle. He'd heard the Widow Caines called the same by half a dozen people since her husband's death. Even his father had whispered the phrase as they watched her walk the lower path, a note of amazement in his voice. Solemn could not imagine two people more unlike in every particular than Imogen and the Widow Caines. Those words surfaced in his mind on the rare occasions he saw them together, if the Widow came into the kitchen to order a task done, if Imogen was called into the sitting room while Solemn was tending the fire. A dirty puzzle. As if they posed the same insoluble riddle to the world.

Solemn fed the animals and mucked out the stalls, he tended the herbs and vegetables started in baskets hung about the kitchen, he kept the fires and fixed up the riddle fence where the winter had bowed it to the ground. And there was still time to sit on the parlour chesterfield and let the jays perch on his head or his shoulders, to feed them oatmeal or pork fat from his hand. The Widow Caines was at the mercantile offices through most of a day's light. In the evenings he would whistle the birds to their cage and close the door after they went to their roost. He went upstairs to the room the Widow used as an office then to ask if there was anything more she needed.

She was always smoking her pipe and rarely raised her head from her work. "Not tonight, Solemn," she said.

The woman was reclusive and aloof and Solemn couldn't help seeing there was something of that separateness in his own nature, a part of himself that stood apart from the world he lived in. All his young life he'd carried that nameless weight in silence, feeling beggared by it and solitary. But there was no sense of loneliness or want about the Widow. She seemed sufficient unto the day and he envied that foreign bearing in the woman.

He counted himself lucky to be in an orbit around her, to be afforded a regular sighting, a word now and then, a half-smile. It made him feel less freakish, less forlorn to know her. Bride accused him of being in love with his employer and he wondered for a time if it wasn't true. But he could see that notion was different and lesser than what he felt. It was something akin to the consolations of the church to be allowed to touch the hem of her garments.

Imogen's warning seemed all the time more small-minded and unjustified. A schemer, his mother had called the servant girl, and he let that dismissal answer her on the matter.

Success overwintered in Poole and arrived back in Mockbeggar in mid-May. It warped to the wharf with a load of lumber and roof shingles and nails and panes of glass packed in barrels of molasses, all ordered by the Widow Caines to construct a hall for the Society of Friends.

The vessel was on its way to Quebec to deliver a shipment of port and was returning from there to Poole. It was a long circuitous journey back to Europe, but the Jerseyman approached the captain about shipping his daughter's body home. The promise he'd made to Anna before she passed had plagued him through the spring and he insisted she be taken aboard this, the first certain trip back across the Atlantic. He paid the captain her passage and extra again to ensure she was sent from Poole to her mother in Jersey at the earliest opportunity.

A driving spring snow covered the deck of the ship and the piers and the roofs of all the buildings in Mockbeggar when the barrel containing the remains of the Jerseyman's daughter was hefted aboard. The cask was lowered into the hold and it felt to everyone present as if they were witnessing a burial. Morels didn't acknowledge a soul, climbing onto his horse when his daughter sank out of view and riding up the lower path toward Caines's gardens, disappearing in the squall's drift before he'd made the road to Looking Glass Pond.

Anna Morels's departure from Mockbeggar was like a breeze across the embers of that story and talk of Abe Strapp's disastrous wedding day flared up on the worksite and in the houses and tilts and the outport's drinking establishments. Strapp seemed content to have the Big House to himself in the weeks after his pregnant wife escaped, happy to be shot of her. But the fresh round of gossip resurrected his humiliation and he occupied himself with drunken diatribes against the Widow's machinations and the gall of his wayward servant-wife to have quit his company without so much as a by-your-leave.

Solemn was helping plane and place the wooden sills of the Quaker meeting house when Abe and Matterface and Heater marched toward the worksite with an odd kick in their gallop. He alerted Aubrey Picco who stepped out into the path to face whatever devilment they might be delivering, but the men walked by without more than a glance in his direction. He watched them carry on a ways, all three drunk but unusually purposeful, as if they were about an errand for the King.

"What is that crowd up to?" Aubrey said aloud.

He sent Solemn to shadow the cruisers and to let him know if they were for trouble and the boy followed at a distance until they reached the gate of the Caines property. He broke into a run, coming through the front door as they hustled toward the kitchen. Imogen Purchase was boiling a pot of ash over the fire to make lye soap when they fell upon her, Abe Strapp grabbing her by the hair and cursing at the girl. Solemn yelling out as he tried to claw his way past Matterface and Heater to get to her.

"Brother," the Widow Caines called.

Everyone turned to her where she'd appeared at the back door, having run along the outside of the house to the servants' entrance to avoid the blockade of bodies in the hall.

"What do you think you're doing?" the Widow said.

"I am taking this low bitch home," Abe announced, though he let go her hair as he said it.

Solemn shook himself free of the two men and was moving past them when Heater buckled him with a dart to the kidneys. He was on his knees, trying to draw breath and Matterface kicked him across the ear.

"Leave off him," the Widow ordered and they backed away a step.

"This one belongs in the house she married into," Abe said. "That's my youngster she's carrying."

The Widow offered her half-smile. "You're certain of that, are you?"

"The slut have said as much, have she not? Dallen Lambe swore as much."

She shrugged. "People will tell all sorts of stories, Brother. If it suits their purpose."

"Mrs. Caines," Imogen Purchase said. She shook her head with her hands over her mouth.

Solemn was just able to breathe finally, taking shallow gulps of air as he got to his feet. His head buzzing so every sound was muffled. He put himself between the Widow and Abe Strapp. Taking in the man who killed his father. The Widow ordered Matterface and Heater out of the house and when they were gone she told Solemn and Imogen to wait in the parlour.

"The girl stays," Abe said.

Solemn left them reluctantly and only after the Widow insisted. Once he was out of sight, Strapp said, "Why would Dallen Lambe make up a story about such a thing?"

"Perhaps he had a soft spot for Imogen," the Widow said. "Maybe he wanted the child she was carrying provided for."

Abe Strapp leaned forward as if trying to see something at the very reaches of his sight, his eyes going wide when he spotted it. "You put him up to it," he said. "You *witch*. You wrote it out and had the noddy set his mark to it."

"Fatherhood can be a ticklish thing to pin down, Brother. Are you sure," she said, "you want to raise a bastard child as your own?"

Abe stared at his sister a moment, at the snotty look of satisfaction she wore when she lorded some contrivance over him. The heartless cold brass of her. He turned on Imogen, slapping at her with an open hand, the servant girl screaming and trying to move out of his range, one arm across her belly to protect the child. She stumbled at the hearth as he whaled on her from behind and she fell toward the fire with her free hand before her, the bare arm sinking up to the elbow in the pot of boiling ash.

MARY ORAM, HER UTENSILS.
THE HOPE. THE BEADLE.

Solemn abandoned his work on the Quaker meeting house after
the accident, staying close to watch over Imogen, to keep her
from picking at the skin which pulled tight and itched like it
was crawling with insects beneath the bandages. He changed the
dressings as he was instructed and he scolded her for the flesh
she was scrawbing raw.

"That won't get no better you don't leave it alone," he told her.

He'd suggested to the Widow he could sleep on the floor
beside the kitchen hearth in case Abe made another visit to the
house. But she shook her head.

"Mr. Strapp has abandoned whatever interest he may have
had in Miss Purchase."

The source of her certainty was a mystery to him, but he
wasn't about to question the woman.

He'd come barrelling down the hallway when Imogen took up her screaming. The Widow hauling the girl into the porch and plunging the scalded arm into the water barrel, laying across Imogen's back to hold her there as she reeled in shock, her mouth open, her eyes wide and blind. It looked to Solemn like the Widow was trying to drown an animal, bracing her weight against the convulsions to keep the arm submerged.

Abe Strapp was gone by the time he thought to glance around.

"Should I go for the Beadle?" he asked.

"The Beadle is away on *The Hope*," the Widow said. "Go and fetch Mary Oram."

There was no one but the Widow Caines could have made Solemn make that run up Oram's Drung, in the same droke of trees where the Catholic dead were buried, to call on Mary Oram. Like every youngster on the shore and a goodly number of the adults as well, Solemn lived in terror of the woman and her reputation for spells and witchery.

It was her queer figure as much as her trade that gave credence to the most outlandish stories about the woman. She was no taller than Solemn's sister and wore a knitted cap over her bald head. She had hardly a lash or brow to her eyes, which gave an inscrutable fairy look to her face. She was said to have no fingernails.

Hers was the only house on Oram's Drung, an ancient cubbyhole hardly fit to be used as a stable. She kept herself alive with the vegetables and salt meat and snared rabbit and firewood people could afford for her services as midwife and healer, and with the fish gifted to her when she went to the waterfront to ask a crew how they'd made out on the water. It was a kind of offering to keep bad luck at bay, gifting her a cod to carry off in her doll's arms. There was no saying what might befall a fisherman who denied her and no one was willing to tempt fate by sending her away empty-handed.

The older youngsters in Mockbeggar dared each other to sneak up Oram's Drung after dark and Solemn had once gotten close enough to see candlelight leaking through the seams of a window's wooden shutter. But every step toward it felt like a descent into the guts of some biblical leviathan and he turned and bolted to save himself being consumed for good and all.

He'd never gone near the place a second time, except walking past it in the funeral procession for his father. He couldn't bring himself to get closer than a stone's throw still, walking into the clearing and shouting for the woman from across that distance. She cracked the door on its leather hinges and peered out into the falling light of the evening. Her bald face looking up at him from the shadows like a moon reflected at the bottom of a well.

"The Widow Caines is asking for you," he said. "Imogen Purchase is in trouble."

"She idn't having that youngster already?"

"She've got her arm scalded to death," Solemn said. The figure in the door frame was small enough he could have picked her up in his arms like a goat.

"You go on down," Mary Oram said. "Tell her I'll be there directly."

By the time he made it back to the house, Imogen's arm was red as the shell of a boiled lobster and the girl was trembling in her seat. The Widow Caines told Solemn to light the kitchen lamps and he set about the task, grateful to have something useful to do. He placed one on the fireplace mantel and the other on the table near where the girl was sitting.

They heard the outer door then as Mary Oram let herself in. Her head not much above the latch as she turned to close the porch door behind her. She was wearing her bright woollen cap and a calico jacket and she carried a leather satchel across her shoulders.

"What's after happening here now?" she said.

"Is the baby going to be alright?" Imogen asked her.

"Don't you worry about the baby," Mary Oram said. "A little scalding idn't going to harm that child."

The Widow said, "Solemn will get you anything you need." And she went back to her office on the second floor.

Mary Oram leaned over the girl's lap and lifted the arm towards her face. After that inspection she removed her materials from the satchel, bottles and jars and cloth-wrappings of roots and dried flowers, a ram's horn. She bidded Solemn about to collect onion and clean linen and linseed while she picked through her pharmacy and she directed him to cut the onions fine as she prepared an oily resin. She scraped a little of the ram's horn into the concoction she set as a poultice on the girl's arm, talking all the while about the burns and scalds and boils she'd seen in her days and who had died of their affliction and who was scarred for life.

A jaw-me-dead, Solemn's father used to call the woman. The boy guessed it was her time alone on Oram's Drung made her tongue run twelve-score to the dozen, the numberless injuries and their various cures coming in a constant stream as she worked. Once she finished with the dressing, Mary Oram had Solemn help Imogen to her bed in the room off the kitchen. She removed the girl's stockings and bound the chopped onion to the soles of her feet.

"She'll be alright then?" Solemn asked.

"If that arm don't go bad on her," she said, "the girl will be fine."

After three days it was clear the arm was going to go bad. The scalded flesh swelled and turned purple and black and it stank sweetly of rot. Mary Oram returned to the house every day and made noises in her throat as she sliced away some of the infection with a knife while Imogen bit down on a piece of leather. She applied sea doctors minced with cod liver oil, and a decoction made of dissolved jellyfish, but nothing improved the situation. At each visit the woman's incessant talking subsided a little more, until the arm was bad enough Mary Oram said nothing as she went about her ministrations.

She never offered a word to Solemn about the state of things but he sometimes overheard her reports to the Widow—talk of having the Beadle take the arm at the elbow, discussions of whether waiting for the baby might be too late for the mother— which made him wish he knew less than he did. He had to steel himself against the smell and the sight of the ruined flesh slough- ing away in strips when he changed the dressing. Imogen staring at the ceiling to avoid the sight herself.

"When *The Hope* comes in from coasting," the Widow told him, "we'll have the Beadle look at that arm."

The Beadle came back into Mockbeggar aboard *The Hope* in the second week of June.

They were sailing with a short crew owing to the winter's losses and the sickness had taken its toll along the coast as well.

Wherever *The Hope* made anchor, they were given reports of people who succumbed through the darkest months of the winter. Clinch was appointed the Beadle at the local Church of England as a young man and took on the task of leading regular services after the death of the clergyman who raised the sanctuary. He'd married and baptized and buried a generation while they waited for, and eventually gave up on, an ordained replacement. He kept track of all births and weddings and deaths on the shore, including the churchless Irish and the few Quakers, recording each in a thick leather-bound volume. As he ledgered the flour and rice and peas and fishing twine, the nails and curing salt and rum and molasses off-loaded at each outlying operation, he kept a careful accounting of the men and women and the occasional child who had perished in their beds.

The Hope was twenty years old, the newest vessel in Cornelius Strapp's fleet. She was built in Poole and sailed to Newfoundland as *The Lord and Lady*. It was the Beadle who convinced his employer to rename the schooner, and he led the re-christening ceremony on the waterfront at Eastertide of her first year in service.

They were the only constants in the lives of Strapp's people scattered among those hundreds of miles of coastline: the Beadle and *The Hope*. Looked for and arriving each spring and fall, as if to remind the lost souls that their names were known and remembered beyond their toehold in creation's wilderness. Those coasting trips to Strapp's concerns were an anchor for the Beadle's convictions. To be a source of respite and sustenance, to be all those isolates knew of the church's consolations.

The Beadle frowned upon gossip among his crew, but the killing of Dallen Lambe and the drowning death of Seamus Fleet on St. Patrick's Day was endlessly raked through out of his hearing.

As was the Widow Caines and the deviant habit of dress she'd adopted since losing her husband. As was the merciless plague that ravaged the shore, taking three of their crew. Setting all the trials and signs together, the sailors felt they might be living through the end times spoken of in Revelations.

The only pillar of their days that had not shifted was the Beadle, their punctilious, sanctimonious prig of a master. They did not like the man and to judge by his manner the Beadle thought little of the people who worked under him and the Christian souls he served. But there was a comfort even in the cold attention he offered and they lived in awe of his North Star steadiness. They tied themselves to the mast of his certainty and sailed on, delivering their dry goods with the news of Elias Caines's passing and the other deaths in Mockbeggar, collecting stories of sickness and loss the length of the coast.

A father and son in one tiny outport. A husband and wife and their infant child in another, leaving behind an orphaned brother and sister, the boy not old enough to shave and the girl younger again. A planter's operation in Break Heart wiped out but for a single green hand who had been forced to spend his first winter in Newfoundland with only the dead for company. The youngster so roary-eyed and desperate when the ship appeared that he hurdled into the water and nearly drowned himself trying to swim out to *The Hope*.

The Beadle made a point of visiting each fresh grave to offer a reading from scripture and a prayer for the deceased before leaving the survivors to their work. Most had already made some sort of peace with their losses and settled into the new season. Even the orphaned siblings pledged to carry on with their parents' miserable enterprise, though it was foolhardy to think they could manage on their own and the Beadle tried in vain to talk sense to them.

The green hand was the only defector on the shore, refusing to leave the vessel even to show where the bodies of his companions were buried or to attend the rudimentary service for fear he'd be abandoned to that horror again. He had lived so long out of his skin that he couldn't even call up his own name. *The terrified one*, is how they referred to him. "Is the terrified one about?" "Has the terrified one eaten anything?" By the time they returned to Mockbeggar, they'd shortened the moniker to Terrified, which was how he was always known, even among those who learned his Christian appellation.

Dozens of people made their way down to the waterfront as *The Hope* made anchor in Mockbeggar, to greet the returning sailors and gather news of relatives and acquaintances in the outer reaches of Strapp's domain. The Beadle watched them lining the finger piers as the anchor was let go and dredged through the holding ground before bringing up solid in the mud. A boat was let down overside to row into shore and the sailors tried to coax the green hand from Break Heart to join them, calling up to him at the rail.

"This is as far as we can take you, Terrified," one man shouted. "You can't live the rest of your days aboard *The Hope*."

The Beadle felt a sudden, foreign hesitance rise up in him then, as if he was a mirror in which the youngster's fear lay reflected in all its naked unreason. A delusional sense that he was safer aboard the vessel, that affliction and strife was all that lay ashore. The Widow Caines ascendant and Abe Strapp like a millstone about his neck. As if God had ordained it so.

He tucked the heavy ledgers under one arm and spoke to the green hand. "You will go down to the boat, and I will follow after," he said.

The authority in his voice was enough to decide the youngster and he climbed overside, with the Beadle close behind. And once these last two settled in their places they rowed away from the ship toward the waiting crowd.

The Beadle sent a man to find Abe Strapp before making his way to the offices where he attended to correspondence. None of the letters that arrived in his absence had been touched and he took an hour to read through the stack of accounts and schedules and proposals, making notes in a ledger as required. There was a letter from the colony's governor that he didn't have the heart to open in the moment. He spent most of what remained of the forenoon writing to actuaries and merchants and clergymen in St. John's and Poole and London.

It was gone to suppertime and everyone else at the office had left for the day when Abe Strapp arrived with Matterface and Heater in tow. Clinch noted the bandolier across his chest, the mud on his buskins and breeches, his cuffs and sleeves halfway to the elbows caked with blood. His companions adorned the same and all three in high spirits.

"You've been hunting, Master Strapp."

"Just in off the barrens."

"How was your luck?"

"None of the dogs got shot," one of his lackeys broke in. "So we counts it a success."

"Oh kiss mine arse," Strapp said.

"Is that an order?" the other asked. "Or just a request?"

"I swear you'll both get a dowse on the chops if you don't give your red rags a holiday."

The Beadle watched in silence as the three men needled and jabbed and picked at one another with the idle buffoonery that passed for conversation between them. He had to remind himself each time which was Matterface and which Heater. Physically they were chalk and cheese—one raw-boned and lanky, one falling a little into flesh, one running to baldness, the other peering out from under a wild copse of hair. But they were so alike in manner and intention that they were virtually interchangeable.

He tried to dredge up what he saw in the two minders to think they could steer Abe Strapp clear of his worst inclinations. They were a year or two above Abe's age and had worked on the shore since they were boys. Both industrious and inexhaustible, both conscientious even as green youngsters. They were never known to shirk a duty and he'd taken that seriousness about their labours for a sign of serious character.

It was still unclear if he'd misread them or if keeping company with Abe Strapp brought some latent idiocy to the surface. But it galled him to watch them lunge and sidestep and parry now like bears trained to dance for an audience.

Abe Strapp was recounting the day's hunt, how the dogs drew upon deer slot out near the Sisters and they circled those hills to sink the wind and come upon the creature unaware. They hooded the dogs when they were in sight of it, a stag almost the size of the Jerseyman's horse, and Abe put a ball through the animal's neck.

Something had changed in Abe Strapp's manner since the Beadle was away. He seemed almost to have forgotten the grievances that coloured their every interaction since his father's death. There was a feckless air of release about him that made the man even more insufferable.

"We chased him a mile or more and had to slip the greyhounds before we could come up close enough to dispatch him."

"A banging fellow, he was," Heater said. Or Matterface said.

"Couldn't raise him off the ground before he was paunched and his head cut off near to the shoulders," the other added.

"The horns on him," Abe said. He spread his arms as wide as he could manage. "Fifty-six points."

It hardly seemed possible to the Beadle that he would be the only one in the room to see Dallen Lambe's blood on their sleeves as they japed and mocked one another.

Clinch had been standing beside Seamus Fleet's drowned corpse, waiting for Mary Oram to come lay the boy out, when he heard the gunshot and ran outside. Minutes later a woman's voice began wailing in the distance and he tracked that sound to the Big House. He kicked his way through the hunting dogs toward the parlour where the three men were kneeling next the fireplace, having carted the body up the path. In the light of the fire and the lamp he could see their hands and sleeves blackened with the dead man's gore. Imogen Purchase was holding her face in her hands and wailing like a nightmare revenant, which made it impossible to take in what he was seeing. The men looked like ghouls performing some satanic ritual.

"What has happened?" the Beadle asked.

All three turned to him, their faces wild.

He raised his voice to be heard over the girl's screaming. "Who is that man?"

"Dallen Lambe," one of Abe's minders said.

"Is he dead?"

"I think he's dead, sir," the same one answered.

"Imogen," the Beadle shouted. "*Imogen.*"

The girl quieted and peered out from behind her hands.

He made a gesture to try and calm her. "Please," he said. He took the pregnant girl by the arm and led her to the servants' room off the kitchen and sat her on the bed. He herded as many of the dogs as he could out the kitchen entrance before he returned to the hellish spectacle at the fireplace. "Who shot Mr. Lambe?"

"Twas Abe shot him," the balding one said.

"Shut your potato trap," the other said.

They could hear voices as people came up the path toward the house. Clinch pointed at the lanky man and told him to stand at the door. "No one comes inside," he said. He hauled the heavy drapes across the windows and knelt back beside the body, peering into the tortured face, the dead eyes.

"Lambe said it was you sent him here to look for Abe."

The Beadle glanced up. "I sent him?"

"To tell Mr. Strapp about the youngster was drownded."

He looked down at the face again, the top lip drawn up over the teeth in a rictus. After Seamus Fleet was well and truly dead, he'd said aloud that Mr. Strapp should be informed. It was Cornelius he was thinking of in that moment, out of decades-long habit. The words were hardly spoken when Abe flashed to his mind and he dismissed the idea. He hadn't noticed Dallen among the people present or that he'd left to deliver the news.

"Where did this happen?" he asked.

"He come upon us on his way down from the Big House."

The Beadle looked squarely at Abe Strapp. For the first time he took in the gash on his face, the eye blackened and nearly swollen shut. "Did Mr. Lambe strike you?"

Abe reached up to touch his cheek as if he'd forgotten falling face-first onto the skiff that afternoon. "So he did, struck me down with his fist," he said. "Isn't that so, Heater?"

The Beadle looked from one man to the other. "Mr. Lambe approached you on the path."

They nodded.

"It was gone to dark, so's we didn't know who it was. He asked if one of us was Mr. Strapp," Heater said.

"He swore he would see me dead," Abe said and he stabbed a finger towards the Beadle to underline the malice in those words. He was angry suddenly, as if experiencing afresh the gall of Dallen Lambe.

The Beadle said, "He attacked Mr. Strapp, without provocation. He struck Mr. Strapp in the face."

"It was Lambe that come at me first, yes," Abe said. "Saying I was to blame the Fleet youngster was drownded. He'd like to of killed me, isn't that so Heater?"

"Mr. Strapp was in fear for his life," the Beadle said and both men nodded. "And Mr. Strapp shot Mr. Lambe in self-defence."

"As God is my witness," Abe said.

The Beadle called to the man at the door. "Is that your recollection of these events?"

"Just so, Mr. Clinch," he said. "And I will swear an oath if it is asked for."

The Beadle turned to Heater. "Go tell Imogen to set water on to boil. And lots of it. We'll have Mary Oram lay out the body when she's done with Seamus Fleet. And I suppose someone," he said to the room, "should inform Mr. Lambe's wife and children."

The servant-bride had already bolted by then, sneaking out the kitchen entrance for her old bed at the Caines house. As far as the Beadle knew she hadn't set foot in the Big House since. He almost asked how things stood between husband and wife now, but thought better of it.

The three men were still discussing the stag's antlers, arguing about where in the Big House the head should be mounted. Each location Abe dismissed as too small or too dark or out of the way.

"The place is not fit for that rack," Matterface said.

"And so it isn't," Abe said. The Big House was the largest on the shore when it was erected forty years before and its name was purely descriptive at the time. But the Jerseyman's residence in Nonsuch was larger and the Caines house was palatial by comparison. "I was years telling Father the Big House was fit only for sheep."

The Beadle stood at the desk, wanting to intervene before that line of thinking drew any more wind. "Mr. Strapp," he said, "I was hoping to have a few minutes of your time with some business matters."

Abe turned suddenly and cocked his head like he was listening for a voice in another room and everyone went still, listening likewise. He ripped a foul, shuddering fart into that quiet, roaring with laughter as his companions fell back from the stench.

"Christ's ears," Matterface said. Or Heater said.

"Go wipe your arse and call that a shit," the other said.

In the days after Dallen Lambe was shot, a corner of the Beadle's heart considered it might change his godson. It seemed impossible to kill a fellow Christian and not be chastened. Or slowed by the weight. If anything, the opposite was true. Strapp told the story of being attacked by Lambe with such conviction that even Matterface and Heater seemed to believe it. He wore the scar on his face like a medal won on the battlefields of Europe. In his mind, he was an innocent victim in the matter and Dallen Lambe being dead didn't go far enough to satisfy his anger. He was often heard wishing Lambe alive so he might kill him all over again.

No one in Mockbeggar credited a word of Abe Strapp's story. But Matterface and Heater swore to the bald facts of it. The Beadle himself stated he'd spoken to Abe Strapp and his two men independently and their testimony did not conflict in any particular. Which forced everyone on the shore to make room for the fiction, to find a chair at their tables for that malignant imp, to carry it in their pockets as they went about their business.

The Beadle expected Abe Strapp would feel beholden to his headman for digging him out of that murdering hole. It was still a surprise to see that the opposite was true—he'd debased himself in the man's service and Abe lorded that fact over him, wordlessly, continuously.

Strapp was minutes caught up in his infantile fit of giggling. When he'd finally recovered himself he said, "I'm gut-foundered, Mr. Clinch. We could talk business over a venison steak if you wanted to join us."

The Beadle shook his head. "There's nothing here that can't wait for tomorrow's light," he said.

After the hunters left he opened the letter from the governor and turned it to the window. His Excellency, at the suggestion of and taking into consideration the good name of Mr. Clinch, was hereby appointing Mr. A. Strapp, owner and proprietor of C. Strapp & Son, as Justice of the Peace for Mockbeggar and Nonsuch and the coastline west and north of said harbours as far as the French Shore, which appointment is to commence immediately and until such a time as Mr. Strapp sees fit to resign the office. The Beadle was instructed to read a proclamation to that effect at holy services every Sunday for a month.

Clinch folded the letter and set it under the lead jigger he used as a paperweight. He looked out the window to where *The Hope* was sitting at anchor in the harbour. "For the good man is not at home," he said. "He is gone a long journey."

As he left the Strapp offices, the Beadle was approached by Dallen Lambe's boy. The Widow Caines had sent him, Solemn said, asking him to look in on Imogen Purchase.

"She is still residing at the Caines house?"

"She won't ever leave it she's saying."

"Is it the child coming?"

"No sir," the youngster said. "She've got her arm in a bad way. Mary Oram couldn't do nothing with it."

Clinch didn't ask about the circumstances of Imogen's injury. The image he had of Abe Strapp in his bloody hunting clothes was connected in some fashion, he knew. The way he'd stretched his arms to map the width of the dead stag's antlers. As if he was holding all the world in that span.

They passed the building being raised beside the Church of England.

"What is going up here?"

"That's the new Quaker meeting house."

"Is it, indeed?" the Beadle said.

The smell of the scarred arm's decay was general in the room where Imogen lay. Clinch turned back the bandages while the girl stared at the ceiling, sucking her teeth. Every inch seemed more noxious, more putrid. The forearm was swollen to the size of her thighs, the fingers were blackened. He stood back from the ferment of corruption.

"Is the baby active?" he said.

"Not so much lately," the girl said. "It was like a young seal one time, I could hardly sleep for it swimming about."

"How long has it been quiet?"

"Since I been able to keep food down."

He turned to Solemn. "Is the Widow Caines at home?"

"She's at work upstairs."

"Would you fetch her for me?"

The Beadle walked through the house to the parlour where he stood near the fireplace, beside the willow cage. The jays swept into the room behind him and offered up their sharp, unmusical calls from their perches as if warning him away.

It was a strange habit to have carried from her childhood, he thought. As a girl the Widow collected all manner of wild creatures, ladybugs and spanny-tickles and frogs and baby birds, keeping them in jars or in dippers filled with water or in boxes lined with grass. When she was eleven, a servant shot a deer behind the outbuildings on Strapp's property. There was a weeks-old calf that refused to leave its dam lying dead on the ground. The Widow had the fawn placed in a crib built for goats where she fed it by hand until the animal was tame enough it followed her around and slept on her bedroom floor like a dog.

But she didn't name her animals or mourn their deaths with childish funerals. She fed the dead frogs and birds to the hunting dogs. Her connection to the menagerie was proprietary, a dominion she curated out of indifferent curiosity. She spent hours drawing the limbs and heads and wings of the animals from various angles. There was no denying the aptitude of those sketches but there was something unsettling about her appetite for dissection. A beak, an ear, the claws, the webbed feet. As if there was some truth that could be discerned only by taking a creature apart and examining one element at a time. As if the sum would prove greater than the whole in the end.

She had an unnatural desire for learning as well, taking up reading and writing at an early age. She was seven years old when her mother died giving birth to Abe Strapp and her whole life turned to books and study, as if there was consolation for losing a mother in them. She attended the school on her father's property each day and went from there to the mercantile offices where she occupied herself by copying the hand and signatures of Cornelius Strapp and the Beadle and the mercantile officers she found in company correspondence. It seemed a harmless pastime, like sketching or cross-stitch or knitting, and her talent for that ventriloquism amazed everyone who witnessed it.

Over time she became more interested in the numbers in the company ledgers. To avoid her relentless interrogations, Cornelius had a junior accountant teach her credit and receivables, payables, margins, loans and interest. Her understanding outstripped her tutor's in short order and at fourteen she set to work at the business in earnest. She never completely abandoned her habit of sketching and she dedicated part of each day to drawing in a leather-bound book. But the business of numbers and their relations became her main preoccupation.

Everyone but the Quakers looked upon the girl's mercantile education as an abuse. Even the elder Strapp suspected he was doing his daughter a disservice.

"I expect she will never find a suitable husband," Cornelius admitted to the Beadle.

Clinch pursed his lips. He was of the same mind but had never happened on the chance to say so. "She could be a fine house-wife, as long as she's kept in some awe," he said. "She will need a husband who can govern the greatness of her spirit."

"I wish the poor man luck," Cornelius said, "whoever he may be."

"It might serve her," the Beadle said, "to be put in charge of her brother's welfare, rather than spending her days among the ways of the world."

"You've given this some thought, Mr. Clinch."

The Beadle had never reconciled himself to the girl's presence in her father's place of business. She arrived each day with the tame deer in her wake like a royal ascending a throne in a great hall, taking a seat among the men she looked upon as serfs and vassals with the dumb beast attending. That absurd pairing seemed designed deliberately to mock the world as it was ordered and ordained and Clinch finally insisted the animal be left outside, the two arguing the matter with a fierceness that suggested it was the girl herself he wished to ban. Which they both knew to be the truth of the matter.

Even though Cornelius took the headman's side in the dispute over the deer, the girl's imperious tendency of thought grew in her like a malignancy. Her impulses were all contrary to a woman's character and given the opportunity Clinch couldn't resist suggesting a radical corrective. "Your son is long past the age to begin his education," he told the elder Strapp. "His sister would be a fine tutor. And it might spark a maternal interest more becoming in the girl."

"From your lips," Cornelius said, "to God's ears."

Her brother was raised by servants instructed to indulge his every whim. He was wet-nursed by a young mother and insisted on taking the teat until he was four years old when the woman finally refused to carry on. For months afterward he grabbed at the servants' breasts, trying to haul down their aprons and blouses to suckle, sending the house up with a tantrum when they fended him off.

He'd never taken much to table manners or even to wearing stockings or trousers. He had been sent to school with other children his age but he would not sit still for two minutes at a time and chased the girls around the schoolhouse, holding his bald cock like a pistol and squealing as he tried to piss on their skirts and shoes. Even though her salary was paid by Cornelius Strapp, the teacher refused to hold classes with Abe in attendance and eventually he was kept home.

He had no interest in any bookish undertaking or instruction. The only discipline he respected were his sister's sketches, which he looked upon as a kind of magic that he demanded to be taught. The infantile and cockeyed figures he could manage infuriated the boy. He despised his sister for holding the talent to herself, as if she'd stolen something that rightfully belonged to him, and he defaced her sketches with charcoal scrawls or burnt them in the fireplace. She retaliated by holding him by the ear and driving the alphabet into his head as if she was hammering nails through a board.

They each saw in the other the antithesis and obstacle of all they valued and wanted from the world. Each day was a contest of wills that descended into physical confrontations, the sister holding the upper hand at first by dint of her size, despite Abe's fondness for kicking, for using his nails and teeth. He would pinch her tender breasts between a thumb and forefinger and hold on for dear life as she beat him across the head and shoulders.

She went to her father repeatedly, asking to be returned to her old life. But he insisted, almost sorrowfully, that it was her duty to be a helpmeet to her brother. Even then, she recognized the Beadle's words in her father's mouth.

Clinch argued it was in the best interest of both children to stay the course. It would teach the daughter humility, he said. And his godson might learn something of use in the struggle. On both fronts, he was disappointed. At the end of the arrangement, Abe could do little more than sign his name with a pen. What he knew of numbers and maths he learned elsewhere, playing at cards and dice. And his sister's masculine arrogance showed no sign of abating despite her circumstances aligning more closely with a woman's nature and due.

By the time Abe was eleven, he largely absented himself from her lessons. He was introduced to firing the flintlock and pistols and he wandered the backcountry in search of something to maim or kill. The deer his sister had raised from a fawn was full-grown by then and Abe shot it dead one winter morning in response to some pedagogic humiliation. The balance of power between the siblings had reversed and Abe left his tutor with bruises on her arms and legs and breasts, with blackened eyes.

Cornelius Strapp called a halt to the arrangement to avoid permanent injury to one or the other of his children. The Widow returned to the firm's offices where she proceeded to make herself indispensable, working through accounts with a speed and prudence that seemed second nature, offering opinions whose reason and soundness couldn't be denied. She seemed preternaturally sensible to the mercantile possibilities of every circumstance, to every individual's economic use, like a spider at the centre of a web, attuned to the quiver of each silver ring. It seemed to the Beadle almost an infernal talent.

She worked there six days a week until her brother's sixteenth birthday, when her father legally changed the firm's name to C. Strapp & Son Co. Ltd. New signs were placed over the offices and the warehouses on the waterfront. She never entered the doors of those buildings again, but for the day she was invited to attend the reading of her father's will in which the daughter was left nothing, a significant dowry having already been paid out to her husband.

Shortly after she left her father's business, the Widow abandoned the Church of England to attend Quaker meetings. People saw it as one more sign of her obstinate nature and, later, as a calculated move to bring herself within the orbit of Elias Caines. The Beadle couldn't dismiss either notion, but he knew her antipathy toward him was a factor. Refusing even to look upon his face during Sunday services, to listen to the word of scripture from his mouth.

He heard her on the stairs and turned away from the jays as she came into the room. They hadn't been in each other's company since the Widow orchestrated Abe Strapp's marriage to Imogen Purchase. She was still brazenly adorned in the green jacket and waistcoat, as if she had the heart and stomach of a man. She took her place on the chesterfield without offering him a seat.

"You are raising a hall for your congregation," he said.

"It was my husband's wish."

"Was it also his wish to place it beside the Church of England?"

"He did not specify a location. It seemed as likely as any other place in the harbour." She offered her evasive half-smile.

"Is Mr. Strapp aware of his wife's condition?" he asked.

"He has divided his house with his wife, Mr. Clinch. He has all the inside and she has all the outside."

He nodded. "You must have foreseen this marriage would come to no good."

"I was well able to see what a marriage between my brother and Anna Morels would come to. Of the two options, I felt this one was preferable."

"You have sacrificed the life of an innocent girl to your own ends."

"You were perfectly willing to sacrifice the Jerseyman's daughter to yours."

"Mrs. Caines," he said, as evenly as he could manage. "I have only ever wanted what was best for your father's business."

"What was best for my father's business," she countered, "was me."

Every meeting with the woman confirmed the Beadle's earliest suspicions. The sulphurous pride and ambition he'd seen in her as a child she paraded now like an animal on a leash. For all his godson's mulish bluster, his pigheadedness, Abe Strapp could be shifted left or right with the proper leverage, with the application of enough force. But the Widow was quicksilver and inscrutable, impossible to pin down or herd. He sometimes felt it was the Adversary he heard speaking through her, the Dark One's cunning and subtlety. Even these few moments in her presence was bracing, a rebuke to his misgivings, the temptation to doubt his own convictions.

He said, "I'm very much afraid Mrs. Strapp's child is no longer quick."

The Widow nodded. "Mary Oram suspects as much."

"She will have to lose the arm," he said. "The sooner it is dealt with, the better."

"We'd best waste no more time in conversation," the Widow said.

Imogen Purchase was laid out on the kitchen table, the dome of her pregnant belly like the cover of a massive serving tray. It was nearing the solstice, but the day was quickly fading and lamps from several rooms were lit and placed about the crude operating theatre. The arm's infection had reached the elbow and the amputation was to be made several inches above the joint, a tourniquet reefed tight about the bicep. Solemn stoked the fire high and the Beadle set an iron poker to heat among the coals.

Aubrey Picco and his wife were summoned to assist and along with Solemn they pinned the girl's limbs to the table when the operation began. Solemn holding her shoulders and her forehead, his eyes closed to avoid watching the saw as it bucked and jammed in the bone. Imogen screaming into his ear, the sound muffled by the leather bridle between her teeth. They were all dripping with sweat from the heat of the fire and the exertion of keeping the girl's arms and legs tethered. Her eyes rolling into the back of her head when the poker was applied to the raw stump.

"God have mercy," Relief Picco whispered.

They all stood back from the girl, stunned by the violence and intimacy of the procedure. The amputated arm lying a little removed from its host on the table. It had the air of a hopelessly ruined shoe, inanimate, divorced from its utility. The Beadle placed the desolate thing on a length of rag and wrapped it tight. He looked into Imogen's face, the breath through her nostrils laboured and unsteady. He reached to remove the leather between her teeth but couldn't budge it. And the girl's water broke as he tried to wrestle it from her clenched jaw, the rush of liquid dripping onto the floor.

"It appears we have induced her labour," the Beadle said.

"God have mercy," Relief Picco said again.

Clinch turned to Aubrey. "You'd best make a report to Mrs. Caines. Solemn, go and fetch Mary Oram." He raised the package in his hand. "Mrs. Picco, if you would stay with the girl, I will dispense with this."

A DELIVERY.

THE BOWELS OF COMPASSION.

It was pitch dark by the time Mary Oram stepped into the Widow's kitchen, the light of the lamps casting shadows over shadows that made the room feel crowded and close. Relief stood from the chair where she'd been holding Imogen's hand on the far side of the table.

The fire had burned back but the heat inside was stifling and Mary Oram had Solemn stand the door to the servants' entrance open for a breeze. She approached the table, the floor under her feet slick with blood and the girl's water. Imogen turned her head, her eyes wide as if she was surprised to see Mary Oram. Or any living thing. She shook her head and started to bawl helplessly around the leather in her mouth. The strange woman leaned in close to the girl, placing a hand on her tortured face.

"You've had a hard go of it," she whispered.

She reached to ease the soaking leather from between her teeth. She asked Relief Picco to bring water and to help prop the brutalized child up enough to drink. Imogen buckled into a contraction before she finished and they held her until it passed. Mary Oram wiped down her face and neck and washed her sweat-soaked hair with hot water. She took up her leather bag and began laying out her utensils, knives, needles and thread, a handful of crude-looking iron instruments that to Solemn's eye seemed designed to harm or mutilate a body. Mary Oram caught sight of the youngster who she'd forgotten was in the room, his eyes wide with fright, and she ordered him outside till he was needed.

"Now," she said, "let's see what we got in store for ourselves here." She passed a lamp to Relief Picco and they stood at the end of the table between the girl's legs, Mary Oram probing with the fingers of one hand, the other pushing against the belly to guess at the baby's position beneath her palm. She sighed heavily. "What have Abe Strapp got done to you," she said.

Imogen's head and shoulders lifted a foot off the table as another contraction took her over.

"Breathe now," Relief said. "Breathe through it."

The girl shook her head savagely, as if she was refusing the advice. "It's not his," she said through her teeth.

"Not whose?"

"Abe Strapp," Imogen said. "It's not his." She was lying flat again, sucking air through her nostrils.

The two women stood still a moment.

"You said Mr. Strapp was the father," Relief said.

"It wouldn't true. God help me, it wouldn't."

"Did you ever lay down with Mr. Strapp?"

She shook her head. "It was the Widow's notion to say so. She said he was too drunk betimes to deny it. And it would see the youngster looked after."

The two women looked at each other again. Relief went to the back porch to close the door and then stood at the girl's side. "Imogen," she said. "Who is this child's father?"

"Dallen," she said. "Dallen Lambe."

"God have mercy," Relief whispered. "You're certain?"

"I never lay with no one other."

"You told the Widow this?"

"She made me confess to it," the girl said. "And she had Dallen make his mark on a paper said it was Mr. Strapp. The Widow swore it would settle everything out."

"Why would you do such a thing?"

"Dallen begged me," she said. "To keep it hid from Mrs. Lambe." She was sobbing again, a ragged breathless weeping that made her body clench and shake.

Mary Oram hushed her and leaned over her face. "There's no sense throwing snot about now," she said and she insisted the girl follow the rhythm of her own breath to loosen the knot of her lungs, her belly.

Once Imogen Purchase found a little release and eased back into the wood beneath her, she said, "You can't tell a soul, Mary Oram." She seemed not to know Relief was present, though she'd answered her questions seconds before. "For the love of all that's good," she said.

"I got no one listens to me anyway, child," the midwife said.

The delivery lasted hours longer. The baby was dead and lay wedged sideways in the womb, so fixed in its place Mary Oram couldn't shift it though she leaned all her weight into the effort and had Relief Picco working in the opposite direction. The trauma of the amputation made Imogen oblivious to most everything that was happening which Mary Oram considered an awful sort of blessing. To save the girl's life, she took the child from its mother's womb one limb at a time, her fingers looping a length of fishing twine around the legs at the hip by feel and then working the line to sever the pulpy joint.

The midwife cajoled the girl during each contraction, calling on her to push while working with her hands to maneuver what remained of the baby inside her. When the torso and head finally rushed clear, the decaying skin sloughed off in Mary Oram's hands. She wrapped the dead thing and its disparate parts in linen and set it inside a bassinet of alder branches Imogen had fashioned for her baby. She massaged the girl's belly to release the afterbirth while Relief set about washing Imogen clean and when the placenta passed, Mary Oram laid it on the fire.

She went out through the back porch where Solemn Lambe was asleep on the steps. She called the boy inside and together with Relief Picco they moved Imogen to her bed. They settled her under the covers with the stump of her arm propped on a rolled blanket and they left her there, somewhere between the worlds of the living and the dead.

Mary Oram urged Relief home, telling her there was nothing more to be done for the girl. But the kitchen was as foul as a slaughterhouse and Relief refused to leave until it was scoured. They hadn't said a word to one another about Imogen's confession and they each avoided the other's eye as Relief went about douting the lamps, the glass chimneys blackened with soot.

Solemn was watching the two women from the door of Imogen's room. "What's happened to the baby?" he asked.

The Widow Caines appeared in the hallway entrance, dressed for the day. She said, "The baby is dead, I expect."

"That isn't so?" Solemn said.

"What have you done with it?" the Widow asked.

Mary Oram tipped her head toward the bassinet where it stood against a wall. "Solemn," she said. "That water barrel will have to be filled if this room is going to be put to rights."

The boy nodded uncertainly and went off toward the brook with his buckets and iron hoop. The Widow Caines walked over to the alder cradle and crouched to fold back the linen. She stared at the livid creature curled there—patches of skin crimped away from the flesh, the tiny hands tucked under the chin. The legs placed beside it like utensils in a drawer.

"What happened here?"

"It wouldn't coming out of that girl in one piece."

"Was it the injury to Imogen's arm did this?"

Mary Oram said, "That child has been dead a long time. The skin let go wherever I touched it."

Relief Picco stood with her back to the room as she polished the glass shades of the lamps, ignoring the Widow's inspection of the tiny corpse, her disinterested interrogation.

"It doesn't look natural," the Widow said.

Mary Oram was washing her utensils in the last of the hot water. "I been a rabbit catcher long enough to see the queerest kind of phys come through that gate," she said. "Birthed a child in Mistaken Cove had a tail was six inches long. Didn't it have little bones same as a dog's tail and these stiff hairs down the length.

I crimped it off with a splitting knife and burnt it in the fire before anyone saw it, for fear they'd tie a rock to the youngster and drown him in the harbour. He's still fishing up there now. Nothing to show for it but a little scar above his arse."

The Widow Caines stood from the bassinet and watched the midwife skeptically.

"Your mother never told you about your tongue, I expect."

"No," the Widow said warily. "My tongue?"

"You couldn't latch on to the breast when you was born. Everyone expected you might starve to death before I thought to root around in that maw of yours. The underside of your tongue was warped tight to the floor all the way to the gums so's you couldn't lift it to suckle. I had to slit the bob-stay free like I was cutting the sound bone from a cod fish."

The Widow straightened her waistcoat with both hands, tugging at the hem. She was moving her tongue involuntarily, imagining that predicament, thinking of Mary Oram's nailless finger probing about in her mouth.

"You would never have managed to speak a word if I hadn't been at you with that knife."

"Well, as I have full use of my tongue, I suppose I should thank you."

Mary Oram made a face as she wiped her hands in her skirt. "I wonders on times," she said, "if I hadn't better left well enough alone back then."

The two women watched each other, both so still they might have been a single figure reflected in a mirror. Until the sound of Solemn Lambe coming into the back porch with the water buckets broke through, like a bell being rung. Relief walked between them on her way to the door and again bringing a bucket to the fireplace to pour water into the iron pot, swinging it on its crane over the flames. Solemn came in to reclaim the empty bucket and was brought up short by the strain in the room, a feeling like a ship holding sail and lying on its beam ends in a gale. All three women turned to stare at him.

"I just," he said. He pointed. "I was after the bucket."

Relief handed it across the kitchen and he clattered away for another spell of water at the brook.

For seven days Imogen remained in a mending way, suffering with the pain in her stump and the after-effects of Mary Oram's ministrations, but seeming every day slightly better. The Beadle came to examine the site of the amputation and pronounced himself satisfied with the progress.

Solemn Lambe had given up on the notion of taking a full share in the boat, throwing in permanently as the Widow's house-man, planting and tending her farm gardens, cutting and hauling firewood, keeping the two cows and the chickens, the goats and sheep. And between his round of chores he waited on Imogen in her sickbed, sitting a few minutes with her each evening before leaving for the day. The girl propped on pillows, the lank sleeve of her blouse pinned to her shoulder.

Almost nothing was said during those visits. The whiskey jacks sailed in and out of the silence, landing on the bed or the dresser or Solemn's outstretched hand before bustling back through the kitchen toward the parlour, waiting to be settled away in their cage. And Solemn's memory of holding Imogen to the table while she screamed and the handsaw grated through bone flitted in and out of the room like the jays. Imogen never spoke of her dead child or her missing arm and he hoped the girl's grasp of that time was somehow hazier than his and beyond recovery.

The door to the back porch opened while he sat there and Mary Oram came into the room for her daily examination. Solemn had still not made peace with the woman's preternatural presence, with her childish figure and ageless face. With her fingers which he could plainly see were without nails, or her endless trawling through decades of treating the sick and dying on the shore, describing injuries and diseases by turns grotesque and alarming and implausible. She seemed every moment about to announce something a person would be happier not knowing. It was only Imogen's own discomfort around the midwife that kept him there and they suffered through her visits together.

Mary Oram's departure was his cue to leave as well and in the moments before he got to his feet Imogen looked intently at him, as if she felt he couldn't see her and she was free to take him in without guarding her own expression. He endured those bald inspections in silence for days, until his curiosity got the better of him.

"What is it?" he asked.

She said, "I'm sorry about your father, Solemn."

It seemed an odd thing to offer condolences weeks after she'd offered them the first time. "I knows that," he said.

She turned her face away from him, looking angry almost. As if he'd missed the point altogether.

The next morning, Solemn found Imogen Purchase suffering through a fit of ague. Mary Oram was sent for and as her condition continued to worsen the Beadle was sent for as well. He bled her of ten ounces of blood and still there was no improvement.

The girl suffered periodic seizures and a high temperature and complained of severe pain in the missing limb, crying out at times as if the amputation was still in progress.

The extravagant fever endured a week, increasing in its severity each day so that she was rarely conscious and rarely in her right mind when she was. The last time she spoke with any coherence was during a visit from the Beadle when she looked up from her bed and asked if her child was entered yet into his ledger.

"Your child?"

"Yes," she said. "Is his name in your book?"

Clinch didn't know for certain if the dead infant was even a boy. He said, "Your child was stillborn. It has no name."

She shook her head. "I give him one." She lifted a hand as if she was about to write it in the air, though she could neither read nor write. "Dallen," she said. "That's the boy's name."

"Dallen," the Beadle repeated.

Imogen stared at him, her face flushed with the exalted fever that was about to kill her. "Please, Mr. Clinch," she said.

He nodded then, to offer at least that little peace before she died.

Her funeral was held in the Quaker meeting house. The Widow claimed it was at Imogen's request, but the Beadle saw it as her way of preventing him having the last word on the girl's life. Forcing him and Abe Strapp to sit dumbly among the circle of mourners in that bare room where they had no particular standing, listening to the unlettered and the ignorant claim to speak in the spirit.

The service lasted an hour, most of that time in a prayerful silence. Near the end, Aubrey Picco stood from his seat and turned to look at every face in the circle, as if seeking permission to speak from each. Relief sat in the chair beside him, staring at her hands in her lap.

"The loss of Imogen Strapp," Aubrey said, "reflects upon us all. It asks us to examine the ways we may have abused her, or misled her, or used her to our own purposes, rather than seeking to lead her in God's light."

He turned to Abe Strapp, who was present and relatively sober at the Beadle's insistence, and then he turned to the Widow Caines, waiting each time until they returned his gaze.

"Her death asks us to look in the mirror and see ourselves anew. Strife," he said, "begets strife. In the death of this innocent, God implores us to lay aside wrath and malice and revenge and to put on the bowels of compassion one toward another. Otherwise we are lost."

"Amen," Relief Picco whispered.

Solemn walked the Widow back to the Caines house after the burial. He'd almost refused to enter the hall when he saw Abe Strapp present in the room and it was only the Widow nodding him ahead that convinced him inside.

"Your brother as good as killed Imogen," he said to her as they crossed the harbour. "The same as he killed my father."

"I couldn't argue that conclusion."

He started crying silently. "I got no right to sit among the Friends," he said.

"Why would you think that, Solemn?"

"What Aubrey said. About malice and wrath and such."

She watched him as they walked, taking in the struggle playing out on his face. "You would not be human if you didn't wish my brother ill," the Widow said.

He turned toward her, her features a starry blur through the tears.

"Nor would I," she said.

The Beadle went straight from the cemetery to the firm's offices. Before closing up at the end of day, he opened a leather-bound book where he made note of Imogen's name and the date of her death. And thinking on the girl's final request of him, he added her stillborn baby to the ledger.

Dallen Purchase, he wrote. *Bastard child of Imogen Purchase.*

To anyone with eyes, Abe Stapp's appointment as Justice of the Peace was encouragement to corruption, a licence to defraud and intimidate and steal without repercussion. But the first months of Strapp's tenure were marked by a surprising level of restraint, as if it was enough to have the imprimatur of the Crown attached to his name. His first official act was to name his lackeys Matterface and Heater as constables and the trio spent their days swanning about the harbour, people said, like their shit didn't stink.

There had never been a formal jail in Mockbeggar. There had never been much need for one. Occasionally a servant was accused of stealing a pair of stockings or refusing to work, or a man on a bender threatened to kill his wife or his master, and they were barred in a stable or a fishing room until they sobered up or until the matter was resolved with a beating or some other reparation. But Abe identified the absence of a prison as a mark against the town. Any settlement that could support more than one tavern, he said, must be in need of a jailhouse.

After the fishing season clewed up half a dozen men were recruited to construct a lockup near Looking Glass Pond, a bare structure of unpainted spruce boards with wooden bunks nailed along three walls and a single tiny window with iron bars. It sat mostly empty for months then. The building's sparseness and the expectant silence that occupied the room earned it the nickname "Quaker Hall."

The Beadle had tried to dissuade Abe Strapp from the clown-ish project. But seeing the man would not be brought to his bearings, he'd suggested a licensing fee for the alehouses and grog shops in Mockbeggar and Nonsuch as a way to cover the expense. Licensing those lawless establishments had long been advocated by the Beadle and there was a general feeling on the shore that Clinch would be a moderating influence on Strapp's worst instincts. There were a handful of resolute doomsayers, but most were content to let the matter be as the winter settled in.

When *The Fortune* made anchor in Mockbeggar the following spring, Abe Strapp seemed to lose interest in his judicial position altogether. The brigantine was a new American vessel taken by the British Navy the previous summer and purchased for C. Strapp & Son at auction in Poole. It carried enough curing salt to distribute to fishermen the length of the shore. But it was the ship's non-mercantile cargo that took all of the magistrate's attention.

Putting up the jailhouse in the fall had rekindled his desire to build a home worthy of his position and authority on the shore. He still hadn't found a proper place to mount his prize deer rack and he vowed to put that right, ordering the necessary lumber and materials for a residence that would be the largest and most expensive on the island outside Harbour Grace or St. John's.

The Beadle objected to the undertaking. Raising the house Abe envisioned would take a large crew the better part of the season. Meanwhile the plantation in Break Heart sat idle and every other outfit on the shore was in need of more hands.

"Well, get more bloody hands," Abe had insisted. "You are the headman of this operation. The operation requires bodies. I trust you will figure it out."

He was as willfully short-sighted as the Beadle feared, averse to counsel and immune to common sense. Talking to the man was like arguing with the tides.

"There is one thing I could suggest," he said.

"Don't suggest. Just find me the men I need."

"I insist on telling you," the Beadle said, "that your father refused to consider this option."

"My father is dead," Abe Strapp said.

Abe went down to the waterfront as soon as *The Fortune* made fast to the warehouse pier to oversee the handling of his materials. Half the men in Mockbeggar were engaged in off-loading the rafter timbers and cedar shakes, the pine planks and window panes and chimney bricks, the massive purple flagstones for the hearths in the kitchen and dining room. The other half of the town's residents were on the waterfront to watch the endless extravagance as it was winched from the ship's hold and transported to Cornelius Strapp's property where it was stored in the schoolhouse that had been sitting unused since the elder Strapp's death, or stacked under tarpaulins against the dirty spring weather.

The Beadle supervised the transfer of curing salt taken on in Lisbon to the warehouses, and then went in search of the brig's captain. Moses Cheater led the way to a low windowless structure near the stern that stank of offal and penned animals. The door was barred on the outside and the captain removed the bolt to swing it wide, the rank hum of the enclosure spilling into the open air.

A flurry of chickens scattered through the door, followed by half a dozen sheep complaining their way onto the deck. Then a vaguely human figure crawled into the day's light. Then two more on their hands and knees, and behind them a fourth. They stood with the slow arthritic movements of ancients, their eyes watering against the bright as if they were just cured of a lifetime's blindness. Two of them were without shoes and they were all outfitted in what amounted to patches and rags. Their faces and clothes were filthy. They looked to Clinch like root vegetables just pulled from the earth.

"Names," Moses Cheater said and they rhymed off in order, Lynch and Trapnell and Webb and Price. Lynch was the tallest and oldest of the four. The last three were mere boys and Price the youngest of them. They were all convicts at Newgate Penitentiary, under sentence of transportation to Australia for seven years before they were offered a commutation in exchange for three years indentured servitude with C. Strapp & Son.

"I asked for ten men," the Beadle said.

"There were ten when we started out. Four jumped ship when we stopped for supplies in Waterford. Two died on the crossing."

Lynch said, "We should all've bought a brush and loped in Bogland. Weeks we been in bad bread here, banged up in a panney with the bleating cheats and cacklers and black cattle when we could have binged avast in a darkmans."

The Beadle turned to the captain.

"They can speak the King's English if you mind to beat it out of them. But they prefer the gibberish lingo of thieves and gypsies."

"And which are they?"

"Thieves all. House-breaking and stealing goods from lighters on the Thames." He pointed to Lynch. "Sly Boots there was an ark ruffian, plundering passengers on boats along the river, stripping them of their clothes and throwing the poor unfortunates overboard."

"I was only ever bummed for a pickpocket," the youngster Price said. He was pale and bran-faced, the freckles thick on his ears and cheeks and his arms and hands. "And I never did more than stand stag upon the safe while the coves was cheving the froes."

"Shut your bloody bone box, Madge," the oldest convict said. He gestured angrily. "You never got lettered just for standing stag."

Young Price slipped his arm behind his back but not before the Beadle saw the brand. All four had a T burnt into the flesh between the thumb and forefinger of their right hands to mark them for their vocation.

"They made the crossing in that stable?"

"Not the entire voyage. But they more than once threatened the lives of my sailors which is why they were confined with the livestock. The little one there—" he gestured toward the talkative bran-faced boy who looked no more than eleven or twelve— "he seems halfways civilized on his own. But the rest are so thoroughly abandoned in their principles I don't doubt they will be hanged if they live to return to England. I will not miss their company."

Lynch nodded toward the captain. "We'll be happy enough to see the back of yon addle plot ourselves," he said.

Cheater smiled and shook his head. "You will have to lay cane upon Abel to make them heel, Mr. Clinch. You may find that someday you are obliged to shoot them in your own defence."

The loss of six of the new servants made Abe Strapp's project a taxing drain on the company's labour pool, but he set about the work with the ark ruffians and his constables and with men the Beadle felt would be the smallest loss to the fishery—green youngsters and malingerers, the addled rescue from Break Heart everyone knew as Terrified, Inez Barter who was the oldest man on the shore and crippled up with arthritis and gout.

Abe had set his sights on a piece of property in a swale of scrub and bog half a mile beyond the Big House. All the proper trees were long ago cut for firewood but their roots still lay in the ground and the swampy areas had to be drained before any outbuildings could be raised. Half of Abe's men were engaged at clearing the root beds and a crew of six set to digging drains in the bog. Eight men were in the woods beyond Looking Glass Pond to cut trees for incidental lumber. *The Fortune* was meant to be sailing for Leghorn to take on a load of lamp oil but Abe commandeered the brig's carpenter and cooper and half a dozen of its sailors to slit the imported planks and mill the local trees and to frame out the windows.

The work crawled along. The blackflies and mosquitoes were so maddening and relentless that Abe was forced to provide a cask of porter to offer some relief. And he hovered and whined and needled about the project and its workers with the same exasperating persistence as the insects, becoming all the time more frantic and unreasonable. Things progressed so slowly and with such a lurching gait that he took it to be a deliberate plot to make a mockery of his ambitions. He cursed all hands as pug carpenters and purblind shankers, brow-beating even the handful of people who knew their trade. No one was happy to see him coming. A month into the shambling project he was too disheartened to show his face on site.

The convicts were the only men deliberately hanging an arse at their work. They sat about in a clutch as if they were above the menial work at hand, speaking to one another in their pedlar's French. Matterface and Heater were assigned to oversee the thieves and, in their fashion, they took on the delinquent habits of their charges, laying about and taking over-advantage of the mosquito porter. They began parroting the lingo they could decipher, referring to the daytime as *lightmans* and the night as *darkmans*, to money as *rag* or *rhino*. They helped dig a pass bank where they were meant to be excavating drainage ditches and spent hours of the day throwing dice. They wagered drams of beer at first, then rum liquor and salt beef and cheese and other peck, then items of clothing.

The convicts had no collateral to ante but Lynch put up the bran-faced youngster, taking bets for use of the boy's muns or his fundament. "You'd have to take off Madge's ears to make his mouth bigger," Lynch said with a wink. "But you'll want some pig grease to roger his feak."

If it was a new arrangement, the youngster offered no protest. His child's face set like someone about to be whipped to unconsciousness at the cart's tail. Both Matterface and Heater took the boy in turns behind a block of granite at the edge of the bog to collect their winnings. And by the end of a week the thieves were all shod and well-fed and rigged out in half-decent gear.

Moses Cheater came to the Beadle with reports about the drunkenness and indolence and gaming among the convicts and their minders.

"According to my crewmen," Cheater told him, "the constables are being altogether too familiar with that crowd."

"I see," Clinch said.

"Especially with the spackle-faced youngster. The one they call Madge."

The Beadle watched Cheater's face a moment. "I see," he said again.

Clinch visited his employer at the Big House the next morning, the dogs mad at the door and he kicked his way inside. He called up the stairs to Strapp still in his bed and he waited near the fireplace where Dallen Lambe had lain dead. Abe came down the stairs half-dressed and pig-eyed with a hangover. He herded the dogs into the servants' room beside the kitchen and closed the door.

"To what do I owe the pleasure," he asked sourly.

The Beadle gave him an account of his visit with the master of *The Fortune* and the talk of gambling and carousing.

"That is quite the cracking crew you have saddled me with," Strapp said.

"There is concern," the Beadle said, "that Matterface and Heater have been engaging in congress with one of the convicts."

"Congress?"

"With the Price youngster, Master Strapp."

"That's the one they calls Madge," he said and the Beadle nodded.

Abe rubbed at his face. He hadn't shaved in days and the rasp of whisker against his palms struck the Beadle as the laboured sound of the man thinking. The dogs were barking at the door down the hall and Abe shouted at them to quiet.

Clinch stared at the shallow-pate before him. Left to his own devices, he expected the man would squander everything bequeathed by his father and it would all find its way into the Widow's hands. The Beadle bowed his head to hide the loathing he felt. He said, "I would be more than happy to see to the situation, Master Strapp."

"What do you suggest?"

"I will anoint them with the oil of gladness."

"I doubt we have any of that balm to hand."

The Beadle glanced up. "A sturdy length of rope will suffice."

The look of anticipation on Clinch's face was so dour and earnest that Abe Strapp was keen to witness it being satisfied. "Rope we have," he said.

They walked to the worksite where the ark ruffians were sleeping off their morning drink at the edge of the field, lying in an untidy weave against the day's chill like a litter of puppies. The Beadle set about beating them across the shoulders and ribs and legs, raining all his frustration and disgust upon them, the rope knotted at the end to add a feral edge to the scourge. He executed the reprimand in such a savage and masterly fashion they all four wound up on their knees with their arms over their heads, begging him to leave off.

Clinch turned to Matterface and Heater who had been sleeping beside the convicts and observed the lashing in a horrified silence, half expecting they would be next. He handed the convincer to the one with the hair. "If they slack a minute of the day," he said, "you will use this rope to set them straight. Or I will use the rope on yourself and your companion."

"Yessir."

He crouched before the two men. "But for this rope," he said quietly, "you will not so much as touch them. Not with your hands. Nor any other appendage of your physiognomy."

Matterface and Heater looked for a moment as if they might offer some protest or contradiction of what the Beadle's prohibition insinuated. But they thought better of it. "Yessir," they said in unison.

Abe Strapp had to bite his lip as he watched the thrashing to stop himself whispering Amen at every stripe. He was revitalized by the ecclesiastical display, as if he'd been cleansed in the waters of the Jordan. He felt almost as if he'd taken the rope to the convicts himself and the men under him felt much the same. There was a noticeable change in the pace of work, a focused seriousness among everyone on the site regardless if they'd received a beating or not. Ditches were dug and lined with beach stones, the last of the lumber was milled and a dozen wagonloads of shale were hauled in from the Nonsuch side of Tinkershare Head and laid as a foundation before the middle of July.

Abe afterward insisted the Beadle make a regular tour of the worksite in his company, to remind his servants of the battle-axe at his bidding. All his life he had resented the scornful, ascetic man's claim on him as godfather and namesake, seeing him as an adversary to be mocked and obstructed. He was shocked to have that formidable instrument aligned with his own design and desire. He walked the Beadle about the property like a dog on a leash, watching the workers side-eye and cower as they passed. It made the condescending prick of a man almost bearable.

~

The ark ruffians were digging the last drain at the north end of the property when they brought up solid on a face of milled wood four feet down in the peat. They carried on clearing the length as Matterface went off to find Abe Strapp. By the time the two men returned all the workers on site were gathered around the trench. Two of the convicts stood at either end of a casket's lid in the black earth.

There was a debate underway about the lumber's origin, if it was oak or ash or teak. The carpenter and the cooper dismissed every suggestion, though they were uncertain what it might be otherwise. The wood was stained by the peat but pristine, the planks solid and untouched by rot.

"Should we bring it up?" Lynch asked Abe Strapp.

"How do you plan to do that?"

Lynch shrugged. "We was resurrection men a few years in London town."

Strapp turned to look at those standing closest. "Does anyone know what he's saying?"

"They was grave robbers, sir," Madge said.

"God blind me. Is that true, Lynch?"

"The anatomists in London paid rum rhino for bodies to slice open," he said.

"They did what?"

"It was a study they made of their insides, sir. Digging out their lights and livers and arse-ropes and such to make maps of them. They was always short of volunteers to sit for a portrait."

Abe had never heard of such a thing. "Hell and the devil," he said.

"It did no great harm to the morts," Lynch offered, "so far as I could tell."

Abe Strapp looked down at the thief who was shading his eyes as he tipped his head to the light. His filthy hair silver-laced with lice. A black T marking the flesh of his hand.

"You had a run at every manner of badness, I imagine."

"Many's the time I let my anchor go to the windward of the law. But the mooring never seemed to hold."

"Perhaps this time, then."

"Please God," Lynch said, without conviction.

Strapp motioned with his hand. "Bring it up," he said.

By the time they'd dug out the sides and shimmied lengths of ship rope beneath the head and foot of the coffin, half the people in Mockbeggar had arrived and crowded about, like a misshapen wheel around a seized axle. More gawkers were arriving every minute, including the Beadle who pushed his way through the crowd as the eternity box was raised from the bog.

The Fortune's carpenter bent over the casket, brushing the peat away from seams and joints and discussing details with the cooper. "That's hemlock wood for my money," he announced finally. He tugged at a corner and the lid started away from the frame where the nails had mouldered to rust. He said, "That's been in the ground since Noah was a boy."

"Let's have a look," Abe Strapp said.

The Beadle spoke up to say it was a desecration to have disinterred the coffin and it would be sacrilege to open it to satisfy the lurid curiosity of the gathering.

Abe said, "We don't even know if the unfortunate before us is a Christian soul, Mr. Clinch. And it will do no harm to take a peek." He glanced at Lynch. "We idn't going to slice the poor creature open to measure his guts or the like."

"The body will have to be properly reburied," the Beadle insisted.

"I'm not about to settle my arse in a cemetery. You're welcome to add it to the congregation in the churchyard if you like."

He nodded to Lynch who yanked the lid free to allow sunlight to shine upon the dead man's face—skin drawn so tight to the skull and cheekbones it seemed polished, the sparse hairs of his beard and eyebrows still in place. He was dressed in a doublet with white cuffs halfway to the elbows and an extravagant white ruff about the neck, which several in the crowd claimed was the ancient costume of the Puritans or the Pilgrims. There was a long discussion of the difference between the two sects while Inez Barter was called for and brought up close to the coffin.

No one knew the rights of Inez Barter's age. Inez himself could only say he was as old as his tongue and a little older than his teeth. He'd lived on the shore since the Seven Years War and had acquaintances among the Red Indians who knew his name and left him gifts of deer meat and carved bone relics in the days before the last odds and ends of that race were hounded into the country. He was considered an authority on any question out of general memory and the old man was asked if he recognized the corpse's duds or recalled talk of the grave in his early days in the harbour. But he only shook his head, looking on the deceased with the solemn cast of a man gazing upon his own near fate.

Someone pointed out the skeletal hands were folded over a black leather-bound book. "That's the Bible, I'm guessing," Abe Strapp said and he moved to take it up when Inez Barter laid a hand to his arm.

"That's not for us to be touching, Master Strapp," he said.

Abe shook himself away from the servant's grip.

"Nothing is to be touched," the Beadle said. "This man is a Christian. He will be buried in the churchyard in the condition he was found."

Abe was staring at Inez Barter, though the old man wouldn't meet his eye. He said, "You are the soul driver on the shore, Mr. Clinch. Buried he will be."

The wheel of spectators made a slow, untidy revolution around the open coffin then as everyone pushed in for their turn to see the corpse and to speculate on his origins and the mystery of how he came to be buried there. The Beadle had the cover set upon the casket when the day's light began to fail and he ordered Matterface and Heater to keep the corpse company through the night.

The next morning, Bride Lambe came into the kitchen of the Caines house and announced the Widow was not in her bed.

"She's awake already?" Solemn asked.

"She's not there, I means."

"You idn't serious."

"She didn't say a word when I knocked," Bride said. "So I poked my head in. She's not there, Solemn."

Solemn's sister was taken on as maid and cook after Imogen Purchase was buried. She was eleven years old, as able and industrious as any woman who served in the house since the Widow arrived as a newlywed. She didn't move into the servants' room, preferring to stay at home with her mother who spent her days sitting before the cold fireplace or in bed, speaking only when spoken to and eating only what was set before her.

Bride was wary of sleeping under the same roof as the Widow besides, uncertain what to make of the family's employer who was silent and severe and seemed neither fish nor fowl in the girl's eyes. But for Bride's hatred of Abe Strapp chiming with the Widow's feelings for the man, she doubted she would have stepped foot in the door. She rose early enough each morning to walk to the Caines house and boil the kettle before the Widow woke, bringing a tray of tea to the office and then knocking at the bedroom door. She and Solemn ate their own breakfast in the kitchen before the woman appeared in her husband's wide-brimmed hat, the youngsters standing as she offered instructions on the day's chores.

Her absence was so unlikely and disconcerting that Solemn and Bride watched each other in silence a few moments.

"She must be up there, Bride."

"I looked for her, so help me. Could she be gone to the out-house?"

"Not all this time," he said.

They heard the front door then and a wash of lamplight moved along the hallway toward the kitchen. The Widow stopped still when she saw them there.

"We missed you gone," Solemn said.

She douted her lamp and stood it on the table.

"Your tea is on the desk upstairs."

"Thank you, Bride," she said and she ran through their day's chores and asked that all the rugs be brought outside and beaten of dust. Solemn was to go to the mercantile offices at eight to tell Aubrey she would be taking the morning at home. They both nodded and the Widow walked down the hall and up to her office where she pushed the door closed.

~

The first hint of the morning was at the window but it was still too dark inside to read or sketch and she sat waiting for the light. Her heart racing, the pulse knocking in her temples. One hand clenched at her chest.

The casket's guards were asleep when she came upon them on Abe Strapp's property. They'd emptied a bottle to deal with the nip and damp of standing stag in the open air and in her lamp's flickering shoal of light they looked like bodies of the drowned on the sea floor, mouths wide and their limbs adrift.

She'd turned to the coffin, setting the glim at her feet to push the lid clear, letting it tip to the ground on the far side. At first glance the interior was so dark it seemed empty and bottomless and a chill of recognition passed through her. It was a tremor that was almost pleasurable and she let it travel to the ends of her fingers and toes, to the roots of her hair, before she raised the light from the ground to take a view of the corpse.

The deep shadows in the sunken eyes and cheeks, the sparse, spidery hairs of the beard, made the face seem a crude likeness made to mock a living person. The wide white ruff at the neck added to that impression, as if the head was separate from the rest of the sham figure, placed atop a straw effigy meant to be burnt over a bonfire. It wasn't until she saw the bony hands that she was convinced it was a real person lying there. The knuckles protruding under the gaunt. The dull nails at the ends of the fingers. The black leather book the hands folded over was invisible against the dark cloth of the doublet but the spark of a gold ring caught her eye in the glaze and shadow of her lamp.

She brought the light in closer and could see the ring was engraved. She reached to touch it, turning it slowly on its flesh-less spindle until she had centred the skull stamped into the gold.

A winged death's head. Her breath caught in her throat at the menacing beauty of it. It was something like desire she felt, that heavy mantle settling like a force outside herself, anointing her whether she willed it or not. A kind of greed that she mistook for love. She set to working the gold band up over the wasted finger.

"Sister," Abe Strapp called behind her.

She whirled away from the casket, lifting the lamp high.

"Give you a fright," he said.

"You're awake early, Brother."

"The dogs were on the high ropes when you walked past the Big House."

"I didn't think that was enough to stir a sleeper such as yourself."

"I'm surprised the racket didn't wake our friend in the coffin there," he said. "I saw your light and thought I should see who was making a visit at this hour."

"You didn't trust your constables to look out to a dead man's welfare?"

"What are you doing here, Mrs. Caines?"

"The same as everyone else in Mockbeggar," she said. "But I was hoping to skip the carnival of it all."

Abe Strapp stepped up to the casket. "You looked to have your peepers on he's book."

"What book?"

Abe laughed. "Playing the innocent has never suited you, Sister."

She leaned in beside her brother. The black leather of the Bible barely visible still though she managed to spy out its contours against the doublet.

Abe looked askance at the Widow. "You thought to sketch the man's visage, I imagine."

She shrugged, her mouth puckering against a sickly feeling in her gut to see that Abe Strapp knew her better than she thought him capable. She said, "How long has he been buried there, do you think?"

"Time out of mind, I'd guess."

They stared at the dead man, both thinking all the time of the blood standing at their shoulder. Feeling cursed to be bound to the other's muck, that hobble chafing at their flesh.

"The only thing you'll take from the dead man here is his likeness, Sister."

"And that I have already," she said with her infuriating smirk.

She headed down the path to their father's house and past it toward the harbour. Abe Strapp watching his sister go as far as he could see her, her shadowy raft of light rolling and dipping in the dark as if she was travelling on the ocean's swell.

In her office she sat circling a thumb around the band of gold she'd spirited away from the gravesite in her palm. Trying to decipher the letters engraved there by feel alone as she waited for the sun. She poured tea and filled and lit her pipe. Thinking on the face of the corpse, its uncanny, inhuman expression, and the terrible hands folded over the Bible like creatures from a nightmare. Macerated by time and still at the outset of that endless pilgrimage into the dark.

When it was light enough she brought the ring to the window and held it to the glass. Taking in the skull framed by its wings and then turning the band slowly to read the inscription as it came into view a letter at a time. *Death Conquers All.* She closed her fist around it a moment, then opened the hand to be surprised again by its elegance, its simple uncompromising message. Beauty and truth. The awful loveliness of the thing made her heart lift, as if the eyeless creature in her chest was framed by wings of its own.

She went to her desk, unlocking the drawer where her sketching ledger sat next the magistrate's official seal that she'd spirited from the Strapp offices after the reading of her father's will, while her brother was cursing and turning over chairs and everyone in the room was preoccupied with removing Abe from the premises. She lifted the ledger to the desk and spent half the morning drawing versions of the death's head, shading the wings and the skull's dark sockets in different degrees, bringing subtle variations to each rendition.

There was a knock at the door and Bride looked in to ask if she wanted anything more from the kitchen.

She gestured at the tray on the desk. "I'll have more tea," she said. "And a roll if you've any ready."

Bride reached for the tray and paused, seeing the open ledger and its iterations of the flying skull, the lightless slots of the eyes. The Widow reached to close the book and held her hand on the cover until the girl left the room. Minutes later Bride was back with the tray, setting it on the desk. Her face bright red, as if she'd recently walked in on her mistress naked.

"Thank you, Bride," the Widow said. Feeling a queer embarrassment herself to see the morning's sketches through the girl's eyes. All of them seeming suddenly childish and inept. She'd been working up to trying a likeness of those strange folded hands in the hickory casket. Wanting to snare the truth they contained and set it on a roost in her ledger, to tame it for her own. She'd put off the attempt all morning, afraid any version she managed would fall short of the fact of them.

It had always seemed a cruel joke to her, not to be able to capture the whole contained within a thing. She drew creatures in fragments as a girl, making sketches that were incomplete by design. For a time it made her feel the lack was a deliberate choice and not a congenital deficiency. She fell into the world of numbers and finance largely as an escape from that shortcoming. Profit and loss, payables, receivables, debt and interest. They simplified things in a way she found calming.

She placed the ledger back in the drawer with the government seal and she placed the pilgrim's ring beside them. Then she locked the drawer with the key she carried on her necklace of keys.

All the world and his wife attended the interment of the ancient Pilgrim at the Church of England cemetery. There wouldn't have been a larger gallery, people said, if a public hanging preceded the burial.

The Fortune's carpenter nailed the coffin lid shut with new nails and everyone who walked as far as Abe Strapp's property was given a shot of rum to send the Pilgrim on his way. Three different sets of pallbearers spelled off on the procession down through Mockbeggar to share the surprising heft of the casket, the crowd in the churchyard parting before the dead man's caravan as if some royal sovereign was riding upon their neighbours' shoulders. The day was clear and oddly windless and the entire ceremony proceeded in a solemn quiet. Everyone felt this second burial was more final than the first, a confirmation that made the Beadle's promise of the kingdom to come seem little more than a conceit to ease the deadweight of living.

"The departed shall be in everlasting remembrance," he said, though the nameless man before them spoke against his testimony.

The coffin was let down on ropes beside the resting place of Imogen Purchase and the congregation waited till it was covered and the earth tamped down with the gravediggers' shovels before they wandered off. Most of the fishermen walked from the churchyard to their twine sheds on the water where they talked quietly about the Pilgrim's peculiar garb and what became of his people to bury the man at the far edge of the world as if he belonged to nothing and no one. Fearing the same fate for themselves above all others. The women who returned to their houses and dirt-floored tilts to see to the needs of their youngsters felt themselves adrift in the same mauzy fog. Though they never spoke the questions aloud or even let them take on flesh in their minds.

HER VISITORS. THE DEVIL'S SWORD.
ENCHANTED CHRISTIANS.

The summer maundered on through spells of rain and drizzle and fog, through occasional hailstorms and choleric gales of wind that threatened to swamp the fishing boats or kept them off the water altogether, the hellish weather interspersed with large, cloudless days and a brassy heat that briefly made the coast seem a tropical outpost in the North Atlantic. On big fish days the crews were up putting away the catch past midnight, every stage in the harbour aglow with slut lamps and torches.

Acres of drying flakes occupied the real estate around the mercantile properties and every day that didn't promise a downpour saw the green fish laid out to cure, dozens of servants setting the waterhorse that had been stacked to drain overnight onto the wooden platforms, placing the salted cod in rows tight as city cobblestones.

At the end of September month, men who had been on the water all summer were recruited to Abe Strapp's property in a push to finish his new residence before winter set in, earning a few shillings' credit for setting the flagstones and bricking the three flues of the massive kitchen fireplace, framing in the upstairs windows, shingling the roof with cedar. The building like a great ship stripped of masts and rails in a storm being busily mended by a crew spidering across the rooftops and walls.

The summer's volatile weather and the season's shift toward fall made little difference to the servants and their mistress at the Caines house. Six mornings a week the Widow left for the firm's office before her pocket watch marked eight. The property was left to the youngsters the better part of the day and they wandered tame about the house much as the whiskey jacks did. The hush in the rooms made the siblings quiet with each other, never speaking louder than needed. Solemn milked the cows and fed the chickens, he dug the potatoes and carrots and turnip and filled the wood boxes and the water barrel. Bride went back and forth between the Caines house and their own tilt, helping harvest the gardens and washing the linens and scrubbing the wood floors, bringing food down to place in her mother's lap.

Even when the Widow was at home they rarely laid eyes on the woman, marking her presence mostly by the smell of pipe smoke. She spent her time in the upstairs office, taking her supper at the desk where she entered numbers in an account book or wrote to merchants and actuaries abroad or sketched in the leather-bound ledger she kept locked away in a drawer. Bride put the kitchen to rights in the evenings while her brother settled the cows and sheep and hens and that summer's pig. He whistled the jays to roost and went upstairs to report to the Widow on the day's happenings before he and his sister went home to their mother's silence.

The riddle fence that surrounded the property seemed to separate the place from the rules and rhythms that governed the world beyond it. No one but the Widow's headman ever darkened the door and that so rarely it seemed an edict had been proclaimed to stay clear unless called upon. They were so accustomed to the house's privacy and calm that when a knock came on the front door that fall neither youngster seemed entirely sure how to respond.

"Who is it out there?" Bride asked.

"I don't know," Solemn said.

They heard the knock a second time.

"What do they want, Brother?"

The Widow called from upstairs, telling Bride to answer the door. And even so, the girl seemed uncertain.

"Go on then," Solemn said.

It was the headman's wife. "Hello, Bride," Relief Picco said.

Bride nodded, still holding the doorknob.

"Ask her in," the Widow said from the top of the stairs.

It was a cold early October evening. Solemn offered to lay a fire in the parlour but the Widow brought Relief into the kitchen instead. She sent the Lambe youngsters home once the jays were caged and she set about making tea, gesturing Relief to a seat at the table where Imogen Purchase had lost both her arm and her baby.

Relief sat thinking of the girl's confession about the father of her child, of Mary Oram cutting the Widow's tongue loose. It seemed impossible the Widow didn't relish the thought of serving her tea on the boards Relief had scrubbed clean of the poor girl's blood and afterbirth and shit. As a kind of punishment for knowing those stories. For a moment she regretted not accepting Aubrey's offer to come with her.

The Widow placed the cups and the teapot and the bowl of sugar on the table. "To what," she said, "do I owe the pleasure?"

Relief Dowse was fifteen when she arrived in Mockbeggar to teach in the one-room schoolhouse. The Widow was eleven at the time and nearly the teacher's equal in reading and writing and arithmetic. For the first time in her life, Relief was away from her home and the strangely adult girl took her under wing. She was already tending the fire when Relief arrived at the school each morning. She stayed after classes to take on extra reading or sums or simply to talk. They sat together during services at the Church of England. They held hands and walked the paths with the tame deer following at their heels.

They went as far as Looking Glass Pond on calm evenings and weekends, the water reflecting the surrounding hills and grassy beaches and the sky above in perfect detail. The girl using a stick to draw waves or hillsides or intricate patterns of her own design in the sand as they sat talking. She was self-possessed and pre-ternaturally confident. She seemed never to be surprised by the world, never at a loss. Relief felt a peculiar sense of stillness and safety in her company, as if the motherless child was her guardian. There were moments they held each other's gaze and the young teacher saw herself twinned in the girl's eyes. Her best, most con-tented self reflected there, as calm and contained as the image of the world on the pond's glassy surface.

Relief said, "We haven't had a teacher at the school since your father passed, as you know. Aubrey has secured a girl from Harbour Grace to take it up and we hoped she would start this fall. But Abe," she said. "Your brother. He won't free up the old school for the purpose. Aubrey and me. We thought the Friends' Hall would serve in its place."

"That seems sensible."

"The bigger problem," Relief said and she turned her cup in its saucer, a quarter at a time, bringing it full circle. "Your brother tells us he will not be paying the teacher's salary as your father had done."

"Can the Church of England not cover the cost?"

"I brought it up with the Beadle," she said. "They already supply the slates and chalk and provide the firewood. And they are raising funds for a church bell besides."

"To redress the presence of our Meeting Hall, I expect."

"That would be an uncharitable interpretation."

"Uncharitable does not mean incorrect. What about the Friends?"

"You know yourself. We are a small congregation. And most of the local Friends are servants of little means."

"Of course," the Widow said. "I wonder if you might prevail upon the Jerseyman to contribute?"

"He is not keen to fund a teacher here when Nonsuch lacks a school."

"You've already spoken to him about this?"

"Well," Relief said. "I."

"You went as far as Nonsuch to speak to the Jerseyman about paying a teacher's salary in Mockbeggar? So I am the very last person you thought to approach on this matter."

Relief understood how the girl might be hurt when Aubrey Picco began his awkward, earnest courtship. How first the engagement and then the marriage curtailed their time together and altered their connection. Even the church Relief attended changed. But the girl's vehemence shocked her, the unalloyed poison of it. She was at the schoolhouse with the fire lit before Relief arrived still, but she wouldn't acknowledge her. As if the teacher was a phantom in the room, as if the school rightly belonged to the student. She sat with her back to Relief during lessons and went about her own reading and writing and sketching.

Aubrey Picco couldn't see how such a passive affront sabotaged his wife so completely and she was helpless to explain it. It was completely irrational. Or impossible to render in rational terms. For months she barely slept. When she realized she was pregnant, Relief resigned her position. It was impractical to carry on in the circumstances, she said. But she was afraid to remain in the girl's company was the truth of the matter. As if the malice was airborne and too long an exposure to the vapour might harm the unborn child.

They barely laid eyes on one another in the years that followed, before the Widow unexpectedly began attending Quaker meetings. Aubrey Picco was so innocent of a woman's interior life he expected they might rekindle their friendship. He didn't see a match was being made between Elias Caines and Cornelius Strapp's estranged daughter until Relief pointed it out to him. She watched the woman turn the same face to Elias she'd once offered her teacher. Elias leaning over that pool to take in his own exalted reflection.

"I have wasted your time," Relief said to the Widow. "I'm sorry to have troubled you."

"Not at all. This is no trouble. You know what real trouble looks like, Relief. You have seen it in this kitchen. On this very table."

"It was an awful night."

"The longer I live, the more it seems to me that having children is the end of a woman's life."

"Imogen was unlucky."

"My mother likewise. But even where a woman is lucky, there is a death of sorts. A sacrifice of the mother's life to the child's."

"I have never regretted the choices I've made."

"That would number you among the few," the Widow said. "But you are not dead yet."

Relief forced herself to smile again. Appalled ever to have fallen for the veneer of the woman.

The Widow brushed her hands lightly over the table's surface. "I've often wondered what sorts of things Imogen Purchase spouted in the throes of it here that night. She must have been out of her mind altogether, I imagine."

"Imogen was remarkably coherent, all things considered."

The Widow nodded. "I understand a husband and wife will share things," she said. "Things that are not spoken of in more public circumstances. No one could condemn such intimacies."

Relief stood to leave and the Widow stood as well, raising a hand to hold her. She said, "In memory of Imogen and her child, I would be happy to pay the teacher's salary. In perpetuity. But I would ask my role be kept a confidence between us. And Friend Aubrey, of course."

The two women stared at one another. It was a mistake, Relief thought, to hope the woman might be capable of an untainted human exchange. It had gone to dusk in the kitchen and she could see only the featureless outline of herself in the Widow's eyes. And what seemed bottomless wells of darkness beneath.

~

There was a second, even more unlikely visitor to the Caines house that fall.

On a wet Sunday afternoon in mid-October, Mr. Morels led his horse through the back gates of the Caines property and stabled it out of the rain with the cows and the pig and the goats. He went to the servants' entrance and knocked. He waited a goodly length of time and knocked again and finally the Widow Caines appeared in the porch.

"I'm sorry," she said. "The servants are home on Sunday afternoons."

"Yes," he said. He was wearing an outfit of the oiled cloth fishermen used against the elements but was soaked through regardless. He held his arms out from his sides. "I am very wet," he said.

"Of course," the Widow said and she backed away from the door to allow him into the porch. "Come in to the fire."

The Jerseyman shucked out of his sopping gear and pulled a chair up close to the fireplace in the kitchen.

"Can I get you some tea?" the Widow asked.

"If you don't mind." Morels rummaged in a leather pouch he'd carried in with him and brought out a bottle. "I expected I would need to supply my own. I hope you are not offended."

"You are free to live your life as you see fit, Mr. Morels."

The whiskey jacks flew into the room to investigate the new arrival as she brought a glass and took a seat beside him. The Jerseyman watched the birds flick about the room as he dripped onto the floor and drank off several fingers of rum.

"I apologize for imposing," he said.

They'd seen little of each other since the day of his daughter's near marriage to Abe Strapp and she was struck by the change in the man. He was barely forty and had always carried himself like a youngster, the same ease and vigour about him as there was about his horse, an animal's inbred grace. He had aged, she thought, and then corrected herself. He'd faded. His face and hair had thinned. He was collapsing in on himself like a house abandoned to the elements.

"I wanted to know," he said, "if you would be interested in purchasing my horse?"

She laughed at the notion, thinking the man was already drunk. "What will you do for riding in the spring if I buy your horse?"

"I am not coming back in the spring, Mrs. Caines. Or the summer or fall."

She watched him closely. "You didn't strike me as a quitter, Mr. Morels."

"I was not a drinker once upon a time," he said. "But circumstances change. People change. My horse is for sale." He shifted his chair to face her directly. "As is the firm in Nonsuch. And my properties and interests on the shore."

"We've been through a rough stretch, I know. But even with the crews shorthanded we've all managed to remain solvent."

"You have done more than remain solvent as I understand it, Mrs. Caines. I hear talk of expansion to harbours on the Northern Peninsula?"

"There is always talk."

He smiled at her. "Modesty does not suit you," he said. "Not even your father would have made as much of these circumstances."

"You are nowhere near folding, Mr. Morels."

He shrugged. "I have lost the stomach for the fight. I'm leaving for good, that much is decided. The question that remains is what will become of my interests. Needless to say, I do not relish the thought of all I own falling into the hands of your brother."

"You seemed perfectly happy with the notion a short time ago."

He made a face, as if he'd touched his tongue to a canker sore in his mouth. "Circumstances change, as I said."

The Widow got up from her chair and took down a second glass. "May I?"

"Live your life as you see fit." He lifted the bottle from the floor. "If you are planning to expand, would it not make sense to take over existing operations rather than starting from nothing?"

"There is a difference between adding two or three modest plantations and doubling in size overnight. Five years from now, I would be in a position to consider it."

"Opportunity does not follow a calendar."

"Don't condescend to me, Mr. Morels," the Widow said.

He raised his hands above his shoulders. "You are right to be wary," he said. "It will be a risky undertaking. But if you do not buy me out, the Beadle will ensure that Abe Strapp does. And it will be a matter of time before Caines Mercantile is taken over by C. Strapp & Son. Which is why you raised your objections to our merger at the church two years ago."

The Widow sat with the notion a moment. There was no arguing the math. She sipped at the rum and then sipped again, trying to sort the possibilities from the danger in the man sitting beside her.

"May I speak freely," the Jerseyman asked.

She lifted her glass.

"This," he said and he gestured toward her. "What is the purpose of this uniform you insist on wearing?"

"Does it offend you?"

He tilted his head left and right, as if physically weighing that question in his head. "I am not offended," he decided.

"You are confused."

"Clearly."

"Uncertain?"

"Yes."

"Uneasy?"

"Somewhat."

"Vexed?"

He nodded and smiled to admit her point. He said, "Could you not make me feel these things just as well in more customary dress?"

"Would the uncertainty not lie in a different sphere altogether if I were wearing a fucksail? If I may speak freely."

The Jerseyman's head ticked back several inches. "I am not familiar with this word," he said. "Fucksail."

"I may have coined it just now."

"The devil's sword is our keenest blade," he said. He raised his glass and they both drank.

"Would you consider a merger, Mr. Morels? And maintaining a share as a sleeping partner?"

He laughed and shook his head. "I'm sorry," he said. "These terms. Merger, sleeping partner. I apologize, I am a little drunk." He refilled her glass, still laughing to himself. "I would prefer," he said, "to sell outright and be shot of Newfoundland altogether."

"This is because of your daughter," she said.

"This place," Morels said softly. He shook his head. "This place has nearly killed me." He drank off the rest of his rum and refilled his glass. The jays who had been foraging about the kitchen floor started up and arrowed down the hall, the Jerseyman watching after them.

"It is a sin against nature to have them cooped up here," he said.

"We all live in one cage or another," the Widow said.

He looked her up and down. "You seem free to do as you please."

She raised the glass to her mouth, holding his eye all the while. "We had an Irish servant in the house when I was a girl. This was before my mother died. The servant can't have been older than ten herself. If she was upset or frustrated by something she would whisper 'Piss and corruption' under her breath." The Widow smiled at him. "I admired her for that transgression, small as it was. I took up the phrase myself, just for badness."

"How old were you?"

"Four? Five? The girl was discharged for her malign influence on me."

The Jerseyman laughed. "That seems a harsh punishment."

"After my mother died, I spent much of my time in my father's premises on the waterfront. And I used to sneak into the warehouses to listen to the men. Without them knowing I was there, you understand."

"I can imagine what you heard."

"Rank filth," the Widow said. "There was no place in my life I could conceive of speaking as those men spoke, no person I could imagine speaking to in such a manner." She shook her head in amazement. "They had nothing to their names, those servants. And I envied them." She said, "All my life I was like a bird in a cage, with objects I desired on every side but could not touch or obtain. It made me want to kill something. Or someone."

The Jerseyman watched her, trying to judge the sincerity of that claim. "Now you are free to touch what you wish," he said, "I hope you have been cured of that urge."

"I am hardly free, Mr. Morels. But I am somewhat less encumbered when I reach for things."

"Perhaps this is a chance to have more of what you want, Mrs. Caines. With luck you might even make a play for C. Strapp & Son."

"You are a patronizing knight of the blade," she said dismissively. But the thought of swallowing the firm gifted to Abe Strapp passed through her so visibly the Jerseyman couldn't mistake it.

"A better route to that result will never come your way," he said. "And you know it."

She nodded and looked up at the ceiling, considering. "Aubrey will be against a buyout," she said. "But he can be convinced. Myles Taverner will threaten to resign his position to protest such a reckless proposition. Which is not a mark against the undertaking."

They spent most of an hour running through Morel's holdings and properties then, his ships and servants and buildings, arguing their relative values against the firm's outstanding debts and receivables. There was nothing argumentative in the back and forth, just a quiet probing and countering on both sides that was collegial and candid and oddly intimate. It was obvious to the Jerseyman the Widow knew as much about his holdings as he did.

"I feel as if you have seen me naked," he said wryly. He raised his glass. "Repeatedly."

She presented a detailed breakdown of international politics then, running through the myriad ways the alignments and disputes among kingdoms and countries the world over might affect the price of salt and provisions in Portugal and Ireland in the coming years, the interest likely to be charged on borrowed money, the markets for Newfoundland cod in Spain and Greece and the West Indies.

Morels refilled her drink. "I have always admired your head for business, Mrs. Caines. You've made more of the firm than your husband managed, in less than ideal conditions. Every operation on the shore would be under your thumb had you been born with a plug tail rather than a woman's commodity."

"My *commodity* has been a regret to me as well," the Widow said and she smiled back at him. "But it needn't be so in every circumstance."

The Jerseyman straightened up in his chair, not quite able to credit the implication. She was surprised herself in the moment, to feel the rum's mercurial heat pooling at her centre.

She said, "Where is your horse, Mr. Morels?"

"It is stabled with the other animals."

The Widow stood from her chair and leaned over the Jerseyman, reaching for what she wanted. Feeling his yard rise against her palm as she cupped it. "I am prepared to make an offer," she said, "to purchase your horse."

She straightened and went to the door of the kitchen where she looked back at the man. "Once you sail for the continent, you will never lay eyes on me again. It would be a shame to pass up such an opportunity."

She paused then, watching the man drunkenly consider the proposition. She said, "Do we have an agreement in principle, Mr. Morels?"

He rubbed his hands along his thighs and stared into the fire. "This place," he whispered before getting unsteadily to his feet.

That summer's season, like the season that followed the pandemic, had been marked by abundance and prodigal catches the length of the shore. Even Inez Barter couldn't recall seeing fish in such numbers. And in all the months after Imogen Purchase was laid to rest, the only burial recorded was the interment of the anonymous Pilgrim in the Church of England cemetery. Not a single death was reported on the coast from disease or injury or drowning, from fire or starvation or the warping deprivations of age. As if to redress the grim run of mortality they'd been forced to endure, as if some balance was returning to God's creation.

There was an exuberant air of relief about the outports and plantations on the shore and the Christmas festivities in Mockbeggar resumed the tradition of dismal anarchy they were known for. Late on Christmas Eve, the members of each household stood at their doorways with a rifle or pistol, firing powder shots at midnight to mark the day of the Lord's birth. Even in the poorest houses a dram of rum was shared out to each inhabitant to toast the day's advent and the harbour rang with a choir of voices offering three cheers like the crew of a British man o' war sailing broadside of a French vessel. They retired out of the cold into their houses then and proceeded to get roaring drunk on spruce beer and swish and calibogus, spending the long hours of the night in singing and quarrelling and blind punch-ups.

The celebrations went on into Christmas morning and continued through the length of the day. Pisswigs too young for drinking wandered the paths, stopping at every house for biscuits or syrup or figs. Those children and the handful of Quakers were the only people on the shore not altogether corrupted with liquor and lewdness and minor depravities.

Cornelius Strapp always marked the day by presiding over a feast for employees and servants who had no family of their own in Mockbeggar. Abe surprised everyone by reviving the tradition that Christmas, to make a show of his new residence. Strapp Manor, he christened it, the name carved into a wooden plank fastened above the main entrance. He'd lived without servants in the Big House after Imogen Purchase abandoned him, but he hired three local women to cook and wash and keep the new house in trim.

He treated the bachelors to rum and brandy and a gin called Strip-Me-Naked, to veal pie and rice pudding and roasted beaver haunches. The celebrations in the massive dining room were overseen by the branching antlers of the stag's head that the room had been built to accommodate. "Sixty-five points," Abe declared when he pointed out the rack above them and the guests raised their bumpers and toasted it with three cheers as if it was Christmas Eve all over again.

He attended his guests with animation and good humour that a stranger might have mistaken for a general kindliness of spirit. He checked around the table to be sure everyone's drink was full and to ask if they were ready for another helping. Old Inez Barter had as much as licked his plate clean but for his cut of roast and Strapp made a point of asking about the oversight.

"You have a stomach too delicate for the beast, Inez?"

"I seen him eat the head cheese of a bear," Matterface offered. "We should all have a stomach as delicate."

No one but Strapp and the Beadle remembered the old man's subtle reproach, placing a hand on Abe's arm to stop him touching the dead Pilgrim and his materials. But Abe and every other soul in Mockbeggar knew Inez Barter's feelings on beavers and beaver flesh.

"If it isn't your stomach," he said, "why are you refusing my food?"

The old man shook his head. He said he had never trapped or shot or eaten beaver as it was his belief those mortal creatures who stood upright on their hind quarters and held their dexterous front paws before them as if in prayer were in fact enchanted Christians.

Strapp threw his head back laughing and even Inez Barter smiled at his plate with the two or three teeth left in his head. But most others at the table were wishing he'd leave the old toast in peace.

"You won't eat them," Abe said, trying to catch his breath, "because they are men like you and me?"

Inez nodded. "Such is my belief, Master Strapp."

"You think," he said, suddenly serious and pushing his plate away to lean over the table. "You think I am serving the flesh of Christians to my guests, Inez. On the day of the Lord's birth."

The quiet room went quieter still, Inez Barter still smiling stupidly at his plate.

"You think every manjack at my table is a barbarian cannibal, is that your claim here today?"

The Beadle spoke a few words in the servant's defence then, but Abe raised a hand to stop him. Inez began making his excuses to leave, standing from his seat.

"You bring your arse to anchor, Mr. Barter," Abe said.

When the old man sat down Strapp moved to claim the chair beside him. He took up the fork and knife and carved the beaver into bite-sized portions. He proffered a forkful to the old man.

"So help me God," he said, "you will eat the meat before you. Or I will cut off your ears and serve those to you instead."

The guests watched in mortified silence then as Inez gummed and swallowed his plate of roasted beaver, weeping over every appalling morsel. When the meat was gone, Abe Strapp put his arm across Inez's shoulders. He patted the traumatized ancient's stomach with his free hand. "Your man," he said, "hath gone to a better place."

He poured his glass full and topped up every glass within his reach and had the table cheer Inez and his appetite and then cheer him again. "Enchanted Christians," he shouted with his drink raised high and the revel which was on the verge of capsizing rolled back onto its keel. Everyone at the table but Inez Barter came to feel themselves in on the joke from the start and forever after told the story as if they were.

The Beadle left shortly afterwards. He stepped out into the winter darkness without announcing his departure, grateful for the stillness and the bitter cold. He was stunned by the performance he'd just witnessed, by the sour cleverness of it. He would have thought it beyond Abe Strapp to choreograph the steps of that dance or to make his way through them with a delicacy and patience so at odds with his reputation. It made Clinch wish his employer was as buffle-headed and gormless as he once believed.

The Christmas sky was choked with stars and the relentless frost made them feint and blister overhead. The Beadle could hear voices in the houses and shacks around him as he walked through Mockbeggar, people singing or cursing at one another or bawling unintelligible nonsense. It was a passing thought he dismissed as self-pity, but for a moment the senseless noise struck him as the eternal music of the spheres.

TAKING THE TRADE. A LOOKING GLASS.

The day the Jerseyman's vessel left for the continent, Solemn came
to the door of the Widow's office. He pointed through the window behind her. "The Jerseyman's horse is in the stable," he said.

"I purchased his horse."

"It wouldn't there when I left for home last night."

"We will have to build an addition to the stable to house it
properly," she said.

The Jerseyman had spent part of every night before his departure at the Caines house. The Widow waiting at the servants'
entrance in her mother's fucksail with no articles worn beneath
and he took her over the kitchen table in his riding boots, before
they stripped out of their clothes and did everything they could
think of to crawl inside one another. Morels made his way to
the stable in the small hours, riding back into Nonsuch ahead
of the Lambe youngsters arriving to light the morning fire.

The horse was all the farewell the Widow wanted from the man. She spent the day at the firm's offices while crowds walked to the waterfront in Nonsuch to wave their goodbyes. The paperwork and banking documents to finalize the buyout sailed with the Jerseyman to be registered in the London financial sector.

Myles Taverner was also aboard the vessel, having resigned his position rather than be party to what he called a dereliction of fiduciary duty. He refused even to wait for a Caines ship in the spring, booking passage with the Jerseyman to return circuitously to Poole after seventeen years in Newfoundland. He travelled with his family and all the possessions that could be packed into trunks and a condescending letter of commendation from his employer lauding his accounting expertise and tireless devotion and obedience.

The Widow insisted the buyout not be announced until the financials were completed in London and most on the shore heard nothing certain of it for months. Even when rumours began making the rounds in the early days of the new year no one reacted with panic or dread, given the late abundance of fish on the coast, given the fact Morel's headman was staying on to oversee the operation in Nonsuch. The Widow offered her wry, stoic face to questions about the transaction and its consequences any time she found herself in company. But in her heart she was suffering enough panic and dread to serve the coast and its entire population.

She leveraged almost all she owned to close the purchase and every passing day that transaction seemed more ill-considered, more demented. She spent her time running the numbers, altering one variable or another to gauge how easily she might be ruined in the coming years. Easily enough, that was clear.

It was a foreign experience for the woman, to be overwhelmed by doubt, to fixate on hypothetical circumstances over which she had no control. She couldn't sleep without the aid of several fingers of rum, which she had Solemn buy at one of the grog shops and smuggle into the house, making her the only wet Quaker on the shore. She woke every morning to nausea and gut-rot that was almost enough to put her off the drink. At times it was bad enough she couldn't stomach a morsel of food before suppertime. Solemn slaughtered and butchered the pig in mid-November but just the thought of the meat in her mouth made her urge. The pig's hams and ribs and hocks were hung in the garden's smoke-house and the Widow chinked the window and the space below the office door with cloth to keep the stench at bay. Even the smell of her pipe made her want to vomit.

After Christmas, Solemn raised his shy concerns for her health and suggested she might submit to the Beadle's attentions as a precaution. She dismissed the notion until the second month of the new year when it occurred to her she'd not suffered her regular visitor since the fall and all her recent afflictions took on a different cast.

She sat three days in her office without a fire or food during the coldest stretch of the winter and it was impossible to imagine anything growing in that bitter season. But there was no denying the ineluctable fact of her condition finally. Which induced a different sort of panic and dread.

On the fourth day of the vigil she called Solemn to the office. "This evening," she said. "As soon as it is dark. You will go to Mary Oram and ask her to come to me directly."

"Wouldn't you rather see the Beadle?"

"This is not something the Beadle will be any help with. You will wait for her and bring her back down to the house. Take the Upper Path," she said.

Solemn set off when the stars came clear over Tinkershare Head. The wind dropped out when the sun went down but the cold was fierce and the packed snow as hard as stone. He headed toward Looking Glass Pond and took the Upper Path that circled above the harbour. The trails were well beaten and the walking easy until he reached Oram's Drung where an iced-over track no better than a goat path twisted into the lightless crevices among the trees. He thought he'd passed by the woman's tilt and almost turned back several times before he caught sight of it, a huddle of black in the woods and a weak flicker of light through the log walls' ancient moss seams. He wanted to call out to her from a distance as he'd done before, but his hands and feet were burning with the cold and he steeled himself to knock instead.

Mary Oram opened the door, her face mousing into the open air. "Who is it there?"

"Solemn Lambe," he said. "The Widow Caines sent me after you."

"The Widow ought better look to the Beadle for help," Mary Oram said.

"I told her as much myself," Solemn admitted. "But she says it's only you can look out to what's wrong with her." The strange woman took a moment to consider that statement. He said, "I'm to wait and carry you back with me." She didn't answer still and finally he said, "I'm half froze to death out here, Mary Oram."

She stepped away from the door to let him pass and he ducked his head under the ceiling to cross the room and crouch before the poor fire, the back of the fireplace made of wattles clayed over and a blackened wooden chimney hanging above it. He could still see his breath as he knelt there and it seemed hardly warmer inside than out. The woman was rattling about in the dark behind him, collecting bottles and jars and plants hanging from the log rafters.

"How long have she been sick?" Mary Oram asked.

"Months now it seems," Solemn said. "She can't hardly keep a thing in her stomach."

The woman made a noise in her throat and he looked behind to see her tying rags around her ragged shoes with string. "Is you ready?" she said.

"I'm happier moving than sot still like this."

Mary Oram knocked the fire apart before she covered her colourful woollen cap with a knitted length of wool that she tied under her chin. She picked up her satchel and they stepped out into the bleak. When they reached the Upper Path, Solemn started across toward Looking Glass Pond.

"It's half the time to go down through Mockbeggar," Mary Oram said.

"The Widow Caines says we're to take the Upper Path."

"Do you do everything the Widow says, Solemn?"

He didn't know what to make of the question. "As I'm meant to," he said.

Mary Oram made the noise in her throat again. "There's not a soul about on a night like this," she said. "There's no one going to note us passing, whatever road we takes."

She started down toward the houses around the harbour and he watched her go. The wind had come up again and it rattled at the iron hinges of all his bones. And he followed after her, running a ways to catch up.

"You would do well to remember this," Mary Oram said to him. "If you plans to stay in her employ."

"All right," he said. Though the youngster was so clipped and raftered by the cold he wasn't sure exactly what he was meant to remember.

They found the Widow at the fireplace in the kitchen at the Caines house. She'd moved the jays' cage from the parlour for the warmth and it hung beside her, covered in a blanket. The fire was roaring and she was settled close with a glass of rum. She motioned Mary Oram and Solemn to join her at the hearth and they stood unwrapping themselves and opening their outer layers to let the heat in.

"I sent Bride down to see to your mother," the Widow said. "You should go on yourself once you've taken off the chill."

"I likely won't never be warm again," Solemn said. He had his hands over his ears, trying to rub some feeling back into the dead flesh.

"Bring a chair for Mary Oram."

The tiny woman hopped onto the wooden seat, her legs dangling above the floor like a child's and the three of them stared into the fireplace, as if the flames were a dumbshow put on for their entertainment.

Finally the Widow turned to Solemn. "Leave us to it now," she said.

After the youngster went out the door Mary Oram said, "He seems a right devoted one."

"Solemn?" The Widow shrugged. "We have made a good fit," she said. "I'm lucky to have him."

"I'm sure he thinks the same," Mary Oram said quietly. She stared into the light of the fire where the flames seemed to dance over the wood without touching it, as if they were merely witnesses to that slow consumption. "How far along is you?" she asked.

"Since the end of the tenth month."

"October then." Mary Oram swung her legs idly as she turned that detail over in her head. "It's the Jerseyman's doing, I'm guessing."

"It was my doing," the Widow said and she sipped at her rum. Then she said, "How did you know?"

"You got no doubt how far along. And that's when Morels left the shore."

"That's when Myles Taverner left the shore. You didn't think it could be him?"

Mary Oram smiled at the fire. "Why did you have me brought down here this night, Mrs. Caines?"

"You know very well," she said, "why I asked for you."

"I thought you was against taking the trade?"

The Widow looked across at the diminutive figure. "You said yourself it might just as soon kill Imogen Purchase as cure what ailed her."

"She had the stomach to take that chance but for you speaking against it."

The Widow turned back to the fire.

Mary Oram said, "Weighing the risks is a different task from this end of the scale, I imagine. But you seemed happy having a girl to parade around the church with her belly full when Abe Strapp was getting married, offering up your oaths and papers and such."

"A person in your position ought not to be looking for trouble, Mary Oram."

"I got no position to speak of, Mrs. Caines. I'd be just as happy sitting at my own fire as this one."

After a long silence the Widow said, "When should I start?"

"Today would be better than tomorrow."

"Then we'd best waste no more time in conversation," she said.

Mary Oram spent a few minutes in lamplight at the table measuring out the toxic remedy.

"That doesn't seem enough to do what I want done," the Widow said.

"We'll both be grateful it idn't too much," Mary Oram said.

She offered to spend the night but the Widow refused, shaking her head and stamping her foot against the violent aftertaste.

"I don't want to start any talk with you staying here."

"Well you oughtn't be left alone," Mary Oram said. "I'll go by young Solemn's on my way and send him up." And she presented a list of symptoms and circumstances that would warrant having the youngster fetch her back from Oram's Drung.

After the woman left, the Widow sat beside the fire with the trade at work within her. Waiting for the first sign to announce itself without the slightest notion what that would be. The grievance she'd held to a simmer all her life scalded up like hot oil over a flame, a disgust for the circumstances she was born into, for the cockeyed rules that governed the world's standards and proceedings and transactions, setting one thing over another against all sensible measure.

She threw her empty glass into the fireplace, a gesture so useless and impotent she was more livid every second. She stood and paced the dark kitchen. She faced the cage a long moment and stripped away the cover, the birds rustling and cocking their heads and turning about before they settled again. The Widow opened the door and reached inside to clutch one of the drab jays, the panicked creature clawing and pecking at her flesh. She clamped her free hand around its head, twisting the neck until the living thing went limp and she threw the corpse onto the fire, watching as the feathers leapt up in flames. She turned back to the cage and reached inside again.

Solemn noticed the jays gone when he thought to let them from the cage the next morning. He whistled softly as he walked the rooms of the house, guessing they must have escaped when Mary Oram left to fetch him back, though he couldn't imagine why they'd be roaming free at that hour. He went to both doors and whistled into the dawn light and he wandered around the garden calling to them. When he came back to the house, Bride showed him the charred remains she'd found among the dead coals in the fireplace, the bones blackened and cracked so they were barely recognizable.

"She's dicked in the head," Bride whispered.

Mary Oram came to the Caines house every night, listening to the woman breathe and asking if she felt anything at all in motion, good or ill. She left for her tilt on Oram's Drung before light each morning, in a mocking echo of the Jerseyman's clandestine visits before he sailed for the continent. Two days in, the Widow demanded a second dose and against her better judgement Mary Oram administered it. By the fourth night the Widow was puking and flapping about in the bed like something possessed, adding weight to Bride's diagnosis. Though the fever and the racks of pain seemed real enough.

It wasn't until the end of the first week that the truth of the woman's sickness came clear to them. Bride was sitting with the Widow's chamber pot in her lap when Solemn arrived that morning. He stood near the table, trying to figure a sensible reason his sister would be in the kitchen, cradling the Widow's thunder-mug in her arms. Afraid to go any closer.

"Brother," she said.

It struck him then how their father had always called the chamber pot a looking glass. As a joke, to say the mess in that porcelain bowl was a likeness of the person who produced it. Chasing his wife and his children around the tilt, pushing the container of shit and piss into their faces, shouting "Look upon thyself and tremble!" All of them in hysterics.

"Is the Widow alright?"

His sister shook her head. She lifted the pot helplessly.

He walked around the table toward her. Not wanting to see what lay in her lap, but feeling it was his duty to witness it.

There were large black clots of blood and among the livid muck an alien figure about half the size of a newborn piglet. Something small enough he could have held it in his palm. It looked like a drawing you might make with a stick in wet sand. Primitive but eerily suggestive of a living creature. The nearly translucent skin showing dark spots where the eyes would be.

Bride said, "You have to bring it to Mary Oram."

"She'll be by again tonight."

"You have to go now, Brother."

He looked down at the bloody mess in her lap. Feeling his sister's urgency to have the unearthly thing out of the house.

Bride fished it from the muck and washed and wrapped it in a linen rag and again in a square of brin and tied it up with string. Solemn hid the nearly weightless bundle inside his coat as he walked up to the pond and took the Upper Path to Oram's Drung. He knocked at the door before letting himself inside, his head tilted sharply to clear the low rafters. Mary Oram was sitting under a cloak of blankets beside the fire.

She said, "Is the Widow still with us?"

He opened his coat. "This is what come out of her."

"Why did you cart that all the way up here?"

"We figured you'd know what to do."

"The doing of it is done," Mary Oram said.

He proffered it towards her. "Should we bury it then?"

Solemn hacked away at the ground behind her tilt with the fireplace poker, which was the only iron instrument Mary Oram had that he could dig with. He placed the knotted brin in the depression and covered it with chunks of frozen dirt and he hunted around for a flat rock to set overtop.

"Should we say something?"

"You're a Quaker now, is you?"

He shrugged. "I don't know what I am."

"Either way," the woman said. "It's best to be silent sometimes. I'll be down to look in on the Widow after dark." And she went into her tilt and closed the door behind her.

The next morning, the Widow woke to a burning pain in her right arm and took a fit of the ague. Each day afterwards her condition grew worse. Solemn and Bride traded off nights at the Caines house, taking away her sick and mess in the chamber pot, wiping her forehead and face with a cold cloth to ease the fevers.

In the heights of her delirium, the Widow pointed an accusing finger at anyone who came within her sight. "You did this to me," she hissed at the elfin woman and the youngsters who waited on her hand and foot. "You did this!"

Mary Oram offered an apologetic look to Solemn and Bride. "Don't mind her now," she said. "She idn't herself."

For days she suffered violent convulsions and they did what they could to hold her arms and legs and writhing body to the bed. All the time expecting the Widow to curl up and die and Mary Oram offering nothing to contradict that expectation.

The seizures and fever continued into mid-March and she was weakened enough she didn't leave her bed until a week beyond St. Patrick's Day when she dressed in her green jacket and waistcoat and spent an hour or two a day in her office. She asked to see Aubrey Picco and he became a regular visitor, bringing letters and bills and contracts to be signed. But it wasn't until she began smoking her pipe again in the first week of April that Solemn and Bride thought she might survive the ordeal.

The youngsters never spoke of what they'd witnessed, to each other or anyone else. They took their cue from the Widow who showed no interest in the events she'd come through, acting for all the world as if she'd woken from a nightmare and recalled only a detail here or there that made no sense out of context.

The woman's iron denial was a fearsome wonder to Bride. It made her more uncertain of the Widow to think she could live through the experience and feel nothing at all in the aftermath. She passed her open office with the chamber pot one morning and stopped in the doorway, her heart pounding in her throat. The Widow still looked a death's head on a stick weeks after the worst had passed. She waited there until her employer glanced up from the desk.

"What is it, Bride?"

"Solemn took it out to Mary Oram's," she said.

"Took what?"

She raised the looking glass in her arms. "They buried it out there," she said. "After," she said.

The Widow got up from her chair and crossed to the door. It took everything in the girl not to step back as the woman approached. To hold the Widow's eye as she pushed the door closed between them.

THE KNIGHT OF SORROWFUL COUNTENANCE.

THE SCARRED HAND.

The first vessels from England after the winter hiatus began arriving at the end of April. Once *The Fortune* had anchored and off-
loaded, the Beadle walked to Strapp Manor and waded through
the raft of hunting dogs to make a report on the ship's cargo and
passengers and the news from the continent. He listed off the
salt and dry goods and provisions received. There were a dozen
green hands aboard, indentured servants from Ireland, who would
be divided among the undermanned plantations along the coast.
Even Break Heart would be in operation for the first time since
the pandemic.

Abe was lying on a chesterfield with a dog asleep between his
legs. He seemed hardly to be listening to the headman's report,
idly stroking the animal's head.

Stories of Caines Mercantile purchasing the Jerseyman's firm
had reached them early in the new year and it rattled both men.

That the woman had left her father's house and inveigled her way into Elias Caines's operation was one thing. To have her in a position to challenge the place of C. Strapp & Son on the shore was something other. The Beadle expected Abe was too plodding and unimaginative to picture it, but it was clear to him the Widow would not rest until she usurped her brother's firm and buried him. Which would spell the end of the Beadle's world as well.

Abe was chiefly concerned with how the changes made him look in the eyes of others. He'd demanded a strict accounting of the Widow's expanded circumstances and how they measured up to the holdings of C. Strapp & Son—which firm boasted the most planters and servants, the largest overall tonnage of vessels, the largest square footage of warehouse space, the highest average gross weight of fish sold overseas, the largest profits. Abe pored over accounts and figures, demanding additional information on this or that element with the same infantile cloddishness he'd brought to overseeing the construction of his house. Had the Widow been his brother, people said, Abe would have ordered an examination of her bush-rusher to assure himself he had the superior member. The fact that C. Strapp & Son remained, on balance, the largest mercantile operation on the shore was little consolation to the man, given how narrow the margins had become.

All spring he'd clanked about in the iron chains of his sister's success as if he'd been cuckolded. Even the Widow's prolonged illness was more torture than comfort. The possibility she might die while practically his equal in business felt like a lethal humiliation. But her survival as proprietor of the expanded Caines Mercantile seemed worse than her dying a rich woman. He railed against the understrappers at his office and his actuaries in Poole as cork-brained calf-lollies, as noddypeak simpletons. The only maidservant at Strapp Manor not already driven away by his bullying and harassment gave her notice and he occupied his days with solitary drinking and listless acts of self-pollution that were often soured by a niggling sense the Widow and her maddening smirk were observing from the room's shadows. He trolled the backcountry with a rifle in search of creatures to bring down and butcher, sick at heart and sullen and murderous. The knight of sorrowful countenance, people called him.

When the Beadle completed his inventory of goods and materials just arrived on *The Fortune*, there was a silence that lasted long enough Abe looked to his headman. "Is there something more?"

The Beadle said, "Master Cheater has brought some news about the Widow's purchase of the Jerseyman's firm."

Abe turned his head away in disgust. He kicked the dog off his legs and sat up to rest his face in his hands. "I am not prepared to listen to talk of the Widow," he said.

"According to Myles Taverner, the Widow Caines wagered her entire worth on buying out Morels, Mr. Strapp."

Abe lifted his head. "Everything?" he asked.

"Cash reserves on hand. And she mortgaged much of what she owns besides. If what Mr. Taverner says is true, she couldn't get a new suit of clothes now but on credit. At unfavourable terms."

"Well," Abe said, "it's handy she's so fond of the one she has."

"To be over-extended in our venture, Mr. Strapp. If things do not go exactly to plan for her, it may offer us an opportunity in the future."

"The *future*," Abe said dismissively. "God's blood," he said.

But he was gambler enough to like the odds their volatile business might ruin the Widow and force her to surrender her holdings to the highest bidder. Each day the possibility seemed more likely and in short order he convinced himself it was all but inevitable.

He was like a creature kept in a cage who discovers the door unlocked. He charged around in a roil, rolling in whatever shit he found lying on the paths. He doubled the fees on alehouses and grog shops and he shuttered the establishments who refused to pay it. He sold himself a licence and opened a tavern in the Big House, selling alcohol confiscated from the shops he'd closed down.

He tasked Matterface and Heater with collecting the outstanding debts of livyers who drank on Strapp credit. No one on the shore had cash money in hand and the constables repossessed fishing supplies or tools or food to make up the amount owed. There were confrontations in every instance, men and women and children blocking access to their root cellar or the store, defending the family's boat and their few possessions with knives or rakes or gaffs. The ark ruffians were recruited to bolster the arm of the law and, but for the bran-faced boy they called Madge, they seemed happy enough to bully and cudgel in service to the Crown.

It was only servants associated with Caines Mercantile and the handful of independent ventures on the shore that were targeted by the constables. Some families were compromised to the point of destitution and were forced to leave the Widow's operation, signing terms with C. Strapp & Son instead. There was talk among the livyers of responding to the obvious injustice with force. Even the Quakers debated refusing to honour court summons or rulings.

The Beadle was away coasting during the worst of Abe's affronts to civility and he returned to find a general uprising in the offing. No one doubted Clinch's hand was at work when the Justice left on the next packet boat bound for St. John's.

The Beadle sent his employer off with letters of introduction to the governor and the most prominent merchants in the colony. Abe let it be known that he planned to use the visit to recruit a woman-of-all-work for Strapp Manor, a girl sophisticated enough to cook and serve and see properly to a master's needs without feigning shyness or raising priggish complaints. But everyone saw the voyage for the enforced retreat it was.

A false calm descended on the shore in Abe's absence, a sense of life returning to its proper weights and dimensions. Matterface and Heater retreated to Strapp Manor, not willing to show themselves about without Abe's office to carry before them like a shield. The fishing crews rowed out the harbour before light and the shore crews were busy on the waterfront and in the gardens until dark.

No one would chance the ark ruffians aboard a boat and they were employed in the warehouses and on the flakes of C. Strapp & Son. The freckled youngster, Price, was the only one amenable to work when they weren't under threat of a beating. The boy's general good nature looked to his fellow convicts like backsliding and he became a target of ridicule and abuse, his mates taking it in turn to kick his arse across the warehouse or the flakes whenever he showed an inclination to be civil or useful.

The women on the shore crews tried to shelter the runt of that litter and the youngster couldn't help shifting his allegiances a little in their direction. He refused to abuse or steal food or clothing from anyone who defended him, preferring to suffer whatever punishments might be meted out for insubordination. Eventually the Beadle took the knotted rope to Lynch and his comrades to warn them off the boy. And he shifted Price out of the shack where they slept, to keep him beyond their reach.

Aubrey and Relief Picco's youngest had recently followed in the footsteps of his brothers, leaving Newfoundland for employment in Poole, and they volunteered to take the boy in. Relief cut his ragged hair and combed the lice from his scalp and sat him to the first real bath he could remember taking. She asked him early on if he had his letters and he extended his right hand to show the T burnt into the flesh.

"Just the one," he said and he smiled shyly at his own joke.

Relief began teaching him in the evenings and on Sunday afternoons he listened as husband and wife alternated reading aloud from the Bible, thinking he might someday take a turn alongside them.

He managed mostly to renounce his habit of canting and obscenity and the reprimands when he failed were so mild and affectionate he didn't know whether to laugh or weep with gladness. There was never a mention of his time in London or among the ark ruffians, no lectures or reproofs or calls to repentance. Any shame for the way he'd spent his days and the acts he'd been party to he discovered within himself and he was surprised by the sudden strength of that feeling.

"You are a Child of the Light," Relief insisted and he wanted with all his heart to believe it so. He sat in silent gratitude before meals and attended Sunday meetings with Aubrey and Relief where all the Friends insisted he refer to them by their Christian names, regardless of their age or station. It was all so strange and unlikely he expected any moment to be tendered a bill he could only settle with trouble or blood. Every day he felt himself more willing to pay it.

"'Madge,'" Aubrey said to him one evening. "Strange for a boy."

They were sitting at the table in the brief lull after a meal.

"It's not your true name," Relief said.

"I been called it long enough it feels so."

"Would you like to be called something else?"

The notion had never occurred to him. "Like what?"

"What is your Christian name?"

"Lazarus."

Relief clapped her hands. She reached across the table toward him. "Lazarus," she said. "Come out!"

Her husband glanced down and shook his head. "Now, Relief," he whispered.

The boy had only the vaguest notion what her words referred to or why they caused Aubrey to look away to hide the smile on his face. But he was shaken by Relief's calling to him. As if it was a voice within himself he was hearing, the word of the inner light the Friends spoke of. He reached out to take the woman's hand.

"Hello, Lazarus," she said.

And he nodded to accept that baptism into his new life with a little rain of tears dropping to the empty plate before him.

Solemn and Bride were the only Friends near the age of Lazarus. The siblings had been attending meetings for months at the Widow's invitation, both feeling it wasn't within their compass to refuse and Solemn not able to resist the chance to spend more time in the woman's presence. He felt immediately at home in

the studied silence of those services, among the uncultivated dec-
lamations when someone was moved to speak, the quiet hand-
shakes that closed a meeting. Bride was less tractable in every way
and maintained a respectful but skeptical distance.

The youngsters were drawn to one another by their age and
shyness among the religious company. The three shook hands at
the end of meetings before turning to the adults in the room.
Afterward they walked as far as the Picco house where Lazarus
shook their hands again with the earnestness of someone aston-
ished to have happened upon unselfish affection. He stood and
watched Solemn and Bride out of sight as they carried on to the
Widow's house.

Eventually Relief Picco invited Solemn and Bride to join
Lazarus in learning their letters of an evening. The youngsters
both looked to the Widow as if nothing in the world could be
undertaken without her say-so.

"I'm teaching for Lazarus anyway," Relief said.

"As long as it doesn't interfere with their duties," the Widow
said. And she smiled in her unreadable fashion. "Or give them airs."

Four nights of the workweek, the youngsters sat at Relief's
table in the last light of the evening, copying the alphabet and
their numbers to one hundred on slates meant for the school. On
Sunday afternoons they declaimed Bible verses Relief wrote out
in chalk.

The true light, which enlightens everyone, was coming into
the world.
My grace is enough for you, for my power is made perfect
in weakness.

After the lessons, Lazarus walked to the Widow's house to help his friends with their evening chores before making his way home in the summer dark.

On Sundays, he and Solemn harnessed and saddled the Jerseyman's horse. The Widow had made a habit of giving the animal a run on those Sabbath afternoons and Solemn took it up after her illness. He and Lazarus rode to the Scrape and down into Nonsuch, Laz sitting with his arms around Solemn's chest. On the way back, Lazarus took the reins. After they stabled and brushed and watered the horse, the young thief ate his supper with Solemn and Bride and their mother.

Other than her youngsters, Lazarus was the only person Mrs. Lambe took any notice of after her husband's death. As if there was a particular odour to childhood trauma that led her to mistake him for one of her own. He sat holding her hand on the edge of her bunk and she set her head on his shoulder, as close to content as anyone had seen her in months. Laz's heart as full as an egg.

For all three, the water around them was deeper than they had the language to fathom or tell. And they seemed to recognize that unnamed likeness, as if they were each seeing themselves in the other. A kindred acquaintance with suffering that made them feel of a piece. And Bride experienced her own quiet conversion in the light of that attachment. Quoting Relief's chalked Bible verses became their way of greeting each other and saying their goodbyes. It was an intimacy that made their connection feel part of an eternal order, something unchanging and everlasting.

"The word is near you, in your mouth and in your heart," Lazarus announced when they met, reaching for their hands in turn.

"The Jerusalem above is free," Solemn would reply.

"And she is our mother," Bride said.

By which they meant to say they were of the same flesh. That they loved each other without reservation, without end.

In the space of a month, Lazarus was disowned by the underworld and abandoned to an honest life.

His former mates shunned him on the waterfront, feeling if they couldn't risk touching him they could at least act as if he were dead. Which was right and proper in the boy's mind. He wanted to be a new creature in the world, a stranger to all he'd known. Everything about his past filled him with remorse and he renounced it all in his heart, keeping himself as far clear of the convicts as he could manage.

The one mark of his old self he felt chained to was the letter, the unalterable brand proclaiming his days of venality and transgression. That badge preceded him each time he extended his hand at Sunday meetings. It was like a letter of reprimand sent ahead to a sailor's every port of call, counselling mistrust and caution.

During his first lessons with Relief, he held the chalk unnaturally in his left hand, burying the right beneath his thigh. He lurched and scrabbled at his letters, like a chicken suffering with bumblefoot. At the start of the third session Relief reached for his right hand. She placed the chalk in his fingers and closed them around it and he carried on copying for her with a new competence, wishing all the while he was dead.

Mrs. Lambe was mostly insensible to the world around her, but even she happened upon it as she sat beside him, running her fingers absently over the back of the youngster's hand when it struck her she was tracing a raised figure there. She glanced down to take in the mark, tracing it again. "Whatever does this mean, Lazarus?" she asked.

He shook his head. "Nothing you need worry about," he said, standing from the bunk and announcing it was time he got home.

Solemn followed him outside and Lazarus was in tears when he came up to him. He lifted his face to the sky, to the first stars coming clear in the dark. "I wish I could cut the bloody thing off," he said.

He was a beautiful creature, Solemn thought. Delicate-featured, the marks on his skin like pale moths on the glass of a lamp. He knew next to nothing of Laz's old life, but he'd heard stories of Matterface and Heater taking the boy to the edge of Strapp's property and having their way with him. Solemn couldn't picture what that meant exactly though it stirred a helpless anger in him, a sick sort of jealousy to be excluded by the boy's experience of the world, by his pain. He took Laz's hand in his own and traced the letter as his mother had. Thinking of the red-hot iron the Beadle used to seal the stump of Imogen's arm after the amputation. "What if we didn't have to cut it off?" he asked.

"What else is there to do?"

"It might be," Solemn said, "we could erase it. Or bury it, like. If you're willing to suffer some."

Laz wiped at his face with his shirt sleeve. "I feel like I was born to that," he said.

The following Sunday they built a fire in the clearing behind the back wall of their tilt where the household's wood was sawed and junked and Solemn set an iron poker among the coals. He'd smuggled half a bottle of rum from the Widow's house during the previous week and he handed it to Lazarus as they waited for the iron to kindle. But the youngster set it aside.

"I can do everything through Him who gives me strength," he said.

He knelt beside the wood horse and Solemn lashed his arm to the frame's top rail. Bride sat astride the horse to weight it to the ground as she watched Solemn take the iron from the fire. The tip glowing molten like an angel with news for the fallen world.

"Do your worst," Lazarus said and he set a leather bit between his teeth.

Bride circled her arms around his neck and buried her face in the boy's hair and she held on as he rocked and shifted and grunted helplessly. It reminded her of trying to hold the Widow to the bed when the fits came over her, the same wild, inhuman upheaval. The stink of burnt flesh struck her then and she lifted her head to see Solemn standing with the poker raised in the air, looking like he'd cast a devilish spell and terrified to see it made manifest in the world.

They untied the boy's arm and plunged his hand into a bucket of seawater they'd put by. Solemn and Bride kneeling beside Lazarus to stroke his head and hold him as he wrestled with the vulgar shock of it. They were all crying in that tight clutch, amazed by the savagery of the moment, the wonder of it. They stayed like that until the worst of Laz's shaking had passed. He spit the soggy leather from his mouth and raised his head to gulp in the air, as if he'd just surfaced from the ocean floor.

"I might," he said. "I might try a drop of that stuff now."

Bride uncorked the bottle and held it to his lips and he nodded against the liquid burn. Solemn took it from her and swallowed a mouthful, trembling himself to have authored that terrible cleansing upon his friend. Lazarus raised his hand from the bucket and turned it in the light to see what had become of the brand. The letter showing black beneath the raw marks scored into the flesh.

"That will look like nothing but noise once the scars set," Solemn said.

Bride took Lazarus's face in her hands. "What is old is passed away," she said.

He plunged the acid sear back into the bucket and sucked air through his teeth. "Amen to that," he whispered.

A BITCH-BEAR; HER CUBS. SODOM OF
THE NORTH. SHIPWRECK.

The Beadle had taken *The Hope* coasting to the firm's outlying plantations and fishing posts when Abe Strapp returned from the capital at the beginning of September, arriving on a packet boat out of St. John's.

He was wearing a new jacket and waistcoat, a silk shirt and a tricorn hat, white stockings and black leather shoes with square brass buckles on the face. Prinked up, people said, like he came out of a bandbox. He seemed to be trying to best the Widow's fit-out with fashionable accoutrements and he had the bedizened look of a child dressed by a senile grandmother. He'd fallen away from a horse load to a cartload during his months of high living in the capital and the spread of his jowls made his head's boxy shape even more pronounced. He sported a chinstrap beard as if to underline that squareness. People nodded their greetings with their eyes at his feet for fear of laughing, which he mistook as a sign of deference.

He sent word to Matterface and Heater to meet him at the Big House and he turned to the gangway to greet a line of women descending, half a dozen in all shapes and states. It was difficult to say by their dress if they were travelling with him or if they were in his employ. He referred to them, oddly, as "my cousins," and they spoke to Abe Strapp with a brazenness that bordered on provocation. They yawned and scratched at their heads and arms and arses as if they'd just been woken from sleep. They spat casually into the harbour and it seemed a judgement upon the place they'd landed.

They all cursed like sailors but for a woman in a black half-cloak with the hood worn up over her hair who spoke with the prim courtesy of a prioress, though she had arms and shoulders and a trunk that befit a bear's carriage and posture. In the eyes of some, the black cloak added to that bestial impression, while to others it seemed more a nun's habit. Her age and manner suggested she held some position over the brood of young girls and she was known ever after as the bitch-bear or the Abbess.

A handful of trunks and bags were off-loaded, along with crates of rum and gin, and Abe directed the men standing closest to carry them up to the Big House. A few minutes later the whole retinue paraded single file off the docks, the younger girls following after the hooded matron like bear cubs in the tracks of their dam.

The tavern at the Big House languished after Abe left for St. John's and closed its doors altogether once the fishing season began in earnest. Matterface and Heater were opening windows to clear the dead air from the rooms when servants began arriving with luggage and boxes. Fires were laid in the dining and sitting rooms and in the kitchen against the damp. There was a makeshift bar in the dining room and once the crates of alcohol were delivered the constables set about serving gin to the girls who drifted about the rooms as if appraising the house for purchase.

Through the sitting room door they could see the Abbess reflected in the mirror above the fireplace. She took a chair and opened her cloak and set her hood back on her shoulders, revealing an extravagant head of curls and a Sévigné bow at her throat.

"This is the house you were raised in?" she called to Abe where he stood talking with the constables.

He stepped to the other end of the bar where he could see her direct through the doorway between the sitting and dining rooms. "I lived here all my years but the latest."

"How many bedrooms are upstairs?"

"Three," he said. "And there's a bedroom off the kitchen at the back."

"The servants' room?"

"Yes."

"It has seen its share of the good old trade of basket-making, no doubt."

Abe stared blankly.

"The blanket hornpipe," she said. "The goat's jig. Clicket. Making feet for children's stockings." She looked out the window and sighed heavily before turning back to the room. "This will do nicely," she said.

Two of the younger girls strolled to the bar to refill their drinks and carried on through the sitting room. Matterface leaned toward the Justice. "Which one is your woman-of-all-work?"

"I imagine I could take whichever I please," he said. "Though there's not a goosecap among them could fry an egg."

"Sure it's only their mutton interests you," Matterface said.

Heater nodded through the wall toward the woman sitting in the next room. "She seems well kitted out."

"The she-napper takes a share of her girls' socket money. And you can tell by the look of her she've been in the trade longer than most."

"I would grind that bitch-bear of a night and happily," Heater said. "Or let her ride St. George."

"You'd suffocate under those kettledrums you put her astride you," Matterface said.

"And die a happy man, I would. She's a lumping penny's worth."

Abe raised his glass. "Here's to the well-wearing of their muffs, the lot of them."

"What are we toasting?" the woman called to him.

"Your health," Abe said and she lifted her drink to join them.

Servants were still carting in the luggage and effects of the women from the wharf, hauling them up to the bedrooms. Abe could see them pass on the far side of the sitting room and he called out to the bran-faced thief as he descended the stairs.

"You," he said. "Miss Molly!"

The boy turned reluctantly to the door opposite Abe, standing with his hands at his back.

"You were above deck a long time," Abe said. "You weren't taking advantage of one of my cousins up there?"

Lazarus shook his head. "I was only talking," he said.

"Is that all you do with that mouth of yours these days? Have you got religion on us, Madge?"

Matterface and Heater offered Strapp a brief account of the youngster taking up the name Lazarus and sitting silent among the Friends in the Quaker tub every Sunday.

"God's blood," Abe Strapp said. "I'm gone a season and the whole place goes to rack and manger. This young malkintrash," he said to the Abbess, "could teach your girls some tricks of the trade if he had a mind. Come in," he shouted to the boy. "You'll have a drink with us. We might save you yet."

Lazarus walked across the sitting room but wouldn't step through the doorway into the dining room, not wanting to get any closer to the constables, refusing even to look at them. About to turn fourteen and a fuzz of pale hair new-grown on his chin. He'd shot up three or four inches since he first stepped foot on the shore, almost a man to look at.

"Here then," Abe said and he stepped toward the youngster to proffer a glass of gin. "It'll do more for what ails you than sitting among those Aminidabs of a Sunday."

He shook his head to refuse the alcohol.

Abe laid a hand to the servant's shoulder and reamed his thumb into the cleft above the clavicle. "You will drink a health to our girls who are putting your mouth and your fundament out of business," he said. "Unless you prefer to go back on the market."

Lazarus reached for the drink and swallowed without tasting, passing the empty glass back to Strapp.

"Good man," Abe Strapp said. "Not so far gone a Quaker we couldn't retrieve you."

"What have he got done to his hand?" Heater asked.

Lazarus set both arms at his back but Abe took his elbow and brought the hand up to his sight. The skin mostly healed, the red crisscross of scars shading to purple.

"What happened here then?"

"I fell into the fireplace."

"This was no accident," Abe said.

"He wishes to hide the mark of his nature," Matterface suggested.

Abe looked the boy in the eyes. "No," he said. "He wants to kill it dead. Isn't that so, Miss Molly?" Strapp shook his head at the vehemence of the disavowal on display. He turned to the men behind him. "I was wrong," he said. "He's a true believer and deaf to our calling." Abe tightened his grip on the boy's arm. "Who was it you were talking to upstairs?"

"She said her name was Nancy."

The Justice shifted a hand up to the youngster's shoulder and dug his thumb into the same tender hollow. "You can do what you like with the women in this house," he said, "if you mind to pay your way. But I won't have anyone closing my cousins' legs to work with talk of religion. By the nails of Christ," he said.

"I only was asking where her people was from," the boy said. He was standing at an acute angle and breathing through his nose against the pain.

"That's how it starts," Abe said. "Where are your people from. And are you far from home. And would you like to take a bath in the blood of the Lord." He reamed into the boy's shoulder with all his strength. "But we won't be having that sort of talk here, Madge. Will we?"

Lazarus shook his head.

"Swear to it."

He looked up with his eyes and shook his head again. "I won't take an oath."

Abe laughed at the farcical seriousness of his conviction. "A true yea and nay man," he said. "You bloody Quakers," he said. He released his grip with a shove that rocked Lazarus halfway across the sitting room. "Go on, get out of my sight," he said. And as the youngster was leaving he shouted, "We liked you better when you were a madge cull and a thief."

The bitch-bear sat witness to the exchange and she tilted her head at an angle almost as severe as the boy's had been moments before. "You said we'd have no trouble with the law or with the church, Master Strapp."

"There's a handful of Quakers is all," he said. "They keep to themselves. The Church of England I will look after myself."

She raised her glass again. She looked out the window and stared blankly, like someone doing multiplication tables in her head. "This will do nicely," she said.

Word of Abe Strapp's return from the capital and the covey of sad cattle he'd settled into his childhood home ran through Mock-beggar and Nonsuch like fire in a field of dry grass. By evening the Big House was full to bursting, the heat inside sultry and oppressive from the crush of bodies, and men stood three and four deep outside the windows to catch a glimpse of the ladies of easy virtue.

Matterface and Heater ran a gambling table of cards and dice in the kitchen except when they were called upon to throw out some obstreperous lush or a drinker who'd run through his money and credit. The Abbess paraded about the rooms to talk up the clientele and suss out those who had the means to avail themselves of the girls' services, escorting them upstairs to the bedrooms, knocking at doors to announce a john's time was done.

Abe Strapp himself was like a gravedigger, people said, up to his arse in business and not knowing which way to turn. He wagered reckless hands at the gambling table or lorded over drinkers at the bar or simply stood in a room to take in the raw rakeshame he'd conjured. He went up the stairs and listened at each room, calling out to urge on the fornicators and hammering at the door as a kind of applause when the enterprise concluded. "Good man," he shouted. "Well mowed."

It was the best night of his life and he wished it might never end.

He woke the next day on the floor of the servants' room. There was no sign of a hangover despite his mad time, as if he was newly immune to consequences. Two girls slept head to tail in the bed beside him, his piss-proud cock standing like a little flagstaff, and he helped himself to the nearest cousin, hauling her shift above her hips and lifting one bared knee to her chest. Spitting into his palm and polishing the head of his piercer to a glisten. The girl slept through the occupation, lying still and silent as a corpse, and that likeness was a tongue lapping at his ballocks. He poured himself into her black joke with a roar that momentarily woke her bedmate before she turned and settled into the wall.

He walked through the house afterward, bawling out for Matterface and Heater before pouring a straightener at the bar. The Abbess was in her seat opposite the fireplace with a pot of tea on a side table. He raised his glass when he saw her there and she nodded her head of curls.

"This will do nicely," she said, with more conviction than she'd managed the day before.

"We might have brought more of the laced mutton from the capital. These few will be wore to rags before long."

"It is a source of continual amazement," she said, "how much a receiver general can set to her ledger. But we will pull some locals to the cause if need be."

Abe threw back his head and laughed. "The handsomest women you'll find on this shore are heavy baggage, to that I can attest. They've all the look of bull beef. And Irish legs besides."

The Abbess tipped a little of the tea from her cup into the saucer to cool it and lifted the saucer to her lips. "In our business, Master Strapp," she said, "handsome is that handsome does."

In mid-September *The Hope* returned to Mockbeggar, riding nearly to the rub-rails with a season's weight of salt fish. The harbour was crowded with brigs and schooners on the north and south sides, a handful anchored in the poor holding ground under Tinkershare Head. It was a tricky job to pilot into the wharf at Strapp's rooms without riding abroad the stern or the rails of one ship or another. Once they'd warped to the dock, the Beadle oversaw the transfer of its cargo into the warehouse, all the time wondering at the vessels set tight together and facing each other across the harbour like checkers on a board.

It was an unusual congregation. The foreign ships rarely stayed longer than needed to load and take on fresh water before heading back to the continent, looking to avoid the storms that blew up from the Caribbean and turned the North Atlantic on its head every fall. The Beadle called down from the deck to young Price on the wharf.

"What's happened to keep so many at anchor?"

He said, "Master Strapp is just now back from St. John's."

There was nothing obvious in that bit of news to explain the circumstances. But the Beadle didn't doubt it boiled down to that simple equation. He made his way to the offices where a junior accountant placed some papers before him and raised his eyebrows as a warning or apology before backing away.

A petition, Clinch read. It was addressed to the island's governor and enumerated the many moral failings and abuses that made Abe Strapp unfit to hold public office. The shooting death of an Irish servant which had never been properly investigated and was considered by many an act of murder. Offering predatory loans in drinking establishments at usurious rates. His use of the court's constables and convicted felons as debt collectors, a practice which was prejudiced and unreasonably violent and forced fishermen into business with C. Strapp & Son, notwithstanding their commitments to other firms. Lastly and most recently, his establishment and living off the proceeds of a common bawdy house in Mockbeggar, to the detriment of all on the shore. "The whole constitution of the town," the petition said, "is corrupted into debauchery, drunkenness, whoring, gaming, profuseness, and the most foolish, sottish prodigality imaginable."

In its tone of righteous anger, in its ecclesiastical cadence and vocabulary, it sounded to the Beadle as if he might have written the petition himself. Even the handwriting could have been his own. He looked across the room, every head bent studiously to their ledgers and figures.

A bawdy house.

The men in the office unable to meet his eye, too demure to acknowledge the subject. Or mortified to have waded arse and doodle into that pond of filth themselves.

The petition had circulated among all the quality in Mock-beggar and Nonsuch. Every Quaker had affixed their names or their mark. Everyone who worked in the offices of Caines Mercantile and the Jerseyman's offices in Nonsuch and several dozen more, the newly arrived school teacher and the owners and managers of the smaller operations in the harbour. But no one who worked in Strapp's offices, he noted, had dared sign on to the call.

The Beadle stood from his desk. "Who delivered this petition?"

The junior accountant with the raised eyebrows said, "The Widow Caines asked it be put into your hands at the first opportunity."

He nodded. "Does anyone wish to add their name?"

One by one the heads turned back to their desks and the Beadle folded the petition inside his cloak.

It was near six o'clock in the evening. He walked the Lower Path around the harbour to the offices of Caines Mercantile where Aubrey Picco informed him the Widow had already left for the day.

"She's at home, then?"

"Is she expecting you, Abraham?" the headman asked.

He despised this Quaker habit, the refusal to acknowledge titles, their insistence on using a person's Christian name regardless of their rank or station. He imagined it was how people were addressed in hell, a world without hierarchy or scale, just a diffuse and catholic torment where every soul suffered equally.

"I imagine she is, Mr. Picco," he said.

At the Caines house, Bride led him into the sitting room where he took his place in front of the hearth. The willow cage stood in its corner, occupied by three grassy birds. They were tiny compared to the jays he remembered from his last visit, with black caps and manic whistles that Clinch found unnerving in the confines of the room.

"They will settle in the dark," the Widow said, coming into the room behind him and covering the cage with a blanket. "They aren't tame enough to be let loose in the house. I don't know if they are the taming kind."

He waited a moment as she took her place on the chesterfield. "You are looking well," he said.

"I am not yet buried," she said. "That is as much as can be said for me or my looks."

He inclined his head as if he was tipping a cap. She did not look well, despite the months of convalescence. Only more attenuated and famished, more formidable.

"You have seen the petition I gather?"

He took it from inside his cloak and unfolded the paper. "A hand very like my own," he said.

"I have always thought it had a certain clerical authority to it."

"And why was it sent to my attention?"

"I was hoping you would be of a mind to sign it."

There was a sudden flurry of motion in the cage, a scuffling and jockeying for position under the blanket, and they watched until the noise settled.

"I was also thinking," she said. "As it was largely your hand which inflicted my brother upon the shore as Justice of the Peace, you would be kind enough to send the petition to the governor directly. It would have more influence coming from you," she said, "than from a lowly widow."

Clinch swung his hands behind his back. "I don't believe it is in anyone's interest to have me insert myself into what is largely, I believe, a family dispute."

The Widow leaned back against the chesterfield. "You took note of the ships in the harbour today, Mr. Clinch."

He nodded.

"Most of them should be at sea. Half are delayed by the inclinations of their masters who have found the new entertainments in Mockbeggar too diverting to abandon. Several of my own vessels are delayed by unexpected damage or impairments that were noways apparent two weeks ago. The repairs are taking twice the time they should as no one is in a hurry to leave."

"Surely there is more to this than some unwashed bawdry drifting ashore."

"For the lips of a strange woman drop as an honeycomb, and her mouth is smoother than oil," the Widow said and she let the biblical quote hang between them a moment. "You are satisfied to have your parish known to the world as the Sodom of the North, Mr. Clinch? To let my brother destroy all you have worked to build?"

It was as if the woman looked into his heart and spoke his thoughts aloud. But he refused to acknowledge as much. He said, "I believe you are overstating your brother's abilities."

"My brother kills everything he touches, Mr. Clinch. My mother being the first of those."

It was an oddly self-pitying appraisal, a rueful womanish sentiment meant to elicit his sympathy but serving only to make him think less of the Widow. He gestured toward her. "You have survived him so far."

She looked down at her hands. "He hath taken away a house which he builded not," she said.

It galled him to hear the words of scripture in her mouth and twisted to her own ends. She might as well have squatted over the Good Book and relieved herself on its pages, holding his eye all the while. "I will not sign your petition," he said. "Nor will I present it to the governor. And I would be unhappy to hear the governor is given the impression I had."

The Widow stood from the chesterfield and straightened the hem of her waistcoat. "Your employer is a flesh broker and a whore master. If you are happy to lie upon your back for him, you ought to wear a different face than the one that is your custom. It will go some way to making you more profitable to the man."

She stood silent a moment, as if listening to the sudden roil in his chest, just as she'd listened to the skirmish in the blanketed cage moments before. A fierce little commotion she counted of no real consequence in the world.

"Bride will show you out," she said.

Every night at the Big House unfolded in much the same way as the first, a crush of drinkers inside and a leering audience at the windows and a long march through deepening states of dissipation and lechery and sporadic violence. More vessels had anchored in the harbour each day in September—merchant brigs and schooners returning with the season's cod and ships from France and Portugal and Spain arriving to bring fish to foreign markets—and they threw new faces and fresh appetites into the boiling cauldron.

Abe's enthusiasm for the enterprise never waned. The nations of the earth were beating a path to his door, proclaiming their allegiance to his spiteful lightheartedness, his relish for the world's puerile and transient pleasures. He gambled at cards with Greeks and Egyptians and Upper Canadians. He threw himself into debates with a braggart's certainty, arguing the use of a deer's brain-matter to cure its hide with a Labrador trapper, the number of angels that could dance on the head of a pin with a Portuguese Jew. He'd made it a personal mission to see every innocent on the shore baptized in the waters of the bottomless pitcher and he hollered encouragement to boys from Indian Burying Ground Cove and Cuckold Harbour and Death's Head Island as they surrendered their innocence to the Mother of All Saints. When the green man they knew as Terrified pleaded poverty, Abe paid for the ceremony out of his own pocket. He led the youngster to his appointment with the Abbess by the collar, the look on Terrified's face suggesting he was walking to his own execution. Abe had a ship's bell installed in the upper hallway and he rang out the sacrifice of each virgin's chastity as they descended the stairs to catcalls and cheers.

As well as his time at the gaming table, Abe wagered on all manner of actuarial oddities, using any form of collateral he could foist upon the drunken roysters in his orbit. When someone made their way upstairs to take a stroke, Abe laid shillings on how often Matterface could sing "Down Among the Dead Men" or "How Stands the Glass Around" before the sated john reappeared. He bet bags of flour and live chickens and powder and ball on who would be the first drinker to flash the hash from overindulgence, on how far a tobacco chewer could stand from the sitting room's spittoon and make the metal ring.

He lost a full round of cheese and a demijohn of rum and a horn of gunpowder in one night to the captain of a French vessel forced into Mockbeggar for repairs after snapping its mainmast en route to Quebec. The captain was near the same age as Strapp, effeminately handsome and refined. He carried a perfumed hand-kerchief in his right hand and still managed to exude an air of virility and frank confidence. Abe Strapp hated the man on sight and his hatred grew with every passing minute. The Abbess and her girls hung at the captain's elbows and cooed over his adorably accented English and molested his clothes or his blond curls. On some unspecified moral or religious ground, the captain refused to gamble for money or a tumble with one of the bitch-bear's cubs. But Abe goaded him to the gaming table eventually, anteing up items about the house, hoping to knock the French bye-blow down a peg or two. Each successive loss added peat to the dirty fire in his gut and made him more reckless.

When he had exhausted everything in the Big House the Frenchman showed the slightest interest in, Abe sent Heater to fetch his father's glass from Strapp Manor. While they waited, the two men fell into a debate about the Seven Years' War and the shifting boundaries of the French shore on Newfoundland's coastline. It was a subject Abe knew only the vaguest outlines of, but he conceded not an inch on any point. They argued whether the fishing rights granted in the treaties were exclusive to the French or concurrent with a British right to fish anywhere on the island. They disputed whether the old French Shore extended all the way across *le petit nord* to Cape Bonavista or only so far as Cape St. John.

"Cape St. John and not a fathom further," Abe said. "I bet my mother's life upon it."

"Please," the young captain said. "I will not allow a mother's life to be stained by such an absurdity."

Abe said, "My mother is dead and buried for long ago."

"My mother is not. Please," the Frenchman said again. "Even as a jest, I refuse."

"You French are all a crowd of queer prancers," Abe said. He raised his foot and set it on the table with a bang that drew the room's attention. "I will bet you my right shoe."

The captain smiled at his host. "One shoe only?"

"Yes! One bloody shoe!"

The Frenchman lifted his own foot, revealing a shoe much like Abe's, the same black leather, the same square brass buckle. "But your device is clearly too small," he said, which set the girls around him into fits of laughter.

"Your mother's life or your right shoe, you whore's kittling."

The captain shrugged helplessly. "I suppose it must be the shoe, Mr. Strapp."

They appointed an arbiter to settle the bet, naming Master Cheater of *The Fortune* who had served in the Royal Navy as an officer and sailed back and forth to Newfoundland for decades past. While Heater was sent to find the man and carry him to the Big House, Matterface arrived with Cornelius Strapp's telescope. It was housed in a cylindrical leather case, the instrument made of polished mahogany with brass fittings. It was an object of such refined elegance that the Frenchman tried to step away from the table.

"It is not a thing to gamble for, this," he said. "It is like gambling for the hand of a beautiful woman. It is something almost *sacrilège*," he said, using the French word to underline his discomfort.

Abe returned the glass to its case and set it in the middle of the table. He said, "One final hand. The glass for everything you've won this evening."

The Frenchman smiled ruefully. "As you wish," he said.

Cheater arrived half an hour later to offer his adjudication on the French Shore issue and the French captain carried away Strapp's shoe with its square brass buckle like a trophy won in battle. Alongside the round of cheese and the demijohn of rum and the horn of powder, he brought Cornelius Strapp's telescope in its leather case aboard the *Liberté* as well.

After he surrendered his shoe to the Frenchman, Abe Strapp walked his rounds in the tavern with a pronounced limp, wearing holes in the filthy white stocking. He was twisted up with rage, like an anchor chain wound around a capstan. He bullied and belittled the girls and his henchmen and his customers. He threw the metal spittoon in the sitting room at the mirror above the fireplace, the glass riven with fissures from the impact. He drank himself into oblivion, passing out on the chesterfield in the sitting room at first light with his big toe sticking through the ruined silk like a sunker showing at low tide.

Which is how the Beadle found him late that morning, one arm a blindfold across his eyes, the other like an oar adrift in its lock overside. There was a heavy-set woman in the chair opposite the fireplace and the shattered mirror, drinking tea from a saucer. A black dress, a head of curls so elaborate that Clinch took it to be a wig.

"You would be the Beadle," the woman said.

"And you would be the mistress of this cunny school."

The woman sipped at the tea in her saucer. "Master Strapp did not mention you had a foul mouth," she said with a smile. She reached her foot and kicked at Abe's trailing arm until he ladled up from the chesterfield, swinging the limb wildly.

It took him a moment to place himself, to make sense of the Abbess sitting with her teacup and the Beadle standing over them both with the face of a boiled boot.

The Beadle said, "Can we speak in private, Mr. Strapp?"

Abe glanced toward the Abbess, then back at Clinch. "I expect she can hold a confidence."

She raised her cup to him and he held her eye as he spoke. "I have heard nothing since my return but news of this," he said. "This." He cast around for the appropriate word. "Abomination."

"Who is it calling my business such a thing?"

"All men of virtue call it so."

"By all men set I not a fart."

The Beadle took a step toward his employer, bowing at the waist to look him in the eye. "Your father would call it such."

Abe stood from the chesterfield to cure the feeling of being looked down upon. "My father is dead this years," he said. "You would do well to remember as much."

A mystified expression crossed his face as a sourceless sense of grievance took him over, a feeling he'd been mistreated or made a fool of. He looked about himself and clapped at his chest and thighs as if he'd misplaced a key and then glanced down at his feet. "Where is my Christly shoe?" he said.

He wandered into the dining room and the kitchen in search of the missing item, slamming around out of their sight. Moments later they heard the ringing peal of Abe pissing into a chamber pot in the servants' room and the Abbess smirked up at the Beadle.

"He won't find his shoe there, I expect," she said.

A young girl wearing only a white shift came down the hall, stopping in the doorway when she caught sight of the Beadle. Her nipples showing through the sheer white material, the well of her belly button where the shift lay tight across her stomach. She turned to the bitch-bear and shook her head. She was close to tears.

She said, "I'm not drunk enough to crawl under old screwjaws here yet today."

The Abbess tipped her head, considering Clinch anew. "I doubt the Beadle is here to lay you on your back, my girl. He looks to have a taste for different meat. Though I have been wrong about these things before."

"Send this child to put on some clothes," he said.

"You heard the man. Go make yourself decent."

"I sincerely doubt that is possible," the Beadle said.

The Abbess laughed suddenly and lifted her tea out over the floor to avoid spilling it in her lap. "Nor did Master Strapp tell me how funny you were," she said. "I believe I have been given an entirely wrong impression of Your Grace."

She went serious then, settling back into her chair. She pointed a finger and wagged it, as if trying to call up the name of someone she hadn't laid eyes on in half a lifetime. "I know that Master Strapp holds some sort of hank on you," she said. "At first blush, I assumed it was your taste in meat. But perhaps you have no appetite at all."

The Beadle turned toward the doorway and shouted Abe Strapp's name, trying to summon him out of the bowels of the house. Abe went by in the hallway seconds later, still tying up his pants. He took the stairs to rummage through the bedrooms, ignoring the Beadle's calling after him.

"It has to be something of the like in these cases," the Abbess said. She seemed happy to continue the conversation on her own. Preferred it almost. "Something dear to you. Something you'd kill for." A sly, shit-eating grin came over her face, as if some alteration in his expression had given the game away. "It couldn't possibly be your little fiefdom at the church? Are you that small a man, Mr. Clinch? Headman for Abe Strapp and Lord of the Church of England in Mockbeggar. This is the ring he has through your nose?"

The woman broke into laughter again, a note of condescension in it that made the Beadle want to eat her without salt.

"You and your women are a stain on this house," he said.

"My girls are every one religious creatures, Mr. Clinch. They just pray with their knees upward."

A racket broke out above them suddenly, men shouting and a girl screaming murder. The Beadle took the stairs to the only room with an open door where he found a naked ark ruffian over Abe Strapp on the floor. Lynch had both hands clamped at his master's throat, Strapp punching limply at the thief's shoulders. A naked girl was standing on the bed above them with her arms outstretched, like an angel hovering over a scene of biblical sacrifice. It had gone oddly silent in the room, as if the grip the thief had on Strapp's throat had choked off every sound.

Clinch crouched down to speak to the naked man. "Let him go," he said calmly.

"I didn't snaffle his bloody stamper," Lynch said through his teeth. He set his weight onto Strapp's neck repeatedly, like he was kneading bread dough on a table.

The Beadle put his hand on the man's shoulder. "You will be hanged on the waterfront this very afternoon," he said.

Lynch glanced up at him.

"I will put the rope around your neck myself, as God is my witness."

The thief let go and fell back against the bed as Abe Strapp hauled in a strangled breath of air. Lynch sat splay-legged on the floor, his face and neck and bare chest splotched red from the effort of choking his employer, his lobcock laying across his thigh like a drowned sailor washed up on a beach. "I never touched his shoe," he insisted.

Abe rolled to one side and hacked up gobs of spittle. "You're a damnable thief," he said. He lifted himself up the wall, turning and leaning against it. Matterface and Heater finally appeared, half-dressed, their faces puffy with drunken sleep.

"Where are your bloody pistols?" Abe demanded.

They glanced at each other and then over their shoulders.

"In our rooms," Matterface said. Or Heater said.

"Useless bloody tits," Abe whispered. He gestured toward the naked man on the floor. "Arrest this shit-a-bed. Lock him up in Quaker Hall till we can raise a gallows."

The two men crowded over Lynch who was twisting away from their hands, the girl on the bed screaming murder again. The Abbess had come to the door, all the women of the house crowding behind her. "Shut up," she shouted at the girl. "Take your clothes and get out. All of you," she said. "Downstairs."

By the time the naked girl gathered her things and followed after the others, Matterface and Heater had a grip on the ark ruffian and were trying to chinch him through the door, Lynch using his feet and knees and shoulders to impede their progress.

"Don't be gentle with him," Strapp said.

The Abbess shouted from the other side of the men wrestling at the doorway. "Mr. Strapp, you lost that shoe to a Frenchman last night."

"I what?"

"You lost it in a wager."

"I bet my shoe?"

The struggle at the door paused a moment, everyone listening expectantly.

"Why in hell's name would I wager a shoe?"

"It was over some argument about the French Shore."

It took Abe only a moment to move past the confusion and take up his anger again. "Well this turdy-gut did not pay for his jig with my cousin this morning, I can tell you that for a fact. And he nearly killed me dead on the floor, for which he will hang."

He nodded to his constables and they turned back to beating at Lynch's legs and ribs to muscle him into the hallway. They inched down the stairs and out the front door, the ark ruffian's bellowing and cursing receding into the afternoon.

The Beadle said, "Now may I have a moment alone with Mr. Strapp?"

"You haven't even inquired about our rates," the Abbess said. "Are you sure you can afford a moment with him?"

"Kiss mine arse," Abe said.

"Not even you can afford that, Master Strapp," she said. "I will knock when your time is up, Mr. Clinch." And she winked at the Beadle as she closed the door.

"I will strangle that miserable shitsack myself," Abe said. He touched his throat gingerly. "And I will piss on his corpse for good measure."

"Mr. Strapp," the Beadle said. "Are you aware of the petition the Widow Caines has been circulating?"

The Beadle spent much of the day talking Abe Strapp through the consequences of hanging the ark ruffian. "The man has a claim to acting in self-defence," he said. "The girl will testify you started the fight."

"The girl is a dirty bunter. Lynch carries the mark of his character on his hand. And I am the Justice on this shore."

"A position you will not hold much longer if you persist. The Widow's petition is damning enough as it stands. Everyone will see the cloven foot in your business if Lynch is hanged, Mr. Strapp. The governor will have no choice but to act."

"I was handy to murdered in my father's house. Am I supposed to let the ding boy walk free?"

"I suggest," the Beadle said, "we walk the middle path."

Matterface and Heater were directed to raise a whipping post in a clearing next the Church of England, overlooking the harbour. The punishment was scheduled for sunrise the following morning. The constables escorted Lynch barefoot and shirtless from Quaker Hall to the post where a crowd had gathered in the fading dark, livyers and the sailors and officers from every vessel at anchor.

Clinch read the charges and the punishment aloud while Lynch stood between Matterface and Heater. Thirty-nine stripes on the bare back at the public whipping post by the hand of the Beadle, for common assault and uttering threats. The Justice, Clinch announced, was willing to forego the punishment if the thief admitted his wrongdoing and thanked Mr. Strapp for his clemency.

Lynch spat at the Beadle's feet.

"I would urge you," Clinch said quietly, "to accept Mr. Strapp's offer."

The ark ruffian spat at his feet a second time.

The Beadle turned to the crowd. He said, "Experience is an expensive school, but a fool will learn at none other."

Lynch took to cursing the Beadle then, along with the church he served and the Justice who waited near the whipping post and the blasted island of Newfoundland and every miserable dromedary who had come from their houses and ships to see him lashed. The Beadle nodded to the constables and they dragged Lynch to the post while he carried on denouncing the colony and all its inhabitants.

Clinch took his place to one side of the prisoner. The light had come up enough he could see the blades of the thief's shoulders under the skin, the ribs like a narrow basket made of saplings. A gaunt layer of gristle and sinew all that covered his bones. Lynch's breath began to hitch and drag as he waited and the Beadle set about the lashing to avoid having to watch him weep with fear.

Abe Strapp numbered the stripes aloud as Clinch laid them on, the thief's back flaying away in strips and a fine mist of blood rising with each stroke. By the twentieth lash Lynch had gone silent, not even grunting as he twisted under the whip. His eyes were wide and glassy and he stared into nothing as he fought to keep his feet. Voices began calling for a halt to the punishment.

Abe hissed at them to shut their mouths. "Twenty-six," he shouted.

At the next stripe Lynch fainted dead away, hanging by the ropes that tied his wrists to the post. Aubrey and Relief Picco rushed forward, followed by a handful of other Friends, placing themselves between the Beadle and the man lolling unconscious by his arms, demanding he be released. Clinch looked to his master.

"Take him down," Strapp said.

The beaten man was given water to drink and Lynch managed to stand with the help of the Quakers beside him. He was shaking along the length of himself, his face slick with sweat and snot. He walked unsteadily toward the Justice and knelt before him. He thanked Strapp for his lenity and his mercy in releasing him from the remainder of his punishment, of which he admitted he was fully deserving.

Strapp looked from the bleeding puppy at his feet to the people huddled beyond the whipping post. "Louder," he said.

And Lynch offered up his grovelling expression of gratitude a second time. Abe Strapp extended a hand and raised the man's chin to look him full in the face. The eyes leaking tears, miry strands of mucus snailing across his lips and chin. Strapp had never despised a living creature more. If he'd had his pistol to hand he would have shot the wretch between the eyes.

The Beadle leaned down to lift Lynch back to his feet, to move him out of Abe Strapp's reach. "I will look after him from here," he said.

After executing his duties at the whipping post, the Beadle turned to scourging Strapp's premises and the firm's ships at anchor.

He walked the warehouse floors and along the vessel decks like Christ driving the money lenders from the temple, his indignation a length of knotted rope he used to flog the servants and sailors and officers who had allowed their bestial appetites to overrule their obligations. Not a soul who witnessed the morning's punishment was willing to challenge the man. Two of the foreign traders loaded with salt cod sailed on the evening tide. Three schooners in turn tied up to the wharf and took on their lading and fresh water and provisions and were ready to make for open ocean at first light. Two days later every Strapp vessel but *The Hope* and *The Fortune* was well at sea.

Caines Mercantile was still behind in sending the season's catch on its way, *Success* late returning from outlying plantations and most of its fleet hamstrung by minor acts of sabotage performed by sailors looking to extend their time among Strapp's fallen women. The summer had been so fruitful that the Widow expected to clear four to five points more on the firm's debt than she had hoped, if she could manage to bring the catch to market. Aubrey Picco spent his time haranguing and badgering on the waterfront in his diffident, ineffectual Quaker way. It made the Widow wish she could borrow the Beadle a day or two and set him upon her underlings.

Half the season's catch still sat waiting in Caines's warehouses the morning people began pointing to sun hounds in the sky. Crews who were out after their fall fish came early off the water. A sudden calm settled on the day. Not a breath of wind and everything alive had gone silent, as if listening for footsteps crossing the floor in an upstairs room. It was so eerily quiet the Widow and Aubrey Picco stepped outside the firm's offices to take it in.

"It's like all the world sat to a Sunday meeting," Aubrey said.

The Widow shaded her eyes to see the ashen circles mirroring the morning sun, pale horses left and right of that bright chariot. "Woe to the inhabiters of the earth and of the sea," she said.

"I expect we'll have to batten down," Aubrey said.

The *Liberté* had completed repairs to its mainmast and was making ready for departure on the morning's ebb tide despite cautions from livyers on the waterfront. Inez Barter sought out the French captain directly, though his toothless admonitions were indecipherable to the young officer who nodded and shook the old man's hand as if he was placating an idiot escaped from a madhouse. Whatever was coming, the French captain told the locals, it was better to ride it out at sea than sit anchored to the sledgehammer of a rocky shoreline.

By the time the *Liberté* disappeared around Tinkershare Head the dark sky had bruised darker again and servants were scrambling to clear the flakes and secure warehouse doors and the boats on the slipways. The ship crews ran cables ashore and set second anchors at their sterns and stowed their sails and anything moveable below decks. An unnatural twilight fell over Mockbeggar before noon when the wind kicked up in gusts and feints and a steady rain began to fall.

When the Widow returned to the Caines house she had Solemn and Bride herd all the animals into the stable built for the Jerseyman's horse, which was the outbuilding most likely to stand whatever was coming. Every creature in that tiny ark skittish and leery but soothed somewhat by the company in those close quarters.

Solemn sent Bride down to look to their mother while he tied up the doors of the other buildings and cellars in the downpour. He stopped in to check on the Widow who was sitting at the kitchen table with her sketching ledger and a storm lamp and the grassy birds in the cage at her feet. The birds were unnerved and chattering, as restless as the animals in the stable.

"They might be happier under their blanket," he said.

"I'll cover them before the weather sets in."

"Will we be alright, you think?"

The Widow had a way of looking at him that stripped Solemn bare, a cold uncompromising scrutiny that seemed to be appraising him against some veiled measure, and she looked at him that way now. A pool of water from his soaked clothes gathered where he stood, as if her gaze was wringing him out like a wet cloth.

"We'll be fine," she said finally. "Thank you, Solemn. For everything."

He nodded at his feet, trying not to look too idiotically pleased.

Men were still working on the waterfront as he wrestled through the weather to his family's tilt. They were hauling nets and fishing boats above the high-tide marks even as the wind bore down and the rain battered at them in waves they had to brace against. The harbour already boiling with white water, the ships creaking and bucking at their chains.

The livyers spent most of the next two days inside as the storm tormented the shore, doors banging loose, roofs lifting and clapping down. The intermittent clatter of flakes or a wharf tearing free and rearing up over the hill toward Looking Glass Pond. Fishing rooms and stages collapsed into the roiling harbour where they were hammered to scrap wood on the rocks. The wind raised tides ten and twenty yards above high water, flooding into the tilts closest to shore, setting chairs and barrels and firewood afloat. Torrential rain bucketed down chimneys and snaked through the layers of wooden shingles and the moss and sod chinked into seams.

Some tilts let go their moorings in the gale, tipping on end before sailing onto their backs, the astounded residents clutching one another as all they owned was chewed up and scattered to the four directions. By nightfall of the first day, two dozen people had lost their shelters and crawled to the Church of England for sanctuary.

Solemn and Bride and their mother sat huddled under a blanket, without a fire or light, the sand floor around them running with rivulets and streams. No one could make themselves heard over the wind and lashing rain. No one slept. They waited helpless in that crucible, not knowing how long the calamity might last or if they would live to see its end. At some point the door tore open and the weather stampeded inside, the youngsters moving blindly toward the breach to try and repair it. Laying hands on a figure in the brawling blackness and Lazarus shouted his name to them.

His appearance out of that maelstrom was so ludicrous, so reckless, they fell into hysterics as they wrenched the door closed and Lazarus joined their huddle on the bunk.

"You could have got yourself killed," Bride said.

"The Jerusalem above is free," he bellowed.

They were no safer with Lazarus in their circle. But they felt something closer to complete in the face of the world's savage uncertainties.

Overnight the lines meant to hold the vessels could be heard snapping periodically and ships rolled their beam ends under and dragged their overmatched anchors. As the hours passed, one and then another was driven ashore and rhythmically beaten to pieces. There was no let-up at daylight and no let-up through the morning or the afternoon. The youngsters ventured out before dark to survey the crippled buildings, the vessels bulged and rolling up on the shore and away like dead whales. They clung to one another in the deranged weather as long as they could stand the thrashing, each of them terrified and transported.

The storm moderated on the second night and the following morning dawned brilliant with a brisk seasonal wind. The Widow made her way to the waterfront where she found Aubrey Picco already inspecting the damage and they toured the harbour together to make a first accounting of their losses. Every stick of the wharves and piers and fishing rooms had blown ashore or was drifting free in the harbour. Half the fishing boats dragged above the waterline had been floated by the surging tides and were never seen again. *The Hope* still sat at anchor on the south side of the harbour but *The Fortune* was run aground where the shore was sandy-bottomed and had been beaten about. On the harbour's north side the sea rolled in unimpeded from head to waterline and only *Success* was still afloat. A second Caines schooner was sunk up to its rails, though it was intact and looked to be salvageable. All their other vessels and their lading lay scattered up over the rocks.

"I expect things are much the same in Nonsuch," the Widow said.

"I expect things are the same the length and breadth of the shore," Aubrey said.

She said, "Verily I say unto you, There shall not be left here one stone upon another, that shall not be thrown down."

And she smiled grimly at the world, as if she had prophesied the event herself.

News of the storm's devastation trickled into Mockbeggar over the months that followed. Every stage and wharf on the coast was washed down and gone. Boats and houses and outbuildings were damaged or reduced to scrap. A British man o' war was reported lost with its crew near Cape St. John. The *Liberté* didn't make port in Quebec or anywhere in the Gulf of St. Lawrence. The young French captain and his ship were never seen or heard from again.

MARAUDERS. THE STOLEN *FORTUNE*.

The rest of that autumn and much of the winter were spent reckoning with the carnage inflicted on the property and materials and livelihoods of everyone in Mockbeggar and beyond. All hands were engaged in salvage and repair. The half-sunken Caines schooner was floated and hauled into dry-dock. *The Fortune* was meant to sail for the continent but the damage it sustained meant a long rehabilitation that kept it in Mockbeggar through the winter. The roof on the largest Caines warehouse had been stripped from the rafters, and the fish still in storage was reduced to a mess of dunnage. Most of the ruined product was dumped into the harbour but for the little fit to feed to the dogs and goats and pigs. The offices of the mercantile firms were taken up with calculations and adjustments and insurance claims and speculation on how their competitors might have fared by comparison. The Beadle cautioned Abe to temper his expectations, but the

Widow's losses were so obvious and general that they both saw her on the road to insolvency.

After spending the storm in their company, Lazarus stayed on at the Lambe residence. As if he was born and raised in the house and belonged nowhere else. There were only two beds in the tilt and Bride slept with her mother while Solemn and Lazarus shared the smaller bunk. The bed was hardly size enough for one and the boys lay there much the way they rode the Jerseyman's horse on Sunday afternoons, one behind with their arms around the other's chest, turning periodically in their sleep as if passing the reins.

Bride was first awake in the house, a habit from her earliest days when she discovered the only truly private space in her life, sitting a few minutes in the stillness while the rest of her family slept. She was in no rush to disturb Lazarus and Solemn, easing onto the edge of their bunk in the dark, laying a hand to one sleeping face and then the other. She was almost fourteen and nothing of a child remained in her nature but her love for the two young men she considered her brothers. But even that youthful alliance had begun shifting under her feet. A baseless irritation was eating at her affections. She found herself envious of the time Solemn had alone with Lazarus when they rode the Jerseyman's horse on Sunday afternoons, of the nights they spent asleep in each other's arms. It felt to her, oddly, as if something was being stolen from her.

"Awake up, my glory," she whispered to rouse them.

"Bride," Lazarus whined and he buried his face deeper into Solemn's neck.

She said, "I myself will awake early."

They both rolled away from her biblical summons and she hauled the blanket onto the floor to let the cold pour over them. "He wakeneth morning by morning," she said, "he wakeneth mine ear."

They both sat up finally, quivering as the chill invaded their senses.

"Weeping may endure for a night," she said.

"But joy cometh with the morning," one or the other would manage. And she kissed them both on the cheek.

Since the age of eleven she'd been fending off marriage proposals from suitors in Mockbeggar and Nonsuch, snot-nosed green hands and widowed fishermen with youngsters near her own age and accountants from every firm on the shore. She was one of the few eligible women among a restless sea of bachelors and their earnestness and desperation in courting her made them all seem equally ridiculous. She offered up one excuse or other for her refusals—he was too young or too poor, she would not abandon her mother, his nose was hooked like a sickle-blade, he was not a Quaker, he was too old—but each time it came down to a simple lack of feeling. She'd begun to wonder if she was simply incapable of giving herself over and was almost relieved to think she might steer clear of the whole sordid mess.

She regretted being taught the difference. It was unpleasant and comprehensive, this new hankering Bride was trying to get to grips with. It animated her the way a hand occupied a puppet, turning her about against her will, and she was ashamed to feel herself at the mercy of something that seemed unnatural, infernal. The girl had learned early on to disguise what lay closest to her heart to insulate her mother from grief. She did the same now, rousting Solemn and Lazarus out the door every morning, leading them to the Widow's house where they lit the fire and set a kettle over the flames, huddling as close to the new heat as they could without setting themselves alight. As if nothing at all had changed between them.

When the kettle boiled, Bride filled the teapot and carried it upstairs where she often found the Widow at the desk, a fire already laid in the fireplace. The woman was quieter and more forbidding than ever that fall. It seemed she never slept, sitting all night at her ledgers in lamplight, trying to will the numbers before her into some configuration that was less disastrous than all the other configurations she'd tried.

It was clear she was wrestling with something unfamiliar and overwhelming, just as Bride was. Something beyond her control. There was the same unnatural set to her face meant to camouflage her desire to cut and run. Bride had never been able to see much past her employer's opaque exterior and the few glimpses she'd managed did nothing to temper her dislike or mistrust. But the helplessness she sensed at the heart of the Widow's steely manner now seemed a perfect image of her own veiled predicament. It occurred to Bride it might be something endemic to a woman's life. Something she and the Widow and all other women were born to.

The days went glassy in the new year, clear and sharp and windless. As if the shore had been placed under a dome of ice. Nothing shifted or changed through those frigid weeks, each morning dawning resolutely brittle and still.

The cold finally moderated in February and there was a stir about Mockbeggar when a sail was spotted in the offing, a vessel sailing past the coastline before disappearing northwards into an icy fog. Even with a glass it was impossible to settle the details. Some thought it sailed under a British flag or a Portuguese or a Danish flag or it flew no colours at all. It was a gunless brig or it showed ports for eight guns or fifteen guns. A ship at sea that late in the winter was unusual enough that the whole population was taken up with speculation, arguing it was a French vessel headed to the treaty shore north of Cape St. John or a crew of mutineers escaping the press and sailing for freedom in Lapland.

The following night, forty-eight armed men rowed ashore with muffled oars, their ship skulking into Mockbeggar's harbour once they'd landed and taken up positions throughout the village. They lit torches and the shock of the vessel's guns firing up over the hill threw the sleeping town into a panic, the livyers running out into the snow in only their shirts, all but a handful of them corralled by the marauders and marched towards the Church of England where they were locked inside without light or fire.

The privateers searched each building, hauling people from twine sheds and root cellars and from under their bunks. Everyone coming over the Scrape from Nonsuch to investigate the cannon-fire was seized and deposited at the sanctuary as well. By the time the moon had set the hall was close with several hundred people packed inside, all in a state of panic or outrage.

Before dawn, a man carrying a torch and a pistol stepped inside and shouted for the masters to present themselves. The Widow Caines and the Beadle and Master Cheater made their way to the light of the torch at the church entrance where they were informed they were prisoners of the *Moriah*, privateer of Boston mounted with twenty 9-pounders and manned by a hundred and sixty men under the command of Captain John Deady.

A voice in the crowd shouted to ask after the whereabouts of Abe Strapp.

"Who is Abe Strapp?" the marauder asked.

"He owns half the shore," someone else called out.

"Is Master Strapp in the hall?"

"He's about somewhere," a third voice said. "I seen him come in."

There was a rustling complaint near the altar, an angry conversation taking place in whispers.

"Brother," the Widow said. "Show your face, for the love of God."

Strapp crawled out from under the altar table, muttering curses as he made his way up the aisle.

The privateer demanded all keys in their possession. He gave permission for a fire to be mended in the church stove for the comfort of those imprisoned before taking the masters down to the waterfront. It was nearing six in the morning but still pitch-black. The *Moriah* had lit all its lamps and that oily constellation shimmered at the head of the harbour.

"Captain Deady requests the honour of your presence," the marauder told them, in his odd gentlemanly manner. They stepped aboard one of the *Moriah*'s boats at the new Caines wharf and were ferried out by a crew of eight.

Abe Strapp felt certain he was being rowed to his execution. "I am a Justice of the Peace," he announced. "A representative of His Majesty, the King. There will be retribution if any harm comes to me."

"We don't care a cobbler's arse for the King," one of the oarsmen said. And they each chimed in to say how little the King and his opinion concerned them. They were all English and Irish by their accents and Strapp said he would see them hanged for their treasonous actions.

"That will be when the devil is blind," the first man said, "and he haven't got sore eyes yet."

They tied on at the *Moriah*'s waist and the prisoners were handed up the gangway, each of the sailors nodding in mock-obeisance and whispering "Your Majesty" to Abe as he passed them. A mate escorted them below decks and into the captain's quarters at the stern, a low room the breadth of the vessel, bright with lamps hung from the beams and warmed by a stove. Deady was standing at the stern windows with his hands at his back. He smiled to welcome his guests. "Please," he said and he gestured to coffee and hot rolls set out on a table. "You must be hungry."

"I am a Justice of the Peace," Abe Strapp said, "a representative of His Majesty, the King." He was half shouting, as if his words were directed to someone listening at the door. "This action is an outrage against the laws of the British Empire and I demand safe passage back to shore."

"At least allow me to serve you breakfast before we discuss terms for your release," Deady said. He was no older than thirty to look at, with the unhurried manner of someone used to entertaining royals and their representatives. He stood at the head of the table, waiting until his guests were seated before taking his own. He asked them to introduce themselves as a rangy youngster with wiry black curls tight to his scalp poured their coffee and the rolls were passed from place to place like a collection plate in church. Deady paused with the tray in mid-air as the Widow gave her name and a brief outline of her properties and holdings.

He inclined his head slightly. "I apologize if my crew mistreated you, madam. As a result of any confusion caused by your dress."

"They have been the very paragons of discretion, Captain. Apart from driving our people into a winter night in their small clothes and locking them in the church."

"Our business requires we take certain liberties we would otherwise abhor," Deady said. "But your people are safe enough if they follow direction. And are not inclined to speak out of turn."

"If that is your measure," Strapp interrupted, "this one here won't live to sunrise."

Deady leaned back in his chair. "She seems perfectly civilized at first blush, Mr. Strapp."

"It's a woman's job to know when to shut her mouth and when to open her legs," Abe insisted. He was in a rage and happy to offer it around. "She has never learned the trick of either."

Deady felt honour bound to speak in defence of women but the Widow was already answering. "Mr. Strapp wants a woman on her tail. I prefer my own two feet."

Abe pointed the tip of his butter knife across the table. "You are the most unnatural creature I ever encountered."

The captain raised his hands to quiet the room, though he seemed mostly entertained by the animosity on display. "From what I've seen of the world," he said, "nature admits all kinds."

"Some of the best hands I ever sailed with were the wives of sailors," Moses Cheater offered.

"A woman aboard ship is no more than live lumber," Strapp said to his plate.

"Some of those women were given prizes for their bravery, Mr. Strapp," Cheater said. "They stood to in storm or battle. They ran powder for the guns in action and never so much as blinked. I once saw a sailor go down at the gun and the girl running powder stepped into his place and served as well as any scaly fish. Till a ball come through the side as she was setting the match to the touchhole. Took her arm off at the shoulder."

"Not true!" Deady shouted.

"May God put out my eyes," Cheater said. "It dangled there by a flap of skin and she staring down at it with the fiercest kind of a look, like someone had torn a rent in her clothes. The match was still burning where it fell and she took it up in her left hand and fired off the gun before walking to the cockpit to have her shoulder dressed."

Deady clapped his hands and shook his head in wonder. He said, "You've seen your share of action, Mr. Cheater?"

"I've spent my life at sea, sir. In His Majesty's Navy, on whalers and traders and such. Three times I've been to China and twice to Africa. I've sailed the land board of America from Nootka Sound to Cape Horn."

The two men traded stories an hour and more as the sun rose through the windows opposite the table. They talked their way through the Holy Lands and Egypt, they touched on the Ethiopian tribes and how superstition made the Portuguese the world's worst sailors. Now and then the cabin boy stepped out of the shadows to bring fresh coffee to the table, pouring their mugs full with the yardarm length of his reach. He had the face and mouth of a cherub but was otherwise all joints and range.

Abe Strapp said, "Does the Duke of Limbs there serve anything stronger than coffee?"

"Of course," Deady said. The captain nodded to the young-ster and he set a glass of rum before Abe Strapp, refusing to meet anyone's eye though they all stared.

They'd settled in their chairs as if it was a social visit they were enjoying, as if they had all the time in the world. Cheater spoke of an old Scotchman from Inverness he encountered in Paita who was bred to the sea and engaged in the contraband trade along the Spanish Main. He was taken captive and shipped to Montevideo and from there to a prison in Lima where he suffered for many years, though he was spared being sent into the mines for his Roman Catholic faith. Eventually a rich Spanish matron procured him a pardon and the two were married.

"His wife was long dead by then," Cheater said, "and he was a wealthy man. He'd fallen sick in Paita and was waiting for servants to take him home overland. I hadn't time to count the number who arrived to collect him. His saddle would have purchased fifty horses. The stirrups were solid gold and every part was laden with it."

"A rich dead wife and a saddle laden with gold," Strapp said. "Every man's dream."

"Please," Deady said, as if the notion was too provoking to go unchallenged in mixed company.

"It would serve you to ignore my brother as much as possible," the Widow said.

"Brother? You are his sister?"

"It is a curiosity to us all, Captain."

"Kiss mine arse," Abe said.

The Widow smiled across at him with a cold disdain before turning to their host who was gaping back and forth between them, amused and incredulous both. "How did you come to your vocation, Captain?"

He was the son of an opulent family in Boston, Deady told her, who were principal owners of the *Moriah*. Her guns, he offered as an aside to the King's representative at the table, formerly belonged to one of His Majesty's frigates which was cast away near Boston. Like Cheater's old Scotchman, Deady said, he was bred to the sea.

"And were you bred to marauding the homes of innocents as well?"

"We live in a fallen world," Deady said with a shrug. "And in every instance, the larger kind eat the smaller."

"That seems an over-broad claim," the Beadle said.

"Name me the exception," the captain demanded. He looked up and down the table. "Master Cheater," he said. "You've circumnavigated the globe in your time."

"Twice over," Cheater said.

"And what in your experience suggests anything other?"

"Very little I'm afraid," Cheater said mournfully before launching into a long discourse on the villainy and inequities that undergird the nations of the earth, Christian and infidel together. Innocents kidnapped on street corners and in taverns and pressed into service in the British Navy. Female chattel in the West Indies who brought them fruit on Sundays flogged from their decks by the Jolly Jumper on Monday morning.

"I've seen slaves on Jamaican estates who had run away and wore iron collars with long hooks to catch the bushes should they run away again. And a one-legged cooper who was chained to the block at which he wrought."

No one in the room so much as glanced at the cabin boy standing in the shadows though everyone's attention inclined in that direction.

"Even where whips and chains are absent," Cheater said, "the rule still applies. The Chinese, now, they are the most oppressed people I was ever among. Every junk has a mandarin on board who keeps order and collects the revenue and tyrannizes over the poor Chinese. Tommy Linn we engaged as barber for the six months we were in Wampoa. He paid seventy dollars for leave to practise on the river. Each new moon all the men must shave their heads or face punishment from the mandarin who lords over their lives entire. They must want even a wife if they are not rich enough to pay the mandarin's tax."

"The mandarin sounds much like our Justice of the Peace," the Widow said.

Abe Strapp had drifted off during Cheater's soliloquy and he was surprised by the sudden laughter at the table and the faces all looking his way. He picked up his glass and drank to cover his confusion.

"The Chinese are clever and industrious and they are excellent copiers," Cheater said, as if he had been granted leave to offer a general treatise on that ancient and obscure race. "But they are not inventors."

Deady shook his head. "That seems an over-broad claim, Master Cheater."

"Nothing I experienced among them contradicts it. The oldest articles you can fall in with are the same make and fashion as the newest. Their houses and their manners are the same today as two hundred years ago. One of our officers sat to have his portrait done and asked only that the painter not make him ugly. 'How can make other than what is?' the Chinese said. He had no idea of altering a single detail to improve upon the object. All was a slavish copy of what was before his eyes."

"There is a skill even in that, is there not?"

"Competence is the lowest form of art," the Widow said.

"You make it sound," Deady offered, "as if true art is not to be trusted."

"I couldn't effectively argue that conclusion, Captain."

"Art and women," Abe Strapp said. "Scratch the surface and an infernal lie shows beneath."

The table went quiet with a wordless animosity toward the proprietor of C. Strapp & Son that Deady couldn't help but join. And that ended the spell of civility they'd been enjoying.

The crew of the *Moriah*, Captain Deady announced, would scuttle every ship in the harbour and burn every building in Mockbeggar and Nonsuch unless a sufficient ransom was paid.

"Hell and damnation," Abe said.

"These actions would condemn our people to starvation or death from exposure," the Beadle said.

The captain turned his palms up on the table. "A regrettable outcome certainly. But I must confess, my men have such a low opinion of the King and his subjects that most would take pleasure in the notion."

"What would your crew require to forego their pleasures?" the Widow asked.

Deady sat back and raised his face to the beams, his head jigging side to side as if he were totting a bill in his head. "We would be satisfied with two thousand pounds."

"Hell and damnation," Abe said again.

"Captain," the Widow said. "Can we speak not of what you would like but what is in our power to pay?"

"We are prepared to negotiate," he said affably.

She offered up a detailed accounting of Caines Mercantile's season, the outlay in salt and provisions and salary and equipment, the quintals of fish taken. "We expected a profit of near fifteen hundred pounds. As a result of damage and lost revenue incurred by a storm September last," she said, "we have posted losses instead. Even after we collect on our insurance, we will scarcely have our heads above water."

"Twas a terrible storm," Abe Strapp said. "We was all lucky to come through it alive."

The Widow said, "My brother, on the other hand, brought his hogs to a fine market. His ships escaped most of the storm's damage and I imagine he has done relatively well on the season."

"Indeed," the captain said. He turned to Abe Strapp who was staring at his sister like he wanted to eat her eyeballs from their sockets.

"He is also the proprietor of a tavern and Mockbeggar's only, what should we call it? Fashion academy? And as Justice of the Peace he collects a tax from all the alehouses and grog shops on the shore."

Deady placed his hand on Abe's forearm. "I see now," he said, "where your opinion of the fairer sex might have its roots."

"I'm sure you know the currency of the economy in this colony is credit," the Beadle offered. "There is little cash money in circulation."

"My good people," Deady said. "I hope my hospitality has not been taken as an invitation to abuse me."

"I have three hundred pounds sterling on hand," the Widow said.

The marauder winced slightly, helpless to disguise his disappointment. "And you, Mr. Strapp?"

Abe shrugged. He looked across the table at the Beadle.

"Altogether," Clinch said. "Just above seven hundred."

Deady let out a long sigh. "My crew has been shut up aboard in the freezing cold for weeks now," he said. "They have become exceedingly restless of late. I doubt I could talk them out of their entertainments for so little."

"Could I suggest one other thing?" the Widow asked.

"By all means."

"Most of the ships on this shore, to be frank, are butter-boxes and nipperkins and all well past their prime. There is one notable exception, however."

"Woman," Abe Strapp said but Deady raised his hand to warn him quiet.

"Master Cheater's vessel, *The Fortune*," she said. "It was just launched out of New England when it was captured by the British Navy two years past. Mr. Strapp's firm purchased it at auction in Poole. I imagine it would be a fine prize to bring back to Boston. Along with the money we have on hand, might it serve as a sufficient ransom?"

Deady asked after its original name, its tonnage and draft and sails, the price paid at auction, Cheater and the Beadle offering up those details while Abe Strapp seethed in his chair like a kettle on a stovetop.

"It pains me to think of depriving a sailor such as Master Cheater of his vessel."

Cheater raised his arms. "A life on the ocean makes no promises, Captain."

"You guarantee our properties will be left whole," the Widow said.

"On my honour."

"Well then. Do we have an agreement in principle?"

"Pending an inspection of the vessel and production of the money discussed," the captain said, "I believe we do."

Abe Strapp called for more rum and the Duke of Limbs stepped forward with the bottle.

"For me as well," the captain said. "We will toast a successful conclusion to our business." When their shots were poured he turned to Abe Strapp and raised his glass. "Your sister is a most formidable character."

Abe lifted his drink. "May you both burn in hell."

A knock interrupted them and Deady motioned the Duke of Limbs to the door where he admitted the privateer who first spoke at the church.

"We have volunteers who wish to throw in with the *Moriah*," he said.

Deady waved them in from the outer passage and the three ark ruffians presented themselves.

"God's blood," Abe said.

"You work for this man?" Deady asked.

"We was bound to him in servitude to escape transportation to Australia," Lynch said.

"I ferried them across the pond two years ago, Captain," Cheater said. "They are the very devils. Not a one of them will louse a grey head of their own before they swing from the gallows."

The captain nodded. "You have just described half my crew, Master Cheater." He turned back to the thieves. "You are volunteering to leave Mr. Strapp's company and serve on the *Moriah*?"

"We would happily blot the skrip and jar it to be shot of this stall whimper. He's the biggest coward ever shat a turd."

"I should have let the Beadle whip you to death when I had the chance," Abe said.

"What would you say to sailing *The Fortune* out from under the man?" Deady asked.

"I would gladly kick his arse to Coventry and back if it pleased you, sir."

Deady pushed away from the table and stood before the three. He had them raise their branded hands to swear an oath of allegiance to him and the vessel and the men who crewed it. "Welcome aboard the *Moriah*," he said.

"They pledged three years' service to me the same," Abe said. "Their word is as close to God's curse as a whore's arse."

"It's been my experience," Deady said, "that an oath is only as good as the man it is sworn to." After the ark ruffians were ushered out, the captain made arrangements to transport his guests back to shore, warning them in his genial fashion against trying to raise a resistance among the locals or making any attempt to abscond with money or property.

"Where would we go?" the Widow asked.

"A fair point," Deady admitted. "But I prefer being as clear as possible in these matters. You will return to your homes with escorts and you will be shot dead if any action suggests you are considering these options. We have your keys and will be collecting the ransom from your premises. If we discover any discrepancy in the amount of money spoken of this morning, you will be shot dead. Master Cheater," he said, "I would like to make a tour of *The Fortune* this afternoon."

"I am at your service," Cheater said.

At the Caines house, the Widow found her birdcage open and the three grassy birds nowhere inside the building. She went upstairs to her office where she was surprised to see the bottom drawer of the desk still sealed. She shut the office door and took the iron poker to the lock. It was the Pilgrim's gold ring with the flying death's head she was after and she held her breath until she laid her hand on it. A chill passing through her at the cold beauty of the thing. She looped it on a leather string and slipped the necklace under her shirt, folding her hands over it as she sat looking out the window.

She lit a fire in the grate and placed her sketching book on her desk. She began drawing features of Captain Deady's cabin boy while her memory was fresh, trying to capture the unusual proportions and symmetry of the arms, the length of his dark fingers knuckled like alder branches. The tight weave of curls against the skull, its peculiar cross-hatch pattern. The full lips of the cherub mouth.

She couldn't say how much time had passed when she heard her escort in conversation with someone in the hall below. Then steps coming up the stairs and a knock at the door. She closed the sketch book on the desk. "Come in," she said.

Captain Deady stepped into the tiny room, apologizing for the intrusion.

"We are at your disposal, Captain," she said. "Apologies seem beside the point." And she gestured him to a chair beside the desk.

Deady took a necklace of keys from his pocket. "We have discovered the locks for all these at Caines's premises and at your offices in Nonsuch and downstairs here. But for one," he said. And he held up the mystery key.

She pointed to the drawer closest to the floor.

"This lock has been forced."

"I assume it was forced by someone among your crew. They also released three birds belonged to me from a cage in the sitting room."

"As I said, Mrs. Caines, my men have been cooped up too long. Has anything gone missing from the drawer?"

She shook her head.

"Really?" he said. "There hardly seems a need to lock a drawer that contains nothing worth stealing."

She leaned forward and removed the government seal. "This was my father's," she said, "when he was Justice of the Peace."

Deady reached for it and turned it over in his hands. "You did not strike me as the sentimental type, Mrs. Caines."

"We contain multitudes, Captain."

He smiled at her. "And there was nothing other in the drawer?"

She sighed. "I ask you, as a gentleman, to take my word in this matter."

"Of course you must know," he said, "such a request forces me to demand exactly what it is you wish to hide."

"And if I do not?"

"You will be shot dead, of course."

The Widow considered calling his bluff. He seemed relaxed, cheerful. Absolutely earnest. She reached to push the book of sketches across the desk toward him.

He took it up and turned it in his hands as he had the government seal, then began browsing slowly through the pages, glancing up now and then to the woman beside him. Nodding his head and murmuring occasionally.

"These are the birds that were released?"

"The jays are long dead. You will find the missing birds further along."

Deady took his time, studying individual sketches for minutes at a time. He lingered over the drawings of a spectral infant's face, the endless iterations of a flying death's head. "You have a great talent," he said.

"I am competent at best," she said. "Which is why I choose to keep the book under lock and key."

"Scripture tells us it is a sin to hide our light under a bushel."

"You did not strike me," she said, "as the pious type."

He smiled again, enjoying the sensation of knocking up against hidden shoals and sunkers in their conversation. "Have you travelled much beyond Mockbeggar, Mrs. Caines?"

"I've never left the shore."

The captain looked up from the book. "Not true!"

"This surprises you?"

"It would not surprise me to think it of your brother, certainly."

"That seems a harsh judgement on our little village, Captain."

He laughed as an apology for the slight. "From our brief acquaintance," he said, "I feel it would be a loss to the world if you never travelled abroad."

"What did you say about the world, Captain? In every instance the larger kind eats the smaller? I would be a fool to venture into a realm so unforgiving."

The marauder watched her a moment, as if taking the Widow in for the first time. "It is a mistake to judge a person's appetite by the size of their teeth," he said. "Some among us are never full. No mettle in nature will overmatch that condition."

He turned back to the book of drawings and came to her sketches of the cabin boy. He made a noise in his throat as he leafed through them, the Widow watching light and shadow animate his face, as if a fire kindled below the surface.

"How long has he been with you?"

"I purchased him in Haiti last spring," Deady said.

"Well. That forfends any need for him to pledge his allegiance."

"I have offered him his freedom for just such a declaration. But so far he has refused to swear any oath." The captain smiled across at her ruefully and she could see he was genuinely hurt by that rejection. "He would make a fine Quaker, would he not?"

The wind had risen through the morning and added a metal blade to the February cold. A dry dwy of snow blew in with low clouds promising storm. Matterface and Heater and a handful of others were missing from Mockbeggar and Nonsuch and it seemed likely they would perish if they'd scattered in through the country without proper fit-outs or tinder or provision. The Beadle requested permission to send a search party for the absent men but Deady refused.

"We will be shipping out on the evening tide," he said. "You can make all efforts you wish once we are at sea."

"The missing will likely be dead by then."

"Our thoughts and prayers are with them," he said.

The weather grew steadily worse as the day passed, with snow and a heavy breeze blowing out to sea. The marauders plundered stores and root cellars for lamp oil and nails and canvas, for salt meat and fish and dry goods. They skinned out Abe Strapp's tavern and the other alehouses and took what livestock they could corral, loading all the pilfered supplies aboard *The Fortune*. Deady left his first mate in charge of the *Moriah* and captained *The Fortune* out of the harbour as a salute to Master Cheater who stood on the wharf, watching his vessel sail to open sea and tack about, waiting for the *Moriah* to follow behind.

It was obvious to Cheater that the first mate was passing too close to Tinkershare Head. He yelled uselessly into the storm's racket as the wind shifted unexpectedly north-northwest and drove the *Moriah* towards the cliffs. All hands were on deck to drop sail and stand to the wheel as they tried to haul her off the rocks, steering past the farthest reach of the head with less than a fathom of water to draw. And as dusk fell, both vessels disappeared into the weltering snow.

The Beadle sent men into the backcountry in search of the missing livyers as soon as *The Fortune* weighed anchor, though the February dark was nearly upon them and the storm the day had promised was settling in. They struck toward Looking Glass Pond and fanned out along the Scrape and inland towards the Sisters and further south and east across the frozen barrens. Within hours all three parties were driven to find shelter, settling for the night in whatever droke or rocky lun they could hit upon in the dark. They cut small trees and branches to mend a roof above themselves and to make fires, but they could scarcely keep them alight for the sap in the green wood and they suffered all night with the cold.

While they were abroad in the elements, Matterface and Heater appeared at the Big House, banging at the door to wake the women inside, both so frozen they were speechless. The Abbess lit a lamp and had the girls kick up the fire and she sent one off to fetch the Beadle. They set about trying to undress the two men but their clothes were barricaded with ice and had to be cut away with metal shears.

They were put to bed by the time Clinch arrived and he examined their faces and ears and their extremities for signs of frostbite, all the while lecturing them for their stupidity and cowardice. He turned to the Abbess who he didn't recognize without her extravagant wig or makeup. "Give them tea and bread," he said. "If they are able to keep that down, warm rum and some venison broth in an hour."

Six other men made their way home in various states of distress through the night and they were wrapped in blankets next to fires and fed by hand like orphaned animals, bawling and bleating as the ravaged flesh of their hands and feet slowly came to life.

In the morning, a search party came upon the last of the missing near a pond beyond the Sisters. The man was half-covered in the night's fall of snow and unconscious when the searchers came upon him. They shook him and called his name until he roused himself and blinked up at them. The youngster they all knew as Terrified seemed to recognize them, nodding at the faces peering down. They helped him to his feet and he walked a few yards until his legs failed him and he was laid out of the wind among the trees that circled the pond. They built a fire and covered the unfortunate in their own coats and he died there without ever opening his eyes to the world again.

The Labrador pack ice arrived in the wake of the *Moriah*'s departure, weeks earlier than expected. There were no open water leads and no patches of loose ice, there was no blue drop in the distance, just a solid sheet of white manacled to the coast, as if to seal them off from the outside world. A circumstance people were grateful for at first.

Even the quality on the shore were reduced to short rations after the marauders cleared their stores and root cellars, and men went in search of seals every day, walking out across the icefield at first light, hoping to land a meal of that rich oily flesh to supplement the little they'd been left to survive on. But weeks passed without sign of hood or harp or round. People fished through the ice on Looking Glass Pond and hunted on the barrens for rabbit and owls and fox. They ate the few chickens and goats left to them. Some killed and dressed their hunting dogs for a meal of what they called bowwow pie. Most nights, most livyers went to bed hungry.

By St. Patrick's Day, the taverns had replenished their supplies with potato alcohol or some other rag water brewed with what was on hand. Abe's house of waste was a turmoil of men mauled by drink. Matterface and Heater were at the gaming table, though both were reduced by their near freezing to death. For a time it looked as if Heater would lose his right foot to frostbite, but sacrificed only a big toe in the end. The dead flesh of Matterface's cheeks and the tip of his nose turned black and he was ever after known as Old Soot.

At the end of March it struck Solemn Lambe that he'd neither seen nor heard a word of Mary Oram since the marauders landed in February. He asked his sister and Lazarus and the Friends at the weekly Quaker meeting, but no one could name the last time they'd laid eyes on the woman.

He and Lazarus saddled the Jerseyman's horse and rode together into Looking Glass Pond and along the Upper Path to the droke of trees that harboured Mary Oram's tilt. There was a line of smoke rising over the spruce which satisfied them the woman was still alive and they considered leaving it there.

"It wouldn't hurt to see she's on her feet at least," Solemn said.

"If you says so."

There was still snow on the ground and the droke was heavy with it, the walking trail an icy cleft in the permanent shade. They rode along the narrow path a ways and stopped at the sound of wood being cleaved somewhere ahead.

Lazarus said, "That's not Mary Oram swinging an axe?"

"I wouldn't put nothing past her."

They dismounted and walked the horse from there, afraid the animal might be spooked by meeting the woman face to face and throw them. The solitary barking of the axe carried on as they came in sight of the tilt.

"Mary Oram," Solemn called.

There was a long deliberate quiet out of their view before Mary Oram answered. "Who is it there?"

"Solemn Lambe," he said. "And Laz Price."

The woman appeared around the corner of the house, her colourful cap tight to her skull.

"You're alright then," Solemn said.

She was watching them with an oddly distrustful look, as if she suspected something might be lurking in the shadows behind them.

"We never saw the first glimpse of you since them marauders struck through," Solemn said. "We was starting to think they packed you aboard as plunder."

"There haven't been no sign of them come back, have there?"

Lazarus said, "Sure they carried off everything worth taking the first time through."

"They couldn't get handy with the ice brought up solid like it is," Solemn added. "They likely sailed for the West Indies by now and good riddance to them."

Mary Oram nodded. "You might as well come inside, you come this far."

Solemn tied the Jerseyman's horse to a tree beside a formidable stack of firewood and they followed the woman into the tiny shack, crouching under the low rafters as their sight adjusted to the sunless dim. An unexpected figure slowly coming clear to them, a strange boy squatting on his heels near the fireplace and watching them with the eyes of a wild creature. Ready to bolt for the clear.

"He showed up here the night they left the harbour," Mary Oram said. "Jumped ship as they was near to rinding on Tinker-share Head and hoofed it in along the Scrape as far as the Upper Path. Wandered up the trail till he happened on this place. Every item he had on was froze solid."

Both Solemn and Lazarus were speechless in the youngster's presence, gobsmacked to find him there and even in the poor light struck by his obvious, uncanny beauty.

"Say your hellos," Mary Oram said. "He don't bite."

They nodded at him and the youngster stood as far as the ceiling allowed, stepping forward to shake their hands.

"The Jerusalem above is free," Lazarus said, for lack of something else coming to him in the moment.

"And she is our mother," Solemn added, with the same awed look.

The youngster smiled at them in confusion and started laughing, which set them off as well, a rolling fit of giggling and guffawing and failed attempts to tamp the hilarity down. None of them could have named what they found funny, other than the strangeness of the world and their own unlikely travels which brought them together, hunched over in a room built for leprechauns.

"You is a well-met crowd of eejits," Mary Oram said. "There's tea made here when you comes to your senses."

He was owned by the captain of the *Moriah* and served most of a year aboard ship as a cabin boy, Mary Oram told them. He seemed perfectly able to speak for himself, but Mary Oram couldn't hold her tongue in company and offered up the youngster's history as he'd told it to her—his months sailing as Deady's property and plotting a way to get clear of the man and his expectations, his demands. She hinted elliptically at things he hadn't been able to speak about directly himself, things that decided him on escape supposing he died in the attempt. Deady's decision to captain *The Fortune* out of the harbour and the confusion aboard the *Moriah* as they nearly wrecked on Tinkershare Head was like someone opening the door to a cage. He slipped over the side into the icy Atlantic and crawled onto the rocks as the vessel scraped by the headland, with no feeling in his arms or legs, his skin burning with a strange heat before the chills set in.

"He was near to dead when he showed up here," Mary Oram said.

"It was lucky he found you," Solemn said.

"I am a lucky person," the youngster said, without a trace of irony or bitterness.

"We half expected they'd come back looking for him. So he been hid out here ever since."

He smiled at her, the teeth on him seeming to glow in the poor light of the tilt. "You have been my saviour," he said.

"Well I'm done with the Lord's work. You got every bit of food I had set by eat up. Time you made your own way now," she said.

"I cannot stay here?" He was blindsided by the announcement.

"I haven't had room to turn about since you come," she said. "It's like sharing a stall with the Jerseyman's horse. These two will take you down into Mockbeggar. See about finding you a situation."

He looked at the two youngsters.

"There's a bed at the Piccos' where you can sleep," Laz suggested.

"There'll be work galore here come the summer," Solemn said.

And after a moment of considering this, seeing he likely had no other option, he nodded.

They led the horse down through Mockbeggar and every soul who saw them stopped to watch as they passed, staring as if they had seen the dead rise from their graves and walk amongst the living. Bride eyed the trio coming across the Lower Path and ran out to meet them, Lazarus lifting her onto the horse's back to ride the rest of the way to the Caines property as Solemn explained the bizarre circumstances they found themselves in. The gangly youngster stood nearly as high as the horse's ears and he glanced toward her occasionally as they strolled ahead.

"What is your name?" she asked.

"Dominic," he said and he smiled up at her. "Dominic Laferrière."

He was the most exotic figure she'd ever laid eyes on. The angel's appearance to Mary came to her mind and a wash of the anxiety that had always accompanied that story passed through her. To think something so intimate could be a secret to Mary, that a stranger might arrive to reveal you to yourself, to change your life instantly, irrevocably. Dominic's smile made it seem as if the horse was suddenly galloping across an open field, she had to push her hands into the mane and hold on.

When they reached the house, Bride let herself into the kitchen to see to the fire while they stabled and fed the horse and the three boys came inside then to warm their bones. They could tell from the smell of pipe smoke that the Widow was in the house and Solemn went upstairs to find her. They all stood when he brought her into the kitchen.

"Oh my," she said. She stared at Dominic so long that he dropped his eyes to his feet. She stepped closer with a half-smile, her cheek twitching slightly. She reached her hand to take his. "I'm glad to meet you under friendlier circumstances."

"Yes, madam," he said.

"Please, sit," she said and she took a chair next to the stranger. "Solemn tells me you have decided you prefer Mockbeggar to life aboard the *Moriah*?"

"He'll be looking for a position of some sort," Solemn said.

"There is no shortage of work. And you are clearly no stranger to work," she said.

There was something unsettling about the way she took in the youngster, a greedy scrutiny that put Dominic in mind of Captain Deady though he couldn't have said the why of it. It was the first time since the storm that Bride recognized the old Mrs. Caines in the woman's face, the avid, assiduous focus she had always turned upon the world.

"I have never seen hair quite like yours," the Widow said. She had one hand suspended in the air between them. "May I? May I touch it?"

"It is only hair," he said as she ran her fingertips across his scalp, his dark face colouring darker with a shame that made the other youngsters squirrel in their seats.

"We ought to get over to the Piccos'," Lazarus said. "I'm hoping they might let him have my old bunk."

"Tell Aubrey I'd like arrangements made for Dominic to be taken on." The Widow ducked her head to look up into his face beside her. "You are most welcome to stay here if Aubrey and Relief are unable to accommodate you."

"Yes, madam," he said without letting her look into his eyes. "Thank you, madam."

The Duke of Limbs's appearance in Mockbeggar was only slightly less shocking to the livyers than the guns of the *Moriah* firing over their heads in the dead of night. Rumour and gossip and speculation overran the shore like a panicked population in their small clothes. To some the youngster was a marauder, deserter or no, and they wanted him tied to the whipping post where they might exact a measure of revenge for their losses. Others were certain his presence meant the *Moriah* would return in search of him and argued he should be hauled to the ice edge and put to sea on a raft.

Even those with less vehement attitudes were taken up with conjecture. He was a blue skin, according to some, fathered upon an Ethiopian by a white man. He was a Haitian prince kidnapped by the American privateers and was richer than James Wibling and his witch. He was descended from a race of cannibals, the Anthropophagi. He had a cock like those of donkeys and his emission was like that of a stallion, he spoke a biblical language understood only by angels and the Adversary himself. The talk was so consuming it made people forget their hunger and worry awhile.

Aubrey and Relief took the youngster into their home as Lazarus predicted and they, in their fashion, were delighted with him. Relief knew some rudimentary French and insisted he speak his native tongue in her company and teach her three new words each day and correct her atrocious pronunciation.

The Widow first suggested Dominic serve alongside Bride as a houseboy but he was so visibly distressed by the notion that she walked it back. As if he was a bird she might tame in incremental steps. He worked in the gardens at the Caines house instead, he and Solemn grooming the Jerseyman's horse and mucking out the stables and puttering at repairs to the fences and outbuildings.

The Widow able to watch at her leisure from the office window. Dominic caught glimpses of her standing above them there and he refused to go inside the Caines house, even to share a meal in the kitchen with Solemn and Bride.

Solemn took that reticence almost as a personal affront and Bride had to explain it was the Widow he was avoiding.

"She don't mean him no harm," he said.

"She looks at Dominic the way Abe Strapp looks at drink," she said.

"There's not one jot of Abe Strapp in Mrs. Caines."

Bride stared at her brother, surprised still by his blind allegiance to the woman, his unwillingness to look past the silvered surface.

"Those two are as close as the rind on a tree," she said.

He wouldn't have been more stunned if she had slapped him. And Bride was almost as taken aback. She'd never till that moment articulated the notion but the truth of it was plain as soon as the words were spoken. Abe Strapp and the Widow Caines viewed the world as a glass to their own visage and nothing within their sight was granted a life independent. Every creature beyond themselves existed only to serve their designs and appetites. For years that knowledge had lived in Bride as a persistent, formless discomfort and even now it was beyond her to outline or offer it in any detail.

"You oughten to speak so about her," Solemn said.

"That woman would eat her own children," Bride whispered.

Solemn stared at her as if he didn't recognize the girl suddenly. "Was it Imogen Purchase told you as much?"

"Imogen?" she said. "Did Imogen tell me what?"

He shook his head in disgust. It seemed a peculiar pettiness the Widow aroused in other women and it galled him to see Bride fall prey to the nonsense. He said, "Abe Strapp murdered our father, Sister." Which was his world's one abiding and unanswerable fact.

The Labrador ice hung on weeks longer than even Inez Barter could recall, stretching away in an unbroken sheet to the horizon through April and into the first half of May. The weather felt months out of season. The ice gave a serrated edge to the onshore winds and people hunched around their chests, as if to keep their hearts from seizing up in the unrelenting cold.

The Widow was almost absent from the life of the town through it all, as if she'd fallen ill with another grievous ailment. She stopped attending the weekly Quaker meetings and worked from home, walking each day in the gardens to watch her latest acquisition at work. She spent part of her evenings sketching the long arch of Dominic's back, the reach of his hands, his eyes as dark as the empty sockets of the flying death's head impressed on the Pilgrim's ring.

Aubrey Picco was her only visitor and they hashed through their options to keep Caines Mercantile solvent through the coming season. The storm's massive losses and the cash money surrendered to the privateers meant kicking their loans up the road and taking on more debt at rates Abe Strapp would have been embarrassed to force on drinkers in the local grog shops.

"It is an unfortunate confluence," Aubrey said. "No one could have foreseen these circumstances."

"If the ice keeps the shore under lock and key much longer the coming season will be something less than we might hope besides," the Widow said.

"We are in God's hands at this point," Aubrey admitted.

And the Widow couldn't say if he meant it as comfort or warning.

As much as possible, people spent those waiting days in industry—hunting in the backcountry, cutting and junking green trees as their stores of firewood ran low. They caulked and payed their fishing boats, they barked their twine and their nets to be ready when the ice finally broke. But they slept longer through the nights and dropped off at odd points through the days as well, setting their heads down on a table and disappearing into dreamless bouts of sleep that more and more seemed a rehearsal for death. Waking after five minutes or an hour and hauling their anemic selves back into the day.

Even the Abbess's girls fell into a kind of languishing, lounging about the Big House half-dressed and silent like pale statuettes in the homes of European nobility. Most of the men who came looking for comfort or release managed only a dry bob or fell asleep in the arms of the girls halfway through the act. Some argued they should be charged half the usual rate but the Abbess was unmoved. "The meal costs the same," she said, "whether you touch the mutton or not."

No one had had time for schooling in the aftermath of the September storm, all ages setting to the work of rebuilding the harbour, and the new school teacher left on the fall's last packet boat without having taught a single class. In that absence, Relief Picco took it upon herself to teach Dominic his letters and numbers and Lazarus spent all his unoccupied time at the Picco house to help with those lessons and to read to Dominic from the Bible. He ate his meals and slept there most nights as well. He sacrificed the Sunday rides to walk into Mary Oram's tilt with the Duke of Limbs, bringing the woman some bit of hard bread or a few potatoes they'd scavenged through the week.

Bride felt Laz's absence from her days as a physical ailment, an ache in her chest or her side. Each time she had to interrogate it—had she slept wrong? did she strike something?—before the cause came to her and the ache shifted, taking up a little more space, finding a more tender spot to settle. In some small way it was akin to mourning, a vague echo of the months after her father was murdered when her heart felt like a bag of sand, the wet heft of it drawing her down to the earth she came from. But setting those emotions side by side in her mind struck her as absurd and shameful and she pushed the complaint aside.

Her suffering would have been invisible to Solemn if it hadn't offered an exact mirror to his own. Watching her walk quiet to the Widow's in the morning dark, the way she paused in her day with a hand to her chest, as if she'd forgotten someone's name and was keeping still until it came to her. It was himself Solemn saw there, his face twinned in her disappointment, in her troublesome, wordless heartbreak. As far as he could measure, he and his sister were both unremarkable creatures. It was no surprise that Lazarus would turn his face to the light of Dominic Laferrière and leave Bride and Solemn to the shadows.

It hurt most to see that the change in their circumstances affected Lazarus not at all. He greeted them with the same familial devotion and enthusiasm. As far as Laz was concerned, their relations hadn't altered in the slightest, his affection for them as animate and central as ever. It was clear to Solemn, and to Bride in her own private torment, that they carried their flames alone. This was the indelible message the angel of the Lord had come to deliver unto them.

Abe Strapp spent most of those stagnant, sluggish weeks in con-
ference with the Beadle, discussing the likely state of the Widow's
mercantile firm, weighing various reprisals as payback for the loss
of *The Fortune*. It was Clinch who suggested Abe make a claim to
the Duke of Limbs as compensation.

"Sue for him, you mean?"

"The Widow is benefitting from the youngster's labour when
C. Strapp & Son has clearly incurred the greatest suffering. On
top of which you've lost three servants and are shorthanded for
the coming season."

Abe ran through those facts among the drinkers at the Big
House as if he was rehearsing a case due to be heard before the
Privy Council. Each time he felt more aggrieved, more certain that
C. Strapp & Son was owed any compensation that came to hand.
And the Duke of Limbs had come to hand.

Everyone in the Picco house had heard some version of the
man's claim as it made the rounds on the shore. But they weren't
prepared for the vulgar intensity Abe brought to stating it in
person, barging in with the constables while they were sat to
their meagre supper. Lazarus and Relief stood from their chairs
and moved behind Dominic to face down the trio that had come
through the door. As if they were seconds in a formal duel.

"Chimney chops there," Abe Strapp announced without pre-
amble, "is by rights the property of C. Strapp & Son."

Relief Picco placed a hand to the youngster's shoulder. "Dominic is not property," she said. "He will work where he chooses."

"Where he chooses?" Abe said. "A beggar will choose his
food, is this what I'm to believe?"

All three men were visibly flawed with drink. The constables were both carrying pistols. Aubrey raised his arms to ask for calm, for civility. "Please," he said.

"I will have a word with the Duke of Limbs and Mr. Picco," Abe said, and he waved a hand to dismiss the two standing behind the youngster's chair.

Laz shook his head. "I will stay," he said. And Relief moved closer again to Dominic.

"God's teeth," Abe hissed. "I see the women are in charge in this she-house, Aubrey."

"They are their own masters under this roof," he said.

"Well outside this hen-frigate, Miss Molly there is a servant of C. Strapp & Son and he would do well to remember as much. And yon dog booby is rightfully mine besides."

"Dominic is already in service with Caines Mercantile," Relief said.

"What, he's taken an oath, has he? I thought oaths were not worth a damn to a Quaker?"

Aubrey said, "He is free to make his own choices in these matters."

"And what of yourself, Aubrey. This is your choice then? To have one of the blue squadron up your wife's skirts?"

Relief took her hand off the boy's shoulder like she'd been scalded. Dominic stood from his chair and Aubrey raised his palm to the youngster. Pleading for calm and civility.

"That black ram is tupping your white ewe, Mr. Picco, or I'm a blind man."

"There is nothing more to discuss on this matter," Aubrey said quietly.

Abe bent forward and squinted, putting a hand to his ear. "Sorry massa," he said, "me no scavey."

"You and your men are welcome to take your leave."

"I will not leave without satisfaction from Sir Duke here," he insisted. He folded his arms above his gut and stared across at the youngster.

Aubrey finally stood from his chair. "Dominic will give your claim due consideration," he said.

"My eyes and limbs!" Strapp said and he swung around to face the constables. "Due consideration!" He turned back to the table and made a sweeping bow towards Dominic Laferrière. "I will await your considered response, m'lord." And feeling he'd made a sufficiently witty spectacle of himself, he led his constables out, the three men laughing among themselves.

Relief was in tears before they were through the door, her hands shimmering with rage. She turned to Dominic but he stepped back and would not let her touch him. He knew enough of the world to see everything between himself and the Piccos had been changed with those few filthy words. The truth of a matter held little water where the alternative was more lurid and satisfying. Lazarus could see the same, the two youngsters avoiding each other's eyes.

It was obvious that Aubrey and Relief were innocent of the fact and for just a moment Dominic despised their childish artlessness. To not know those words would always be in their company on the paths of the town, in the warehouses and twine sheds, whispering from corners to poison all that was good between them.

"There is nothing to his claim on you," Relief said.

"*Néanmoins*," he said.

Relief looked up at him, not understanding.

"Nevertheless," he said.

The breakup when it came was sudden. The prevailing onshore winds shifted out to sea and pushed the ice off the land, the field coming apart in seams and reaches and massive lakes of open ocean, as if overnight the pack had lost the will to hang on one more day.

The harbour was clear for the first time since February and the vessels that had been locked in a months-long vise drifted free on the water's surface. Supply ships began arriving from Fogo and St. John's where they had been forced to wait out the ice. People's barren stores were replenished with flour and rice and peas and molasses, with barrels of salt meat and hardtack and pickling salt. Crates of hens were stacked on the wharves. Sheep and goats and pigs and a handful of cows were goaded down the gangplanks and herded off the waterfront to the bare gardens. Cases of rum and Blue Ruin and kegs of brandy were hefted up to the taverns and grog shops.

Beyond the Beadle's formal prayers of thanksgiving at Sunday services, there was little in the way of celebration to have come through another winter. People were skinned out by months of hard eating and the summer's labour was upon them. They tucked into the fresh provisions and set to work with a purpose, hoping to avoid similar deprivations in the year ahead. *The Hope* and *Success* were readied for coasting to make as much of the abbreviated season as possible.

Over Relief and Aubrey's protests, Dominic Laferrière moved out of the Picco house to sleep in Solemn Lambe's bed while Solemn settled into the servants' room at the Caines house. And Dominic took it upon himself to approach the Beadle about Abe Strapp's demands for restitution.

"I was unaware the Widow had conceded the claim," Clinch said.

"I have asked Mr. Picco to speak with her."

The Beadle sucked his cheek into the gap on the toothless side of his mouth. He had expected a long series of claims and counterclaims to the governor by correspondence, something that would be a thorn in the Widow's side for years without accomplishing anything concrete. It still shocked him to see that Abe Strapp's oafish interventions sometimes achieved all the man wanted and more.

He gathered papers and ink and made out a contract for three years of service. He read it aloud to the youngster standing before his desk to be certain he understood what he was signing.

"After three years you will be free to find other employment. Or to establish your own operation on the shore. This is agreeable to you?"

The Duke of Limbs lifted his long arms away from his sides.

Clinch turned the contract towards him and proffered the quill. "Your mark, please."

And he surprised the Beadle by writing out, in a laboured, childlike script, his signature: *D. Laferrière.*

A request to call upon the Widow arrived the following morning. The Beadle walked to the Caines house and took his place near the fireplace in the sitting room. The birdcage standing empty beside him. Moments later the Widow appeared and took her seat on the chesterfield and they exchanged a few pleasantries, which was the woman's way of acknowledging she wanted something from him.

"Did Bride offer you tea?"

"She did. Bride is how old now?"

"I don't know. Fourteen? I think she's fourteen."

"I'm surprised she is still unmarried."

"The Friends allow a woman more say in these affairs than might otherwise be the case."

"Yes," he said and he looked to the ceiling to show how deeply he disapproved of that particular quirk.

The Widow said, "I was expecting to have heard some word from the governor this spring."

"On what matter?"

"Our petition to remove Mr. Strapp from his position as Justice."

"The governor is a busy man."

"I was wondering if you might have received any word?"

"I don't know why correspondence would be directed to my attention."

"Nor I. Unless, of course, you sent correspondence to advise the governor one way or the other last fall."

"I would not presume to instruct the governor in any circumstance. Nor should anyone other."

She laughed then, but lightly, not wanting to offend him in the moment.

He said, "Mrs. Caines, I would like *The Hope* to sail at the earliest opportunity and there is still much to be done."

"I'm sorry to keep you," she said. She paused, as if reluctant to broach the subject that was really on her mind. "I wanted to ask about the negro."

"Dominic?"

"There is only the one, is there not?"

He nodded. "What of him?"

"He was engaged with Caines Mercantile, Mr. Clinch."

"He came to us of his own accord. Any complaint should be directed to him, not our firm."

"He came to you under duress."

"I am not privy to his motivations."

"Abe Strapp was drunk. The constables were also drunk and carrying pistols."

"That is something you will have to take up with Mr. Strapp."

"I am perfectly willing to file a suit in this matter if necessary."

"As your brother is the local magistrate, it will have to be heard in Twillingate or Bonavista. Or perhaps St. John's."

The Widow glanced to the door, the line of muscle in her jaw clenching repeatedly like she was trying to chew through her own teeth. Uncertain if it was her brother or the Beadle she despised most. More and more they appeared to her to be a single galling entity.

"Forgive me," he said. "I am wanted at Mr. Strapp's's offices."

She got to her feet. "As a dog returns to his vomit," she said, "so a fool returns to his folly."

He bowed deeply. "Shall I tell your brother to expect you, Mrs. Caines?"

She was already on her way toward the stairs. "I will find him at his whorehouse, I assume."

"In all likelihood," the Beadle said, though not loud enough for her to hear.

~

The Widow made her visit mid-morning the next day. It was the first week of June and the harbour was socked in with fog as if to cloak her walk through Mockbeggar from the eyes of others. Her childhood home silent as she approached the door and she let herself in as though she still lived there. A sour reek of alcohol and puke on the floors and in the filthy straw along the hallway.

There was a fire laid in the sitting room and the Abbess was in her chair when the Widow came to the doorway.

"Goodness," the woman said.

"I was hoping to speak with my brother."

"I'm afraid Mr. Strapp is indisposed at the moment."

She looked about the room, the familiar furniture beaten down by months of mindless debauch. The mirror over the fireplace hanging askew and webbed with cracks. "I will wait," she said. The Widow took out her pipe and filled it with tobacco and lit it at the fireplace. She walked across the sticky floor and took a seat on the ruined chesterfield.

The two women had never exchanged a word before.

The Abbess said, "I am Mrs. Valentine."

"I didn't realize you were married."

"It's more an honorary title in my case, Mrs. Caines."

"You are married to your profession."

"I never took a vow," she said. "But enough time has passed that it seems I may as well have done."

"I hope at least it has been a happy union."

The Abbess tilted her head. "It's like any marriage, I imagine. Some mornings I wake in the bed I've made and wish I was dead." She laughed then, to renounce any claim to pity. "I'm sure you know what I mean."

"Men are open books, Mrs. Valentine. It's impossible not to tire of them."

The Abbess rolled her eyes to say she didn't need to be told about a man's nature. She gestured at the Widow then, at her get-up, her pipe. "I can't see why ever you would want to be like them."

"I never wanted to be like them particularly," the Widow said. "I wanted what they have."

"A prick, you mean?"

She looked at the Abbess to indicate she was disappointed in her. "Choices," she said. "Options."

The Abbess watched her steadily, as if she was trying to picture the woman without her clothes. "It is a mystery how you and Abe Strapp could have been sired by the same man upon the same woman. He is the simplest creature I have ever had the pleasure to pleasure," she said with a little laugh. "Stroke his honey pipe or suckle his pride and he sleeps like a baby. I don't know how you and he ever managed to share a house."

"It did not go well," the Widow said. She looked about the room. "It is still not going well."

They turned their heads toward the sound of the front door and seconds later Mary Oram's diminutive frame appeared before them, her bag on her shoulder.

The Abbess sat forward in her chair and clapped her hands. "Now here is a meeting," she said.

"You two is busy," Mary Oram said.

"Not at all," the Abbess said. "We are waiting for Mr. Strapp to present himself." She turned to the Widow. "Can you imagine the face on the man if he were to find us three together?" She slapped her thighs at the notion. "How many have you for us?" she asked.

"There's only a handful been slaughtered since they come off the ships," she said. "But I managed to cobble twenty pieces for you out of that lot." She took a handful of opaque, vaguely leathery-looking envelopes from her bag and handed them to the Abbess.

"I will get you your money."

When they were alone Mary Oram said, "Mrs. Caines."

"What is it you are selling here, Mary Oram?"

"Cundums," she said flatly. "Makes them from sheep gut." She could see the Widow didn't know what she was talking about. "They're like a little tarp goes over the man's tickle tail. Keeps the French disease down." She looked directly at the Widow. "And the babies," she said.

"Most men dislike them," the Abbess said as she came back with a handful of coins. "We generally charge a little more to indulge without. But there's been a sorry lack of materials to hand in recent months." She spoke directly to the child-size woman. "We have a girl pissing pins and needles since the ships from the continent arrived, Mary Oram. Would you have a peek?"

"There's little I can do for that complaint."

"You have worked miracles before." The Abbess looked back over her shoulder as they moved toward the stairs. "I will see if I can rouse Mr. Strapp for you."

The Widow nodded vacantly, preoccupied with the bizarre articles Mary Oram had removed from her bag, trying not to picture how they would be deployed, trying not to imagine such a thing moving inside her. An embarrassment overtook her to be a human creature, to be bound to the vapid degradations of her kind.

She lifted her head to look away from that feeling and caught sight of the mirror above the fireplace, the shattered glass reflecting her back in slivers that almost adhered, the figure there riven and distorted and still undeniably herself. It made her think her instincts had been right all along—the world agitated against coherence, against concord, and the truest portrait a person could manage was fragmentary, incomplete.

She heard her brother on the stairs and she knocked out her pipe against the side table and set it away in a pocket as he leaned against the door frame, looking in at her.

"Are you here after a job, Mrs. Caines?"

She stared without answering.

"You will not be to everyone's taste of course," he said. "But in this business, handsome is that handsome does. And I would be fair tempted to take a stroke, our relation notwithstanding."

"Kiss mine arse," she said.

He walked past her and into the dining room to pour himself a drink. "You know, I have always wondered," he said. He stood in the doorway with his glass. "Did you really do the deed with your Quaker husband?"

"Brother."

"I can't picture old Elias with his dangling hangers between your legs. Though many's the time I tried to conjure the image."

The Widow said, "Can we simply move on to business?"

"If you insist," he said.

"How much do you want for him?"

He looked for a moment as if he meant to profess ignorance, to draw out the drama a little longer. But he couldn't resist twisting the blade. "You want to purchase my negro?"

"If that's how you wish to put it. Yes."

He sat in the chair vacated by the Abbess. "I am shocked to hear this, Sister, you being of the Quaker faith."

"Business, Brother. This is a business proposition. Can we dispense with the theatrics, please."

"God's ears, Sister. You have never known how to enjoy yourself, that is your problem."

"I have many problems. That is not one of them."

"Is that why you have come begging for the Duke of Limbs, then? Are you paying for your pleasures?"

"He is a well-trained houseboy, which is a rare commodity in this world."

He scoffed at her. It was a mystery to him exactly what lay at the root of her hankering. He couldn't imagine it was sexual, though there had to be something of that same greedy urge about it to bring her grovelling in person. He leaned forward, shifting his arse ahead a ways to get as close to the Widow as he could without standing. "You want that creature for your menagerie, is it?"

"Brother."

"He's no different to you than the birds in their cage. Or the tadpoles or the dragonflies you used to bring home and sketch off. He is an exotic specimen, I will grant you."

"He is nothing to you."

"I could care less if he lives or dies, it's true."

"Name your price," she said.

He stood from his chair to make a show of refusing her something she wanted. "The negro is not for sale." He smacked his tumescent belly with his free hand, as if he'd just finished a satisfying meal.

"You were given everything," she said. "Your whole life, everything you have was given you."

He smiled down at her. "You wish me dead, don't you Sister."

"With all my heart."

"But I do not feel the same for you," he said. He headed to the door, turning back with a hand on the frame. "I hope you live a long life. And every moment of it in the same black torment you are feeling now."

Abe was upon the high ropes as he left his father's house, walking out without a jacket and not even feeling the chill as he lumbered down toward the waterfront. Giddy with his little performance and already planning an encore. The cluster of warehouses and fishing rooms around the harbour almost invisible in the fog until he was upon them.

He burst into his offices, calling for the Beadle.

"He's on *The Hope*, sir," one of the desk jockeys said.

"What? Gone to sea?"

"As soon as the fog lifts, sir, yes."

Abe clattered back out the door, yelling the Beadle's name as he went.

The Hope was anchored off in the harbour, loaded with salt and provisions to be ferried along the coast. The supplies were behind their time with the delayed arrival of vessels from St. John's and the continent and no one knew what to expect when they arrived in those isolated outposts, if the fall storm had blown them all to hell and gone, if the marauders had stripped them bare. The Beadle gave strict orders to the crew not to mention a word about Captain Deady and the *Moriah* to the outport servants if they hadn't been set upon. He promised a lashing with the salt eel to any sailor who spoke out of turn. "There is no sense worrying our people about something for which there is no remedy," he said.

He'd slept aboard *The Hope* for an early start but woke to the impenetrable fog which likely meant another day's delay. He spent the morning in his cabin, poring over ledgers, allocating food and dry goods according to how many servants were employed at each operation, calling up occasionally to ask if there was any sign of the fog lifting.

Mid-morning one of his crew showed himself at the door. "There's a boat coming out from the wharf for us, Mr. Clinch."

"You can see the wharf?"

"No sir, Mr. Clinch. But there's someone in the boat bawling out for you."

He sat still and could just hear the voice leaking through the fog's muffle. He sighed and set the ledgers aside on the desk. "Let me know what Mr. Strapp wants," he said. "Show him down if he insists on coming aboard."

He assumed Abe was drunk when he barrelled into the tiny room, red-faced and dressed only in a shirt.

"I was afraid I'd miss you," he said, shouting as if he was still calling out across the harbour.

"We are unlikely to weigh anchor in this weather, Mr. Strapp."

"Right," Abe said. "The weather."

"Is something wrong?"

"Wrong? No, nothing. Nothing's wrong." He giggled to himself.

"Mr. Strapp. You have news? Or orders?"

"Yes," he said and he pointed at the Beadle. "I have orders. The Duke of Limbs," he said.

"Yes?"

"He is to go with you aboard *The Hope*."

"On this voyage?"

"This voyage. Today, with any luck."

"We have a full crew already."

"Not as crew. I want him sent to Break Heart. Or anywhere on the shore, it matters not a damn."

"You want to send Dominic Laferrière to one of your operations along the coast?"

"Precisely."

"It doesn't matter where?"

"Not a damn." Abe stamped his foot, unable to keep still. "Although the more unlikely the better."

The Beadle watched his employer a moment. "Have you spoken to Mr. Laferrière about this? Has he consented to the move?"

"*Consent*. God's ears. I will have Matterface and Heater tie the negro in knots and cart him aboard to keep him from the Widow."

"The Widow came to you about him?"

"She asked me to name my price."

The Beadle brought his folded hands to his lips. He couldn't identify all the forces at work in the drama surrounding the Duke of Limbs. But Abe's instincts for sowing aggravation and misery were rarely wrong. "Our first stop is Orphan Cove. They've been asking for someone to go shares with them for years now."

"Who is that then?"

"The Best youngsters," Clinch said. "They lost their mother and father during the last sickness. They've been running the operation on their own since. I half expect to find them dead every spring."

"That would serve," Abe Strapp said. "And if they be dead, somewhere else. Just be certain our snowball never shows his face in this harbour again."

"I will come in with you to make arrangements."

When they emerged onto the deck they could just make out the shape of the wharves and the warehouses behind them. There was a yellowy tint to the mauze overhead as the sun seeped through.

"The fog is lifting, Mr. Clinch," Abe Strapp said. He climbed overside to ladder down to the boat where it waited. "Perhaps you will get away today after all."

"God willing," the Beadle said.

They were forced to wait for the ebb tide, but *The Hope* set sail that evening with the Duke of Limbs aboard. Lazarus and Aubrey and Relief came down to the wharf and Solemn and Bride, all of them numb with the shock of it. They could see the youngster's unmistakable figure up on the rail as the vessel weighed anchor and made for open ocean, one long arm raised to offer a farewell to the friends gathered to see him off. Knowing they would likely never lay eyes on each other again.

A PLAGUE. CAPTAIN TRUSS & MRS. BRACE.
NOAH'S ARK.

The summer was a season of sullenness and resentments.

There was an unexpected scarcity of fish, the cod migrating further north or off into deeper water or swallowed whole by the ocean—there was no obvious explanation for the sudden lack. The fickleness of the sea they relied on made everyone crooked and unreasonable. Boats drifted from their traditional grounds in search of the meagre cod, encroaching on territory fished by other crews who ran them off with curses and threats, pelting them with the squid and herring going rotten in the bait tubs.

Those disputes were sometimes the only thing fishermen brought off the water, the stages and alehouses alight with a web of grievances and spite. There were constant arguments which led to fist fights which devolved into brawls that resolved nothing. When the courts were called upon to mediate, Abe Strapp inevitably settled in favour of the party associated with his firm and his mercenary bias darkened the bad blood.

The Widow Caines spent those ruinous days in her upstairs office, writing letters to the governor in St. John's, and to the Undersecretary of State and to members of the Privy Council in London, outlining her case for having Abe removed from his position as magistrate. The loss of the Duke of Limbs to her brother seemed to have blinded her to any other issue. All her time was devoted to terminating the abomination that was Justice Abe Strapp, as if that would solve every other problem in her life. Or at the very least inflict a comparable loss upon the man. New letters were written in the wake of each additional outrage, her vitriol increasingly naked on the page.

She met with Aubrey Picco if he insisted on bringing some grave matter to her attention—*Success* had run afoul of shoal rock on its return from coasting and required a new keel, their largest creditor in Poole was threatening legal action to recoup its investment. Where the firm was concerned, all matters were grave. But the Widow was unmoved by even the most dire reports, deferring to her headman each time.

She lost interest in running the household, leaving everything in the hands of her servants. Bride and Solemn by then needed no direction, working side by side and seamlessly as always, but even they seemed uncommonly poisoned with one another. Solemn still hadn't forgiven his sister her equation of the Widow's nature with Abe Strapp's perversity and they spoke as little as necessary and avoided each other when they could.

Both Solemn and Bride had expected Lazarus would move back into their home after the Duke of Limbs was shipped to Orphan Cove or Break Heart or wherever he'd been exiled. The thought of Laz returning to the world as it was before Dominic Laferrière occupied their waking hours and much of their dreams as well, a brief flare of hope that tortured them now. Lazarus stayed on with Aubrey and Relief as a balm for their loss, and every day longer without his company at meals, each night settling into their bunks while he slept elsewhere, was another lash of flesh from their backs.

Solemn dreamt of Matterface and Heater stripping Lazarus naked and holding him to the ground, or else the two Philistines pinned Solemn down and touched him in ways he'd never been touched while Lazarus looked on. Bride dreamt of Lazarus tying her arm to the wood horse and branding her with the glowing tip of a poker, his face angelic and calm as the scorching sensation prickled through her. They both woke aroused and horrified and they carried the grimy aftermath of those visions through their waking hours.

The back end of the season was irredeemably cold and wet. Even when the rain let up the cloud cover shrouded the coast in a permanent dusk. The farm gardens were set late and struggled in the miserable weather and half the root vegetables went to rot in the sodden ground. The green fish was set out to dry in brief intervals between downpours. Hundreds of quintals sat washed and stacked to drain on the stage floors as the rain came over Tinkershare Head in sheets, the piles of waterhorse left for days before it could be spelled out on the flakes. The cod cured and stacked early in the season couldn't be aired through August's wet and most of it went dun and mouldy in the warehouses.

The season promised to be such a failure that even Abe Strapp took notice. He was every day in the firm's offices and on the waterfront, needling and browbeating and complaining, as if the lousy weather and the scarcity of fish were the result of incompetence or laziness. The only thing that gave him any pleasure during those months was the certainty that Caines Mercantile would suffer a good deal more than his own company.

Aubrey Picco came to the Caines house in August and spoke to the Widow of selling the last of the season's catch green though it was worth less than dried.

"Whatever you think is most advantageous, Aubrey," she said.

A young crow was sitting on the back of her chair, its head flicking left and right to take in the headman. It had been her only company since Solemn discovered the unfledged bird in the garden that spring, carrying the drowned-looking creature into the house and presenting it to the Widow like an offering. She'd fed it by hand for weeks and she stroked its head and spoke to the crow as if she expected it might answer.

It hopped onto the Widow's shoulder and turned one blue eye to Aubrey. "Trouble, trouble, trouble," it said, unmistakably.

"Who's a clever bird," the Widow said.

"Piss and corruption," it said.

Aubrey shifted in his chair. He'd never made peace with the crow's presence or its uncanny talent for mimicking human speech. It seemed devilish somehow. He said, "There's no telling how much fish we'll collect along the shore this year or what shape it will be in."

"We will have to hope for the best."

Aubrey leaned forward and touched his fingers to his forehead. The enterprise was all but lost, for the Widow's ambition and an unlikely run of bad fortune. And the woman seemed completely oblivious. His wife had warned him, elliptically, regretfully, about tying himself to the Widow. He'd stayed on with the firm out of loyalty to his friend, Elias, and Relief had acquiesced to his faithfulness. For which it seemed they were about to be heartily punished.

At the beginning of September there was a break in the weather, days of clear skies and a warm breeze. *The Hope* and the re-keeled *Success* and other vessels were being prepared for the fall coasting to outfits on the shore. Most operations weren't expected to cover the cost of materials taken on credit in the spring and Abe Strapp made a point of warning the Beadle against being overgenerous with people in debt to the firm.

"Some will starve without sufficient provision," Clinch said.

"I am not about to cut off my arms to feed them," Abe Strapp said. "Every piece of hard bread is to be accounted for."

"We could bring the worst off into Mockbeggar for the winter."

"We'll have little enough to eat here ourselves," Strapp said.

The Beadle made some noises about Christian charity then, but his employer wouldn't hear it.

"They will have to fend for themselves like the rest of us," he said.

Half the crew aboard *The Hope* were sick with a cough that had been making the rounds through the weeks of working in the wet and dim. A handful of livyers had been brought low enough with fever and chills they were forced to take to their beds where they were bled by the Beadle or treated with Mary Oram's poultices of molasses and bread and lamp oil. But in the avalanche of disastrous circumstances they were travelling through, no one took much notice.

~

By the time *The Hope* returned near the end of September, three men on the crew were too infirm to work and lay all day in their bunks. The Beadle bled them as much as he dared and plied them with James's Powder, though their condition showed no improvement. Everyone still well enough to work was working through bouts of fever and coughs and weakness.

The sickness had taken hold in Mockbeggar and Nonsuch by then as well. Inez Barter was two weeks buried in the churchyard and half a dozen others were all but given up for dead. The Beadle ordered an end to regular services at the Church of England and advised the same for the Quakers. He asked Abe Strapp for a court order closing the alehouses and grog shops.

"What, are we to hide in our houses all bloody winter?" Abe asked.

"Until the worst of the sickness has passed."

"And how are the bitch-bear's girls meant to feed themselves if they aren't able to work?"

"People are already dying, Mr. Strapp."

"Did we run out of room in the churchyard, Mr. Clinch? Is hell full?"

The Beadle shook his head. "Not just yet," he said.

"Well let's have no more talk of it. It will pass over soon enough."

It wasn't until two women in the Big House took to their beds with a fever and several others refused any congress with customers that Abe Strapp made a proclamation closing the taverns and outlawing all public gatherings. He retreated to Strapp Manor with the Abbess and Old Soot and Heater and his pack of hunting dogs while the plague burned through the shore.

The Beadle refused even to hold funerals in the church, performing the services in the churchyard with only family in attendance. Every other day he borrowed the Jerseyman's horse to ride into Nonsuch where the situation was just as dire. In the second week of October he presided at three burials in the local cemetery, the last an infant who had been perfectly healthy two days before. The mother was already hollowed out with the fever and a ragged cough that bent her nearly double and he expected shortly to bury her beside her daughter.

On the ride back over the Scrape he sat the horse when Mockbeggar came into view, looking out across the babble of houses and warehouses and flakes crowding the harbourfront, the handful of vessels like water-striders afloat on the surface of a pond. The world he was ordained to. There were lines of smoke rising from the wooden chimneys but not a soul to be seen on the paths below, as if the livyers had abandoned the outport en masse while he was on the far side of Tinkershare Head.

He lifted his eyes from that unlikely corner of God's kingdom and the flash of a sail caught his attention, a white glimmer on the horizon. He stood in his stirrups, as if those few inches would make the sighting more certain. The ship was travelling from the north with every rag of sail raised, likely a vessel from the French shore or the Labrador coast on an innocuous voyage. But he kicked up the horse and rode by the Widow's house to the waterfront, running into the firm's offices to retrieve a glass.

The spectacle of the Jerseyman's horse at a gallop drew what passed for a crowd to the wharves. People climbed to lookouts around the harbour to try and make out the ship's flag and design. But it had already sailed beyond the reach of telescopes, a pale smudge moving toward Fogo Island, or to open seas and the continent.

Memories of the American marauders were fresh enough that armed sentinels watched through the night. Early the following morning shots were fired to alert the livyers to a vessel making for the harbour, throwing every soul into a scramble for weapons. Men and women assembled with muskets and pistols, with fish prongs and sculping knives. Even a handful of Quakers stood in the early chill, Solemn with his father's old hunting rifle, Lazarus with a sealing gaff, ready to forsake their faith's preaching to spare themselves and their neighbours a repeat of the previous winter's suffering.

When *The Hydra* sailed close enough to glass, it was clear the schooner was limping into port after some disastrous incident at sea. The mainmast and top gallant masts were down and part of the rail at the ship's waist had been carried off. They were making way under the foresail alone and by the time the vessel crawled into harbour and anchored, most everyone on the waterfront had left to see to their sick.

The Beadle and Abe Strapp and his constables and a handful of hangers-on awaited the visitors as a wherry was let down over-side and rowed for shore. A lone figure in the bow looming like some fairy-tale giant as they approached, stepping up onto the wharf like he was stepping over the lintel of a doorway.

"You've had a rough go of things," Abe Strapp said. He looked up into the face of the visitor who leaned on a rifle that stood almost to the man's height with the stock on the ground.

"We ran into a great headswell," he said ruefully. "We have been much delayed recently and were under full sail to make up time." He shook his head to acknowledge his own impatience at the root of their troubles.

"Was anyone hurt?" the Beadle asked.

"We had two men aloft when the masts came down and they were a good deal bruised. But nothing mortal. I would have carried on for Fogo but the wind was against us."

"You have some work to do before getting underway again."

The man's face was as long and wide as a fox's tail, framed by two elaborate sideburns going to grey. "I was hoping to engage some assistance in that endeavour," he said.

"We will offer what we can," the Beadle said. "Many of our people are suffering with a sickness that has kept everyone to their homes."

The stranger's massive eyebrows rose at the mention of the plague. "We were anchored in a cove north of here to minister to a sick girl," he said. "Which was the cause of our delay."

"It wasn't the Best youngsters?"

"The same, yes. The girl was as near to death as anyone I've seen this side of the sod."

"Is she still with us?"

"They were both hale when we left."

Abe pointed to the firearm he'd been staring at. He'd never seen anything the like. "That is a beauty you have there," he said.

"Hanoverian," the stranger said. He looked down at the instrument with a smile he might have turned upon a first-born child. "She has served me well."

"Perhaps we could offer you some refreshment before dealing with the necessary repairs," the Beadle said.

"I have not eaten a proper meal since yesterday morning," the stranger admitted. "My great guts are ready to eat my little ones."

Abe was beside himself with boredom being boxed up with the same handful of faces and their twaddle. "You will eat with us at Strapp Manor," he said.

"You are most kind. Mr. . . . ?"

"Strapp. Abe Strapp."

"Mr. Strapp," he said, reaching a hand near the size of a platter. "Captain Truss," he said. He turned to the wherry where two men sat waiting at the oars. "Bring Mrs. Brace to shore," he said. And he reached a foot to nudge the boat away from the wharf.

Captain Truss was an Englishman from Oxfordshire and for many years an officer in the King's army, rising to the rank by which he still introduced himself. He obtained an ensigncy in Colonel Alderson's regiment in the East Indies where he'd been sent as a young cadet. In Germany he served as aide-de-camp to the late Marquis de Canby, where he had purchased his beloved Hanoverian rifle.

They were seated in the dining room of Strapp Manor where Truss was offering up his autobiography as if he was reading from a script.

After leaving His Majesty's service, Truss spent two years in the Scottish Highlands and nearly bankrupted himself trying to keep two servants and three brace of hunting dogs in meat and out of the rain. Back in England and unengaged, he travelled to Newfoundland with his younger brother who was appointed to serve as deputy commissary of the Vice-Admiralty Court. The abundant fish and game brought him back to the island several years running.

The Abbess interrupted to ask would he like another serving of the hot buttered rolls and venison pie. Truss had already eaten as much as all the others at the table combined and happily accepted the offer of more.

"You are a fine trencher," she said.

Mrs. Brace said, "He plays a good knife and fork, our captain."

The Abbess glanced across at the woman, trying to measure her words. She was introduced to the company as the captain's housekeeper, though she presented herself with a forwardness that suggested there was more to their relationship than that title would allow.

Truss ignored her, forging ahead with his life story. After years of sailing back and forth to Newfoundland, he borrowed enough money to set up an enterprise on the Labrador coast, taking salmon and cod in the summers, hunting and trapping through the winters, trading with the Esquimaux for fur and tusks.

The Abbess turned to Mrs. Brace. "Were you forced to spend time with the Eskimos?" she asked. She gave an involuntary shiver. "The thought makes my skin crawl."

"I can nose the stink of them from here," Abe said. "The same reeking hogo as the Red Indians on this shore in numbers not so long past."

Truss set his utensils on his plate and folded his enormous hands above them, staring at his host.

Mrs. Brace said, "I fear we have put the captain off his food."

"You have a fondness for the savages, Captain?" the Beadle asked.

"He would rather sup with savages than with Christians, is the truth of the matter," Mrs. Brace said, with a brazenness no mere servant would venture.

"The Esquimaux are an ingenious people," Truss insisted. "The men are the most patient hunters I have ever encountered. And the women are forever engaged in industry, dressing sealskin or jerking fish, making boots or jackets. Whenever I had cause to visit, the kettle was boiling in every tent and there was no shortage of belly timber on offer. And they took great pains to entertain me with dancing and singing."

"Whatever else you wish to call it," Mrs. Brace said, "it is not singing. Nor dancing besides."

The captain smiled down at his plate. "I admit I do not admire their tunes," he said. "But many of them had soft and musical voices. As for the dancing, it was difficult to watch with a straight face. One would suppose they had learned that art from the bears of the country."

"I will be happy never to lay eyes on such a one again," the housekeeper said.

Truss took her in with a look that seemed a reprimand. "Mrs. Brace lived years in the same house as my slave girl, Tweegok, and suffered no ill effects. And Indian Jack, who is travelling with us, is a great friend to her."

"He is Montagnais," Mrs. Brace offered. "Which is a different coinage from the Eskimo. And he has British blood on his father's side."

"Is she still with you?" Abe Strapp asked. "The Twee one?" He'd shifted forward in his seat at the mention of a slave girl.

"She was a servant really," Truss said. He was visibly irritated with the turn the conversation had taken. "I purchased her from her father for a bait skiff when she was ten or eleven. She made several escapes back to her mother that first season before she resigned herself to her situation. But I doubt she would have accustomed herself to England."

"She had the most sluttish manners," Mrs. Brace said, "and was of little use besides."

It was clearly an acrimonious subject between the two. All their exchanges seemed coloured by compromises and hostilities that stretched back years.

"You are bound for the continent," the Beadle said, trying to steer them into safer waters.

Truss had received the news of his father's death in the spring and was sailing home to settle the man's affairs. "There is no great estate, a family manor and some property which I intend to sell. The profits should serve to settle the debt I've fallen into during the prosecution of the Labrador trade and will leave enough to live a gentleman's life somewhere outside London's extravagance."

The Abbess turned toward the housekeeper. "And will you remain in the captain's service in England?"

"If he will have me," she said.

"I will miss the hunting most," Truss said, as if he hadn't heard the exchange between the women. In Labrador, he claimed, he'd killed everything from a louse to a white bear that weighed 120 stone of fourteen pounds each. Hunting was the man's darling pleasure and his appetite came back to him as he recounted the staggards and knobblers and hinds, the seals and owls and ravens and seabirds and Arctic hare, the beaver and otter and foxes and wolves and bears he had shot or trapped or bludgeoned in his years on the Labrador. It was a litany that threatened to run into the hundreds and thousands, a Noah's Ark of all species and sizes and descriptions.

"I have so great a dislike for salted meat," he said, "that I would eat the flesh of any creature that is fresh over the finest salt beef or pork."

"I'd be happy to take you into the backcountry," Abe said. "We have bears and medlars and anything you care to name on the wing." He pointed up toward the antlers that framed the fireplace. "And we have deer as you can see."

"Yes, I was wondering who was responsible for that."

"Felled the beast in beyond Looking Glass Pond," Abe said. "Couldn't lift the animal until the head was removed from the shoulders. Seventy-eight points."

Truss sat back in his chair. "It is a fine set of antlers," he said soberly. "But it has nowhere close to seventy-eight points." He got up and crossed to the fireplace. He stood tall enough he could touch the highest branches of the antlers without lifting his heels from the floor. "Unless you are using the German method, of course. The Germans will count anything on which a torn piece of paper will rest as a point. But I count by the old British conditions, as any gentleman would."

"Which conditions are those?" the Beadle asked.

"The watch guard or powder horn test," Truss said. He brushed his fingers across the antlers. "These excrescences are merely offers that could no more hang a necklace than an infant's doodle-doo. There are fifty-odd points here at most." He shook his head. "The Germans make a good rifle, but they are unrepentant braggarts." He went back to his seat, letting that last word hang over the table. "As far as hunting goes, Mr. Strapp, I'm afraid I must see to repairs if we are to sail for England this fall."

"Suit yourself," Abe said. He had gone dark in his chair, as if a curtain had been drawn across the square pane of his face.

"Mrs. Brace," the captain said. "I believe we have imposed ourselves here long enough."

Abe Strapp was in a torment after the meal. He'd never developed the skin to ignore a humiliation and had never been humbled in such a deliberate and unanswerable fashion. He couldn't even pin the insult he felt to any obvious slur. The old British conditions and German braggarts. The slyness of Truss's ridicule was impossible to describe in a way that carried the emotional weight it had in the moment. Which made Strapp more childishly livid. Even the Abbess was at a loss to settle him.

He assigned Old Soot and Heater to keep watch on Truss and his vessel from the firm's offices the next day.

"What are we looking for exactly?" Matterface asked.

"How the hell would I know?" Abe shouted. "Something. Anything. A platter to serve the bastard's head upon."

For all they were keeping to themselves due to the plague, every livyer in the harbour heard of the captain and his housekeeper and of Indian Jack who was Montagnais and accompanying them to England. They knew of Truss's military service and the Labrador plantation he'd run for more than a decade. The captain was said to have raised the Best youngsters nearly from the dead in Orphan Cove and could cure anyone with the sickness and he was repeatedly approached by livyers begging him to visit someone suffering in their bed. Half a dozen times that day, the constables reported, Truss left the ship to offer what help he could.

"Surely someone in Nonsuch must be in need of his doctoring," Abe said.

Heater nodded. "We will make inquiries," he said.

Early the next morning Truss was petitioned and escorted across the Scrape into Nonsuch and Abe Strapp sent the Abbess and two of her most willing tits on the pretence of visiting Mrs. Brace. They carried skin flasks of Strip-Me-Naked under their skirts and instructions to find some circumstance or bit of intelligence Abe could use to fuck with the man.

Mrs. Brace and everyone else aboard *The Hydra* had been told about the Big House and the Abbess's vocation by then. She tried to beg off a visit when the woman arrived, citing the incessant noise of repairs going on above decks.

"I don't mind a little racket," the Abbess said. "It reminds me of my time in London when I was a girl. This is your cabin, Mrs. Brace?"

"It's the captain's," she said. "Although I share the space. There isn't much room to spare aboard a working vessel such as this."

The Abbess nodded at the bunk the woman was sitting on. "I expect there's not much to spare in that bed with a man the size of your captain," she said.

"We have learned to accommodate one another."

"I hope, for your sake, his breach is as well-endowed as his tongue."

There was a cold silence between them and the Abbess tried waving it off.

"I mean no offence. We are women of the world, you and I. Do you mind if I ask what became of your husband, Mrs. Brace?"

"He died."

"I am sorry to hear it," the Abbess said. "And you fell into Captain Truss's service then?"

"I preferred it to going hungry."

"And you and the captain have been close all this time?"

Mrs. Brace stared at the woman seated across from her, their knees almost touching in the cramped quarters. She said, "We have learned to accommodate each other."

The Abbess was wearing a jade necklace and she raised a hand to toy with it as she considered that response. "I swear you have the look of someone tormented by love," she said. She swung the pendant lazily back and forth on its chain. "I am rarely mistaken in these matters. Who might it be if it isn't the captain I wonder?"

A fierce volley of hammering forced them to stare at each other in silence a few moments and a man came into the room just as the racket ended, as if he was delivering the quiet to them by hand. He stopped still when he realized Mrs. Brace was not alone and he looked back and forth between the two women, seeming not to recognize either.

"Yes, Jack?" Mrs. Brace prompted him finally.

"I was looking for the captain," he said.

"I think the captain has gone ashore to see to someone sick," she said.

He nodded uncertainly. He was a young-looking middle-aged man, jet-black hair touched with grey and a wisp of moustache at the corners of his upper lip. His face nearly as brown as the eyes darting between the women as they stared at him.

"I will tell the captain you were looking for him," Mrs. Brace said.

He nodded at her and again at the unexpected guest before turning to leave.

"Indian Jack, I presume?" the Abbess said and she nodded approvingly. "He is a different order of savage altogether."

Mrs. Brace stood from the bunk. "I am feeling out of sorts, Mrs. Valentine, and wish to rest awhile."

"Of course," the Abbess said, getting to her feet. "Thank you for your hospitality this morning." She turned back at the door. "If I run into Indian Jack, I will have him look in on you, shall I? To be certain you are all right?"

"I imagine you will do as you wish," Mrs. Brace said.

On his way back from Nonsuch, Captain Truss was met by Solemn Lambe on the Jerseyman's horse. The Widow Caines had seen him coming across the Scrape from her office window, Solemn said, and sent him out with the offer of a ride into Mockbeggar.

"I am happy to walk," Truss said. He was holding the horse's bridle and stroking its neck as the animal pressed its forehead into his chest. "But I can't refuse a creature as beautiful as this." It lifted its muzzle and nickered, the captain looking down at the horse from his heights.

Solemn trotted along beside the horse and rider as they made their way past Looking Glass Pond and down toward the harbour, answering the captain's endless questions about the town and its industries and his employer.

"You aren't yet married?" Truss asked him.

"There is a dearth of eligible girls on the shore, sir. The fishermen and servants brought over from the old countries is ten men to every woman."

"It's the same in Labrador," Truss said. "There are not enough to go around. I'm surprised to hear the Widow Caines has remained unmarried."

"She've asked you to stop for tea on the way along," Solemn said. "Perhaps it won't seem so unlikely then."

Bride was waiting on the steps to take him inside as Solemn stabled the horse, the captain bowing to stoop under the headframe of each doorway he passed through. The Widow stood from her chair in the parlour as he ducked into the room. He paused a moment as he took her in. "I see," he said softly.

"We have not made much of a welcome to you, Captain."

"You are suffering through unfortunate circumstances."

"It's good of you to take the time to see to the sick while you are here." She motioned him to a seat.

"I have been of very little assistance, I'm afraid. I was just called to see a young girl in Nonsuch who buried her infant daughter two days ago."

"Will she survive do you think?"

"She passed while I was with her," he said.

Bride came into the room with a tray of tea and rolls and cheese and cold meats that she set on the low table before them.

"You prefer fresh meat to salted I understand," the Widow said.

He glanced across at her.

"We live in a very small town."

He was already helping himself to the food and spoke as he ate. "I'm afraid I was somewhat uncongenial with Mr. Strapp during our meal."

"I am sure he deserved whatever misuse he received."

"How such a man could serve as a Justice of the Peace."

The Widow was pouring tea for them both. "You are singing from my hymnal, Captain." And she outlined the man's long history of dissipation and malfeasance and her campaign to have him removed from his post.

A young crow hopped into the room and flew up to perch on the arm of the chesterfield where the Widow was seated. Truss proffered a piece of bread and whistled softly. The Widow had taken out her pipe and she gestured with it, asking permission to smoke while he ate.

"By all means," he said as the crow lurched over her lap toward him and plucked the morsel from his fingers.

"I have sent correspondence to the Undersecretary of State and members of the Privy Council on the matter. But they seem uninterested in the goings-on in the backwoods of a backward colony."

"I can confirm as much from my own experience."

"The brother you first travelled to Newfoundland with," she said. "He was the governor's deputy in Trinity and Conception Bay, am I right in thinking this?"

"Years ago, yes. Before ill health forced him home to England."

"I imagine he wields some influence in those circles still."

"Mrs. Caines," Truss said. "I have some sympathy for your circumstances. But my sharing an unpleasant afternoon in Mr. Strapp's company is hardly sufficient cause to impose this crusade upon my brother. Especially as it may look to an unbiased eye as a squabble between siblings."

The Widow looked at him in silence.

"As you say, you live in a very small town."

Bride came into the room then and the Widow sent her off to refill the teapot. Truss watched as she turned and left the room.

"Is the girl married?" he asked.

"Not as yet, no."

"Your lad Solemn was just telling me there are few girls available in Mockbeggar and here is one right under his nose."

"Bride is his sister, Captain."

"Well then," he said. He seemed genuinely deflated by the news. "A shame for him."

"The Irish servant I mentioned who was shot and killed by my brother?"

"Yes?"

"He was their father. And his punishment for that act of murder was to be sworn in as sole magistrate on the shore."

Truss sat back from the food and rubbed his hands through his sideburns. "I regret having sat at table with the man," he said.

The Widow leaned onto her thighs. "As far as Abe Strapp is concerned, the rules that govern society do not apply to him. And nothing has ever given him reason to think differently."

"You have my sympathies, Mrs. Caines. Sincerely. But we leave for England at first light tomorrow. This is not an issue I can take on with the candour and probity it requires."

She straightened in her chair. "You are a man of honour, Captain."

He smiled across at her. "I almost feel it is something I should apologize for."

"I will admit I have little experience with the idiosyncrasy. You might at least take my letters with you. To be certain they are put into the right hands."

He took up another roll and set it whole into his mouth. "That much I can commit to," he said.

When he returned to *The Hydra*, Truss found half the work he'd assigned unfinished and four of his crew blind drunk about the deck. It meant another day's delay and he took out his frustration on the inebriated servants, kicking them out of their stupors and beating them about the head and shoulders, the men crouching under those enormous hands like they were being set upon by a flurry of hawks. He wouldn't permit anyone to leave off work until the last whisper of light left the sky and he turned everyone out of their bunks to start back in as soon as they could tell a hammer from a shoe in the morning's dim.

Truss hadn't slept a wink in the hours between. Mrs. Brace was awake but uncommonly quiet when he came to their cabin and in a foul mood herself. The Abbess had been to see her, she told him, but the visit was short and the conversation beneath recalling. The woman stayed aboard *The Hydra* the rest of the morning and into the afternoon with her two drabs, polluting the men with drink and likely peppering them with blue boars or shankers or some other venereal disorder besides. On Abe Strapp's instruction, no doubt.

Twice that night Truss turned to Mrs. Brace in the narrow bunk and poured his indignation and pique into her, but he was still too crimped up with irritation to sleep. Or to notice she lay awake beside him the whole of the night as well.

He refused to leave the ship the next day despite calls to see to the sick and dying, overseeing the work to ensure it was completed. All the time eaten up with vexation at Abe Strapp's childish buggery. Matterface and Heater delivered an invitation for Truss and Mrs. Brace to take their supper meal at Strapp Manor and he sent them away with a refusal so blunt he half expected the Justice to arrive demanding an apology. He was disappointed in the end that the man did not and once he was satisfied the vessel was ready to sail, he walked up to Strapp Manor alone. It was early evening and he interrupted the circle of miscreants already in their cups. Old Soot answered the door and led him into the dining room.

"Come in, Captain," Strapp insisted. "I'm delighted you reconsidered my invitation. We've been discussing you and your fine crew all day."

Truss refused an offer of food and drink, refused even to take a seat. "I only wanted to have a word before we sail tomorrow," he said.

"I have some things to bring to your attention as well, sir, you have saved me a trip to the waterfront. But please, you have something on your mind."

Strapp's expansiveness was so mean-spirited, so fetid, that Truss could almost smell it from across the room. He said, "I am here to protest your sending common bawds aboard *The Hydra* to ply my men with alcohol."

"Common?" Abe Strapp said. He turned to the Abbess who affected the look of an innocent accused of a despicable act. "I take exception to this scandalous claim, Captain. Mrs. Valentine and my cousins are every one a cleaver. And some among your crew were only too happy to sample their wares."

"And in all likelihood to be burnt with the clap or some other taint."

Strapp spread his arms wide. "These are risks the lovers among us face," he said. He folded his hands over the massive dome of his belly, feigning a contemplative mood. "Of course, there are other risks for those who dip their toes into that water."

"The pitfalls are many," the Abbess confirmed.

"And here's one you would best take note of," Strapp said. "Men will take a slice off a cut loaf thinking it won't be missed."

There were murmurs of agreement at the table and Truss realized it was a mistake to have come, to expect he might wring any satisfaction from the man. "If you have something to tell me," he said, "I would appreciate it be said directly."

"It is not our place to make accusations that would cause a grievance between masters and servants," Strapp said. "But you may wish to ask Mrs. Brace just how good a friend your Indian Jack has been to her these last months."

"Years, in fact," Old Soot said.

"I will not be turned by idle gossip."

"You are a man of honour," the Abbess said. "And that is noble. But I must report that Indian Jack came by your cabin while I was visiting Mrs. Brace."

"There is nothing untoward in such a thing."

"If there was nothing untoward, why did he claim to be looking for you there? He was with you when you left *The Hydra*, was he not?"

"He was," Old Soot announced. "We witnessed the captain give direct instruction to Indian Jack as he was leaving for Nonsuch."

"Indian Jack expected to have your housekeeper to himself I wager," Mrs. Valentine said.

"It seems Mrs. Brace takes on her men the way Noah took God's creatures aboard the Ark," Abe Strapp said. "Two at a time."

There was a pealing round of laughter at the table and Truss had to shout to be heard over it. "That is a lie, Mr. Strapp."

"Three of the men who consorted with Mrs. Valentine's ladies confirm the fact."

"They were drunk."

"Which makes them pudding-headed and indiscreet. But not liars."

Abe Strapp fairly glowed with pleasure as he watched the captain. The grin on his face made Truss want to shit through his teeth.

"Are you certain we can't get you something to drink?" the Justice asked.

The room seemed to be churning in a gyre suddenly, every stick of furniture, every contemptible soul-case circling the empty space that was Abe Strapp at the head of the table, all of it spinning into that void. Truss had to physically pull himself clear of the riptide, turning without replying and dragging that weight to the door, the current sucking at his heels.

The Hydra was gone before anyone stirred in Mockbeggar the following morning. No one woke to voices in the cavernous silence before dawn, no one heard the vessel creaking as it slipped from the wharf or the sails being raised as it made for the harbour mouth. As if the sea had opened beneath *The Hydra* to swallow the ship and every soul aboard, without leaving a trace behind.

JOB'S COMFORTER. BUNGS FOREVER!
MARY ORAM, AGAIN.

The pandemic faded and flared through the rest of the winter. Coupled with the season's poor catch and the meagre stores on hand in the root cellars, a bright constellation of dread hung over the shore. The sick were too weak to hunt on the barrens or trap in the backwoods and the unaffected spent most of their time nursing those on the verge of dying. Except for the merchants and their closest associates who never seemed much in want, every household suffered the same endless days of lack and distress.

The illness began to ebb for good in March, around the same time the Labrador pack drifted ashore. Aubrey Picco was one of the last to be struck with the sickness. He came through it alive and was back on his feet when ships from the continent arrived in the spring but he was a shell of his old self. He spent each day at the firm's offices but avoided the walk to the Caines house unless he felt it was absolutely unavoidable. He was emaciated and swam in his clothes. He leaned on a wooden cane as he hobbled along, stopping now and then to catch his breath.

Bride answered the door and brought him into the parlour to spare the man having to take the stairs. He was in his early fifties but looked a biblical ancient to the girl's eyes, his grey hair thinned to wisps, the skin of his face and neck hanging in folds and wattles where the flesh beneath had wasted. She took his arm to help him settle into the seat opposite the chesterfield before fetching the Widow from her office.

"Friend Aubrey," the Widow said as she came into the room. He was in the process of trying to get to his feet but she stopped him with a hand to his shoulder. "To what do I owe the pleasure?" she said.

"I'm afraid it won't be a pleasure at all."

"Of course not," she said casually.

"We've had reports from Poole," he said. "Last season was a near total loss. As you know. At this point we are unable to service our debt."

"We will borrow more in the meantime."

He shook his head. "The office in Poole has been making those inquiries all winter. No one will look at us, I'm told. Court action is underway to recoup the outstanding loans."

The Widow took out her pipe to give herself a moment. She turned it over in her hands and then put the pipe away again. An odd clicking sound in the hall drew Aubrey's attention to the Widow's crow descending the stairs one step at a time, as if it preferred walking to flying.

"Where does that leave us?" the Widow asked.

"The Jerseyman's assets will have to be auctioned off to settle the judgements when they come in," he said. "And we will be forced to sell some of Caines Mercantile to raise capital."

None of those details could have been a surprise, Aubrey thought. But it seemed to strike her like news of an unexpected death. She stared into the cold fireplace, seeing nothing. The crow was at the doorway and it spread its wings, launching itself to the top of the birdcage in the corner, but it was too ungainly to settle there and clattered to the floor again.

"This is his doing," the Widow said.

"Abe Strapp is a mile wide and an inch deep," Aubrey said. "He is just clever enough to put his pants on the right way forward. This is simply bad fortune. And recklessness."

She turned toward him so suddenly he drew back in his chair, raising one hand from the cane as if to defend himself.

"There is one thing at least we can take away from the run of bad luck," he said.

"And what is that?"

"Last season's losses were so general I doubt that C. Strapp & Son are in a position to take on additional risk. When they go to auction, your interests will certainly end up in other hands."

"You are a true Job's comforter, Aubrey Picco."

He made a face that was meant to serve as an apology. "We will have to appoint an assignee to oversee the dispersal and sale."

The Widow nodded. "You will look after this," she said.

"If you wish."

They sat in silence a long time then, until it occurred to the Widow there was something else Aubrey Picco had come to tell her. She glanced across at the waning scarecrow, the bony hands folded over the head of his walking stick.

"You are leaving me," she said.

He lifted the cane and tapped at the floor, out of embarrassment or some other discomfort. "I am an old man," he said. "Suddenly, but certainly. All our children live in England. We have grandchildren there we have never seen. And the firm will require fewer hands once the court's adjudication is completed. I won't be missed."

The Widow tugged at the hem of her vest. Furious he could see.

She said, "No doubt this is Relief's idea."

He tapped the cane against the floor again, still mystified by the length and breadth of the Widow's animosity toward his wife. She seemed unable to forgive Relief for having a life apart from her. "Our decisions have always been made in concert," he said.

"I'm sure it appears so to you. But she leads you by the nose, Friend Aubrey."

"I will not hear you speak ill of Relief."

A smile or some imitation of it crossed the Widow's face. She stood from her seat. "In that case," she said, "I will simply thank you for your service." And she left him where he sat, retreating up the stairs.

She could hear Aubrey clumping along the hallway below and Bride speaking to him on his way out. She fished the Pilgrim's ring from beneath her shirt and sat with a fist closed around it. Looking out over the stables and potato drills in the garden and up toward the Scrape. Feeling suddenly beggared and solitary. She squeezed the ring hard enough to score its imprint into her flesh, as if it was the one true thing in the world and she wanted it inside her now. To be certain it would never be lost.

~

In the last week of May, Lazarus made a visit to the Caines house, walking up to the gardens where he found Solemn working around the stables.

"The word is near you, in your heart and in your mouth."

Solemn took his hand. "The Jerusalem above is free," he said, "and she is our mother."

The Jerseyman's horse nickered from its stall at the sound of Laz's voice and he walked over to lean his face into the animal's neck. "My handsome prince," he whispered.

Solemn felt a stupid pang of jealousy roll through him to see his friend stroke the horse's forehead and speak to it so plainly from the heart. Lazarus turned his face from the animal and stood leaning against its shoulder. "It's near the end of the fifth month," he said.

"I know it."

Lazarus said, "I'm soon done my three years with Abe Strapp."

Solemn tried to hold still in his shoes, to keep his voice level. "What do you plan to do?"

"I was hoping you might put in a word with the Widow for me."

"Hadn't Aubrey better do that?"

"He says things didn't go so well the last time they spoke."

Solemn was smiling so broadly his ears ached.

"I'll take anything she can offer," Laz said. Solemn stared with the same stupid expression until Lazarus said, "I could start right away, Solemn. If she knew I was free."

"Yes," he said. And he headed up toward the house.

Bride was in the kitchen when he came through the servants' entrance and she asked what he was grinning about as he clipped through to the hall.

"Those shoes had better be clear of sheep shit," she called after him.

The Widow had seen Lazarus come into the garden and watched the exchange between the two young men, the strange intimacy of their address, and Solemn staring as Laz turned his attention to the Jerseyman's horse. She saw Solemn jog up toward the house and heard his footsteps on the stairs and she turned her chair to face the door before he knocked.

"Come in," she said.

He was too eager to find his words at first, tripping over himself in his hurry to bring Lazarus within the Widow's fold.

"Take a breath, Solemn," she said. "What is it Lazarus is doing?"

"He's near finished his three years with Strapp," he said. "And he was hoping to find a situation with Caines Mercantile. With you."

She nodded slowly. "In all honesty, we are in no position to be taking on additional servants." She paused there, spending a moment with the stunned look on Solemn's face, to be sure of what she'd always known about him. "But as it will certainly infuriate Abe Strapp to lose a good hand to his sister, I think we can find him something."

Solemn had stopped breathing a few seconds and the rush of relief he felt made him lightheaded. He reached for the door. "Laz was wondering," he said. "He was saying he'd like to work in the gardens and the stables if that was something open for him. He've always loved the Jerseyman's horse."

The Widow turned her half-smile on the youngster. "I can hardly afford to keep you and Bride on as it is. We'll have to find him something at the warehouse."

Solemn nodded, trying to be satisfied with the partial victory. "I'll go tell him as much."

She waited until he was in the hall and closing the door before she called him back. "You know Aubrey and Relief are leaving for England in the fall."

"Everyone knows as much."

"Might they ask Lazarus to join them, I wonder?"

She could see the thought had never occurred to him.

"What, leave with them now?" he asked.

She shrugged as if it was a new consideration to her as well. "Now," she said, "or to follow on sometime later." She looked down at the desk and reached to shift things an inch or two. She said, "His working for the firm might not keep him with you, Solemn." She turned to stare at the youngster. "Not the way you want."

The Widow watched as he struggled to reach the surface of the deep water she'd thrown him into. The icy shock of being seen for his true self, to hear it spoken aloud for the first time.

"If he were to marry your sister," she said, "he would always be within reach. Which is as much as you can hope for."

He had stopped breathing again and there were stars pinging across his vision. He stood still until he was certain he wouldn't fall and he nodded toward her. He clung to the banister as he made his way downstairs, keeping a hand to the wall as he went out through the kitchen.

"Are those shoes halfways clean?" Bride shouted as he passed by.

The Hope left on its coasting run in mid-May and sailed back into Mockbeggar in the first week of June. The Beadle was surprised to find Abe Strapp in the firm's offices, sitting at a desk and working through ledgers and bank statements. As if haranguing his accountants and servants the previous summer gave him the impression he was in charge of things.

"These numbers are dismal," Abe said. He was dressed head to toe in a new outfit sent over from Poole, a ruffled shirt and a scarlet waistcoat with buttons that looked to be made of ivory. "The Widow is about to go under and I haven't got two coppers to put on my eyes."

"Most everyone along the shore came through the winter. We stand to right the ship if the fish are plentiful. And the weather cooperates."

"That is a lot of ifs to be placing our bets upon."

"Twas ever thus, Mr. Strapp."

Abe seemed set on making a pricklouse of himself about the office as he waited to see if the ship would find its keel, needling at everyone's business, badgering the Beadle for ways and means to ruin his sister completely and bring her affairs into his operation. Clinch never expressed his doubts aloud, but neither man was quite able to shake the sense the Widow would escape their designs in the end. As if a biblical prophecy they'd set their compass by was turning to ash as they watched.

For all that, Abe admitted no common cause with his headman. He looked upon the Beadle as he would a Judas, as if he was convinced the man was deliberately protecting the Widow.

"It is in God's hands," Clinch said helplessly.

"You claim to have sway in that department," Abe said. "Now would be a good time to make some bloody use of it."

There was no relief from the shit-fire of the man until a thirty-foot bully boat with a gang of Jack tars at the oars rowed into Mockbeggar a week later. They took down their lugsails as they came into the lun of Tinkershare Head and drew up to Strapp's wharf. A dozen or more of His Majesty's sailors among the crew, all of them avid and foul from weeks on the water, all with a look of thirst and devilment about them. Abe led them to the Big House and they proceeded to turn the place on its ear.

The establishment was larded solid by early evening as livyers crowded in for the spectacle. Seamen calling for drink and food and pawing at the Abbess's girls and shouting back and forth in the nearly incomprehensible gammon and patter of sailors. They sang in unison and cursed each other up and down and vomited out the open windows before turning back to the serious work of drinking and fornication. They rotated through the upstairs bedrooms, ringing the ship's bell to call in their replacements as if trading off a watch.

It was almost enough to make Abe Strapp forget what the previous summer's lousy season had done to the firm. The capelin had rolled early on the beaches and the inscrutable cod returned in starry numbers to the shoal grounds along the coast. And the Big House was alight. He stood in a corner with the sailor who seemed to be in charge of the convulsion that had rowed ashore, an affable Scotsman named Warren. He was employed as cooper aboard the *Medusa*, an old East India-man fit more for use as a prison hulk than for Navy service, he said. She'd split her mainmast in a storm the previous spring and limped into St. John's. They'd been ever since in search of a suitable column to replace it.

"I was sent with this crowd of sea crabs last fall to find a length of pine that would serve and we sailed as far as Fogo without luck. We passed the winter there and set out again as soon as the ice moved through. We've been two months now rowing into any likely tickle and river-head on the shore. Every manjack in the boat is thoroughly sick of the country."

"They seem happy enough here this evening."

"They haven't seen a proper cathouse since we left St. John's. I expect I'll have to drag them back to the boat by the short and curlies."

The bell rang at the top of the stairs and Abe nudged his companion. "You haven't dipped your wick yet, Mr. Warren."

The sailor flushed to his eyebrows and he shook his head. "It's a young man's game, Mr. Strapp."

"You're not dead yet," Abe said. "You'll be shod in Buckinger's boot here tonight or I will burn the Big House to the ground, so help me."

One of the Abbess's girls was moving through the room and Abe reached to grab her by the ear, drawing her close. "How does this sow suit?" he shouted over the racket. "She looks a child but she is a coming girl, I can tell you that from experience."

The cooper looked the man up and down, taking in the ivory buttons on the scarlet jacket, the ruffled shirt and silk stockings, the ribands banded at his knees.

"What is your name?" Warren asked the girl.

"Name?" Abe said. "You aren't about to marry the slut."

"Nancy," the girl said. Strapp still held her by the ear and she tilted her head slightly toward him. Her face was powdered and painted and she wore a blue ribbon about her neck like a collar.

"Does Fair Nancy suit you?" Abe asked.

The sailor raised a hand, about to speak, when they were interrupted by a commotion in the crowd, a surge of movement as three of the seamen muscled in to clear a space at the centre of the room. They waved their arms and shouted for attention and everyone leaned in their direction to see what was in the offing.

"It's time," one of the sailors announced, "to mumble a sparrow. Sixpence a try and half a crown to the first man who makes a successful dive."

One of the sailors at the centre had his hands around a grassy bird he'd netted in the woods that afternoon, the creature's head bobbing in terror at the motion and thrum of the room. Its wings were clipped and the sailor who acted the master of ceremonies grabbed a hat from a man standing near him, turning it bottom up and setting the bird in the crown before placing it on the floor. The hat deep enough the bird's head sat just below the brim.

"Who will be first to take a chomp at it?" the sailor called. He reached into the crowd again and dragged one of his crew into the ring, a young tar just able to keep his feet. "Sixpence," the master of ceremonies demanded but the youngster was too drunk to manage his affairs, surrendering to his mate who rooted around until he found the coin he was after. The drunkard's hands were bound behind his back and he was pushed to his knees. He bowed his face toward the hat, the watchful eyes of the bird staring up out of that well.

"A deep breath now lad," the emcee said.

There were shouts and squeals around the room as the sailor dipped and mawed and snagged into the darkness while the creature pecked and clawed for its life. It mauled the sailor's cheeks and eyelids so savagely he was forced to abandon his bid, raising his head to a chorus of catcalls and boos. His skin pitted and bleeding like someone afflicted with the pox.

"Now Jack Nasty Face," the emcee shouted. "The devil has run over your visage with hobnails in his boots." And he clipped the head of the defeated sailor with the back of his hand before untying his daddles and shoving him into the crowd. "Who else among you has the heart to face down this ferocious beast?"

Half a dozen others pushed forward with their sixpence held aloft, lobbying for a chance to bite the bird's head off before it took out their eyes. Each in turn forced to retreat, cribbage-faced with pecks, the crowd abusing them as hen-hearted cowards.

A voice began shouting for Bungs and all the sailors took it up. Ho Bungs! they yelled to the rafters. The entire room began repeating the call, with no idea who Bungs was or why he was being summoned. The master of ceremonies spotted him in his corner beside Abe Strapp and Fair Nancy and he cleaved through the press of bodies to lay a hand on the man's collar, hauling him to the centre of the room. "Ho Bungs," Abe Strapp shouted as his new acquaintance was bound and pushed to his knees, his face and ears purple with embarrassment to be the centre of attention.

"No kissing the bird, Bungs," the emcee shouted. "This is not an assignation with the venerable monosyllable. Unsheathe the sword of your choppers."

He pushed the cooper's face into the mess of spit and feathers and blood and Warren shook his head in the hat like a dog on a hare, coming to his knees with blood on his lips and chin and his eyes tipped skyward. He spat the poor bird's head to the floor, coughing and choking on the feathers stuck to his tongue and the roof of his mouth as a roar went up in the room. The sailors raised him over their heads with his arms still tied behind his back, all chanting "Bungs forever!"

Abe Strapp came looking for him when he was delivered to the ground, clapping him on the back. "And you come through it with not a mark," Strapp said.

"The poor creature was already half-dead. It was a mercy to end its torment."

"Well an act of mercy deserves an act of charity," Abe said. He wrapped his arm around Warren's shoulders, hauling him into an embrace that the cooper did not return. "Mrs. Valentine," Abe called out over the heads of the crowd. He leaned down to the sailor's ear. "I could tell Fair Nancy sparked no fire in you, there's nothing to the girl but skin and grief. But we will get you into a tender bit of beef tonight."

"This one is on the house," Abe told the Abbess as she grabbed the sailor's hand and he followed behind them, bundling Warren toward the stairs by the shoulders of his jacket, ignoring the man's protests. Before they reached the landing, the master of ceremonies stepped in to lay the boom of his arm between Strapp and the cooper.

"Leave off our Bungs," the emcee said.

"Step aside," Strapp shouted. He was trying to push the sailor's arm away without losing his hold on the cooper. "Mr. Warren has an urgent appointment with Miss Laycock and the man who makes him late will pay a price."

"I will pay you as Saint Paul paid the Ephesians," the sailor said, "over the face and the eyes, and all your damned jaws."

Matterface and Heater waded toward the confrontation as the Abbess tried to talk everyone down from the boughs, but it was too late for sense to prevail. Seamen clawed their way from all corners as the pushing and shoving escalated and within seconds the room was in a pelt. The Abbess made her escape up the stairs as half-dressed sailors descended into the pit below, swinging at anyone in their path.

The locals were no match for the Navy crew who were grim and relentless, too drunk to feel pain and fighting for their mates as if for King and country. People scrambled for the doors front and back or crawled through the open windows and ran for their lives. The handful of livyers who didn't escape were beaten to a todge, lying stunned on their backs or under the knee of a tar who flattened their faces into the floorboards.

"Where's that fat commander gone?" the master of ceremonies asked.

Warren bent over Matterface who was in a crumple at the foot of the stairs, using his sleeve to sop the blood pouring from his blackened nose. "Where is your master, good sir?"

Old Soot motioned toward the bedrooms with his eyes and Bungs tapped his shoulder. "I thank thee," he said.

"I am a Justice of the Peace," Abe shouted as he was dragged from under the bed where he was hiding. Bungs and another sailor kicked him down to the first floor and placed him in front of the fireplace and its shattered mirror. "I am a representative of His Majesty the King. There will be hell to pay if you grutnols lay a hand upon me."

The Abbess and her women had all descended the stairs after him and were watching from the banister and the doorway.

"Yon hog in armour thinks he is above us, Bungs," the emcee said.

"It's the rigging gives him airs," Warren said. "He's the type thinks it's clothes that make the man."

"I am a magistrate appointed by the Governor of the Island of Newfoundland," Strapp said helplessly.

"Are we not all the same under the lace and ruffles and ribands, Sir Reverence?" Warren asked him.

"I will have you hanged," Abe said, though his voice had lost all conviction.

Warren took a knife from inside his jacket and he stepped within arm's length of the Justice, reaching to cut the ivory buttons from his waistcoat. The clatter as they struck the floor like the sound of lake ice cracking under a walker's feet.

Bungs stepped back a pace and half a dozen sailors fell upon the Justice, stripping off his duds, tearing them at the seams when they couldn't be wrestled clear of his limbs or torso, and they left Abe Strapp standing starkers but for a silk stocking flagging at one ankle. He was trembling in the dim light, breathing like a man with water on the chest. His shrivelled linky-pinky invisible below the massive gut but for the florid head peeking out below.

"What is that betwixt his legs, Bungs?" the emcee asked. "Is that a toadstool?"

Warren stepped close again and leaned down to lift the member on his knife-blade. "That is the queerest tackle I ever set eyes upon," he said. "The Good Lord should have given the poor man more to work with than this."

The master of ceremonies turned to the women watching from the doorway. "None among you ever allowed this pig to climb aboard?" he said. "Not with that sorry little trumpet? There's not enough money in Christendom, surely."

They all looked away or at the floor, afraid to show how much pleasure it brought them to see the town bull aquiver in his birthday suit. Knowing they would pay for this bit of fun, regardless how it ended.

The Beadle arrived at the Big House with a parcel of armed livyers before they were able to take things further and the Justice fled to Strapp Manor, clutching the remnants of his foppish outfit to his belly, too shaken even to curse the sailors as he went. Warren's crew slept the night at Looking Glass Pond, though they would not acquiesce to being locked up in Quaker Hall. Bungs and the Beadle spent an hour at the water's edge, discussing possible resolutions. In the end it was agreed they would pay the cost of Abe's ruined clothes and leave before first light with a promise never to set foot in Mockbeggar again.

"The Justice," Bungs said. "He won't be satisfied to see us let off so."

"He wouldn't be satisfied if you were all hung by the neck till you were dead. But there is little he can do if you are beyond his reach."

"Do you never tire of tacking against the wind of that blunderbuss?" Warren asked.

"You didn't make the acquaintance of the Widow Caines today, I expect."

"Not so's I remember."

"You would remember," the Beadle said. "She might go some way to explaining my loyalties."

"She must be the very devil then."

"The devil works in mysterious ways, Mr. Warren. Like the Lord."

The pond before them was completely still and its image of the night's constellations glittered up at the sky they had fallen from.

"There is a cove a day's sail from here," the Beadle said. "Orphan Cove, we call it. We have a small operation there. A few hours beyond that, you'll find a river several leagues wide. If you row up that river and hike in beyond the first rattle I expect you will find a tree suitable to your purposes."

Warren nodded. "You will never lay eyes on us again."

"I wish the same were true of others I could name," the Beadle said.

Abe Strapp was apoplectic to learn the gang of sailors had escaped Mockbeggar before he could rain hell upon them. The Quaker House had lately fallen into disrepair and the sailors busted free, rowing out the harbour before dawn, according to the Beadle's report. Hearing they had paid a fine to replace his clothes made him more livid again. As if it was all a simple matter of damaged property. Strapp wanted the sailors drawn and quartered for the Turkish treatment he'd been subjected to and he spent much of his time describing their hypothetical punishments in clinical, nauseating detail. But the sailors were only the figurehead at the prow of that ship.

Something cardinal had shifted in his view. The burnished image the world had always reflected back to him was displaced by the sight of himself naked before his lessers, his cock perched on a blade that moments before had lopped the buttons from his waistcoat. The hedge whores he employed tittering into their hands at the sight of him impoverished by the simple absence of his shirt and trousers. Livyers began referring to the Big House as Strip-Me-Naked, in honour of the gin it peddled they said, though not even Abe Strapp was simple enough to believe that.

In the Justice's eyes, he'd been dealt something near to a mortal injury, an abasement he might never recover from. He wanted to murder the world that jilted him, to stand over its grave and curse the faithless shrew to eternity. And that childish, apocalyptic ambition was the ocean on which he sailed ever after.

Matterface and Heater couldn't avoid the man completely but they kept an arm's length clear of him, wary of the rage he kept at a rolling boil all hours. He shot two of his hunting dogs dead for waking him with their barking and he might have killed them all if the constables hadn't decided to pen the animals outside at night.

The residents of the Big House lived in mortal fear of the man who took their standing witness to his humiliation as proof they'd orchestrated the event for their own amusement. The Abbess tried to blunt his edge with commiseration and sweet talk about his gallant wimble, his jewel-for-ladies. But nothing prevented him shaking the girls or choking them while insisting how ugly or useless or stupid they were. Just the sight of Fair Nancy put him on the high ropes. She tried escaping a room he walked into one evening and he brought her up short by the hair, dragging her across the floor until he tore a fistful from her scalp. He shook that bloody clump in her face while he threatened to take a knife to her brown madam, then whipped it into the fireplace, filling the Big House with the stench of burnt hair.

He was so unhinged during the incident that the Abbess was reduced to asking the Beadle to intervene. But not even Clinch would dip his oar into that water.

At the end of June, Bride dreamt of Mary Oram four nights running, the woman wearing the ubiquitous knitted cap in her bed and discussing the mindless details of her day or the strangest injuries she'd encountered in her time, maundering on without so much as a nod to her company. Most of what she said was forgettable and forgotten when Bride woke. But on the fourth night a handful of the old woman's words were still chiming in her head as she came to herself in the dark. "May earth bear on you with all its might and main," she'd said. And for the only time in those dreams, Mary Oram had looked directly at Bride, pointing a nailless finger as she spoke.

It gave her such a fright she sat bolt upright in bed, waking Lazarus beside her and he reached a hand to her back. They had just moved into the servants' quarters in the Caines house, to have a room to themselves after standing to make their declarations at Meeting and being officially recognized as husband and wife.

It was a shock still to find themselves married and neither could trace their path to it exactly. Solemn declaring Bride to Lazarus in quiet asides—in love with him, Solemn said, sick with it almost though there was nothing to say so at the surface. Laz looking afresh at the girl and Bride feeling herself taken in by him for the first time. It was provoking to him to discover late how she felt and how long she'd managed to hold it to herself. Their every interaction like coins Laz knew only one face of and he spent days turning the opposite sides to the light. Surprised now and then to find something of his own heart hidden there. From nothing, it had the sudden weight of something fated and inescapable. He felt hopelessly thick to have missed it so long.

It was Solemn's idea they move into the servants' quarters at the Caines house. Bride refused the notion at first though she couldn't explain her hesitance. She had always hated the thought of being asleep in that house, of lying defenceless within the Widow's sphere. It seemed too obscure and juvenile an objection to put into words. And there was nowhere else they would have their own room with a door to close themselves behind.

The first night in the servants' room the newlyweds were impossibly shy with one another, both sleepless, both keeping torturously still. The next evening, Bride climbed aboard Lazarus for fear of spending another night on that rack. Her head resting in the hollow of his neck, his hands cupping the rocking weight of her. Both of them alert to the Widow's presence upstairs and working to keep silent. Lazarus rolled Bride onto her back and they lay face to face, breathing each other's breath, as they fell into a rhythm so simple and penetrating it seemed a consecrated thing.

"Oh Jesus," Bride whispered. "Oh Jesus."

Bride dreamt of Mary Oram for the first time that night and again each of the three nights that followed. She started to think the woman's appearances were somehow connected to the physical pleasure that flooded through her before she slept, as if the dreams were an emotional hangover, the hag extracting payment for her happiness. Or as something conjured by letting her guard down in the Widow's house, as she feared.

"What is it?" Lazarus asked.

She lay back and burrowed into his heat. "Just a dream," she said.

They were lying naked in the bed and young and new to contented pleasure and Bride lifted herself over Lazarus to take him inside her again, both of them half-asleep and blissful.

Solemn arrived at the house before light each morning and called to the newlyweds as he made a fire and set water to boil. The three of them sitting at the kitchen table to eat after Bride delivered the Widow her tray as if nothing at all had changed between them.

Lazarus asked after the dream that woke her and Bride described Mary Oram's recurring presence and her strange declaration which seemed a warning or an awful sort of blessing.

May earth bear on you with all its might and main. Solemn thought it might be something from the Bible and suggested Aubrey or Relief would know its provenance.

"It sounds like a witch's spell," Bride said.

"There's no telling with Mary Oram," Lazarus said.

And they stared at one another.

Solemn and Lazarus rode the Jerseyman's horse down through Mockbeggar on their way to Oram's Lane. Both of them carrying Bride's visitations in their minds, both filled with dread.

They passed a group of men outside the Church of England where a newly arrived brass bell was being installed. The church had no steeple and a low belfry was being raised beside the front doors, the men gathered there looking up to nod to the youngsters on horseback as they approached.

"Miss Nancy," Abe Strapp called out, walking clear of the knot of volunteers he'd been haranguing.

"Just keep going," Lazarus told Solemn.

"Madge," he shouted.

"'Mr. Strapp," Laz said as they came up to him.

"I thought the Widow would have fitted you out in a dress by now." He was walking alongside the horse to allow more time to abuse the whore's bird who felt himself too good to work for Abe Strapp. "She has a skirt or two to spare," he said.

"Better to wear a dress than to be stripped naked before company, Mr. Strapp," Solemn said.

"You impudent bastard," Abe shouted, skipping to stay abreast of them.

"Keep going," Laz said quietly.

"Speak up, Miss Nancy. What sweet things are you whispering to your indorser? Have you married the wrong Lambe then?"

"Kiss mine arse," Solemn said.

Strapp ran a few awkward steps, reaching to grab the bridle. The horse shied to one side and Solemn kicked at Strapp's arm to keep him clear.

"Go on, now," Lazarus said, digging his heels into the horse's ribs, and they spurted ahead and down the path with Abe cursing them in their wake. When they were out of range of Strapp's bellowing, Solemn reined the animal in and they rode in silence a spell. The Jerseyman's horse was trotting sideways under them, wanting to gallop on, and the riders were in the same agitated spirits. Solemn shaking to have looked into the face of his father's killer up close for the first time in years.

Lazarus said, "You ought not to have provoked him."

"Was I not a Child of the Light," Solemn said, "I'd have beaten his head in."

They went quiet as they turned onto Oram's Lane, walking slow into the droke of trees. There was no wind or sound in the woods and they didn't speak another word before reaching the clearing where the tilt stood smokeless and silent. Solemn called out for Mary Oram and waited a minute before he called her name a second time.

They dismounted and led the horse toward the building, the animal fighting the halter, no happier to be there than they were. There was an abandoned feel to the clearing, like something once human being reclaimed by wilderness. Solemn called one last time.

"I wish she'd say something," Lazarus whispered.

Solemn shook his head. "I think she's done talking, Laz."

The first time the new church bell tolled a death was for Mary Oram's funeral. The mourners taken up with fresh speculation about her age and her strange appearance and where she might have hailed from. Old Inez Barter was the only likely person to answer such questions, but even alive he'd refused to discuss the woman. Just the mention of her was enough to make him leave a room, as if speaking her name was inviting the realms of illness and death that were her trade into the world.

But for her own funeral, she had never darkened the church door and no one could say if she'd been baptized a Christian. The Beadle led the service out of respect for her work among the sick and dying but wouldn't allow the woman to be planted in the churchyard's sanctified ground. The only other cemetery in Mockbeggar was the Irish graveyard which everyone felt was a longer reach again.

In the end the funeral procession carried Mary Oram to the clearing in the droke where she'd been stationed all their days on the shore and she was laid to rest in an unmarked grave beside the remains of the Widow's child, with all her mysteries intact.

Every day after Mary Oram's funeral Solemn and Lazarus expected some response to the altercation with Abe Strapp. But the rest of the summer passed without incident and they'd almost managed to put it from their minds as the season wound toward September. There was prime drying weather near the end of August and *The Hope* and *Success* left on their coasting runs before the month was done.

Days later, Bride spied the constables walking across Mock-beggar from the parlour window at the Caines house. Watching to see what dirty business they were up to without considering it involved anyone belonged to her before they turned toward her mother's house. She ran out the front door, yelling for Solemn at work in the garden. Matterface and Heater were already inside when she reached the tilt and Old Soot stepped up close to stop Bride getting any further into the room.

Bride said, "What do you want here, you long son of a bitch?"

"We are conducting the business of the court," he said.

She pushed past him toward her mother seated on her bunk and Heater grabbed her arm just as Lazarus hammered through the door, come up from the warehouse with half a dozen men who marked the constables making for the Lambe residence.

"We have a writ of attachment," Matterface shouted, spreading his arms wide as if to hold back the tide pouring into the room.

Lazarus pointed at Heater. "Take your hands off her," he said.

Heater smiled at the youngster and gave Bride a shake, like he was taunting a dog with a bone.

Solemn pushed his way through the group of men as Old Soot was digging out a sheet of paper. A raw hatred rose from Lazarus like heat coming off a fire and Solemn grabbed a fistful of his shirt to hold him where he stood.

"We are conducting the business of the court," Matterface said and he brandished the paper over his head. "We are collecting on a debt owed to C. Strapp & Son by the late Dallen Lambe."

"What debt?" Mrs. Lambe asked. She had no clue why so many people had invaded her home or what their business was. "Is Dallen here?" she asked. Bride hauled herself free of Heater's grip and sat beside her, taking her mother's hand into her lap.

Matterface said, "On the seventeenth of March, that being the feast day of St. Patrick, some four years past, said Dallen Lambe made his mark to a loan of sixpence for the purchase of liquor from the coffers of C. Strapp & Son. With interest compounded, the amount owed is ten pounds, six."

"Ten pounds?" Solemn said.

"We have his mark to say as much," Matterface insisted. "We are authorized by the court to repossess whatever goods and chattel in the possession of Dallen Lambe's assigns and heirs would satisfy the loan outstanding."

"Why wasn't this loan called in before now?"

It was the Widow at the door, though she couldn't be seen over the knot of men inside. Everyone stepped clear to give her access to Old Soot.

"This doesn't concern you," Matterface said.

"The law is everyone's business," she said. "Was any attempt made to collect the debt after Dallen Lambe was killed?"

"I am not aware."

"Was notification of the debt ever sent to the family before this moment?"

"It was not," Bride called out.

The Widow said, "We will contest this before the Justice."

"That is your right. In the meantime we will carry out our orders."

"You will not touch an item in this house or on this property," Solemn said.

Old Soot smiled at him. "I thought you Quakers preached the peaceable kingdom, Mr. Lambe."

"We idn't all Quakers here," someone near the door said.

The constables took a moment to consider their situation, the falsehoods of Strapp's claim, the men arrayed against them in the room. Matterface nodded finally. "We will tell the Justice to expect a formal motion," he said.

They started out the door, Heater pausing to look up at Lazarus on the way past. "Your wife is a prime article," he said. "I look forward to handling her more closely in the future."

"Lazarus," Solemn said.

But he was already on the man, dropping him to the floor and slamming his face into the dirt before he was hauled clear. Heater rolling over with sand in his mouth and up his nose, spitting gritty clots of blood.

"This is assault," Old Soot shouted. "This is assault on an officer of the court and you are all witness to it."

Bride was on her feet. "You two get the hell out," she told them. And everyone in the room took it up then, cursing the constables through the door, though the damage was already done.

An armed party arrested Lazarus at Caines's warehouse that afternoon and he spent the rest of the day and the night that followed in Quaker Hall. Next morning he was escorted to the offices of C. Strapp & Son where a courtroom had been jerried up with desks and chairs. Matterface and Heater were called to give their testimonies and Lazarus did not deny laying hands on the constable.

The Widow asked permission to make a statement.

"Do you have evidence contradicting the testimony given here?" Abe asked.

"There are extenuating circumstances to the actions of the accused for which the court bears responsibility."

"But you have no evidence contrary to the testimony offered by the constables and the accused?"

"Not directly."

"Thank you," the Justice said and he turned to Lazarus. "You will be taken from this place to the public whipping post," he announced, "and there receive thirty-nine strokes by the constable's hand."

The Widow said, "The punishment cannot be carried out by the plaintiff or a witness for the prosecution."

Abe looked to his sister a moment and she offered her shrewish smirk. He turned back to the prisoner. "You will be remanded from this place to the jailhouse," he announced. "And at a date to be determined, you will be taken to the public whipping post where you will receive thirty-nine strokes by the Beadle's hand."

The Hope didn't return to Mockbeggar for another ten days and no one spoke of anything in all that time but the trial and Abe's perversion of his office and the travesty of the punishment imposed. Even most of Strapp's servants felt the prickish Heater got only what he deserved. When the date was set and the constables arrived to escort Lazarus from the jailhouse, a crowd gathered at Quaker Hall. The Widow Caines led the onlookers in a procession behind the prisoner. There was a festival air to the proceedings, shot through with a current of outrage. On the Beadle's advice, Abe Strapp had deputized and armed half a dozen men to keep the livyers under control. Even so, they jeered Strapp and the constables as Lazarus was stripped to the waist and his hands tied over his head at the whipping post.

Clinch was not happy to arrive home and find himself saddled with a central role in the undertaking. He'd tried to talk the Justice into commuting the sentence to time served in Quaker Hall, but Abe wouldn't hear of it.

"There is no telling what people will do once the punishment begins," the Beadle warned him.

"Bugger them all," Strapp said. And he spat at Clinch's feet to underline his contempt for that concern.

The sun was up but a nearly full moon hung in the sky opposite, the poles of day and night regarding each other across that expanse like the monarchs of rival kingdoms. Abe nodded to the Beadle where he stood by with his lash. "We will see it through to the end this time, Mr. Clinch," he said. The Justice turned to the heated congregation then and shouted out the charges and the sentence and gave a warning that anyone who interfered with the court's punishment would be charged and treated in like manner. He nodded to Clinch who removed his black cloak, laying it on the ground.

The Beadle looked out over the pageant before him. The Widow standing at the head of the mob in her sharp green coat like the thin edge of a wedge. Abe Strapp beside the whipping post ready to drink the blood of the innocent. Brother and sister circling each other, that corkscrew tightening every season since their father's death. And himself helpless finally to direct it, to slow or alter its grim, unflinching trajectory.

He leaned into the stroke as he was ordered and the icy pitch of the lash shocked the assembly into silence.

"One," Strapp shouted into the sudden quiet.

That call and response plodded on with only the grunting of Lazarus as accompaniment, until he lost his footing and hung helpless by his hands and Bride screamed out for it to stop. The crowd found its voice again, shouting down the Justice and the court and its officers. The Beadle took in that rising wave with the Widow at the crest. She was holding it up for the moment, wanting to see a little more damage done, he thought, wanting the face of the hunters at her back smeared with blood before she set them loose.

"Carry on," Abe Strapp called and Clinch leaned in to lift Lazarus by the waist, giving him that moment to collect himself before rearing back with the knotted rope. Searing another strip of fair skin from his back. The spectators fighting the leash the Widow held, pressing closer with each stroke. Strapp fired a warning shot into the air to keep them off but it served instead as a starting gun, the Widow stepping forward and the rabble rushing past her.

More shots were fired overhead but no one paid them any mind. Abe Strapp and his constables and deputies were forced to back away with their rifles held level at the rioters, people lobbing rocks and curses after them. They cut Lazarus down and put their weight to the whipping post to haul it from the earth, raising it above their heads and cheering its end.

The Beadle reached for his cloak before it was trampled and he put it on as the uproar twisted around him. The Widow stood beside Aubrey and Relief and the Lambe siblings who were trying to shield Lazarus where he lay and Clinch walked over to help them lift the youngster to his feet. He turned Laz around to inspect the cross-stitch of desecrated flesh.

"I'll have to see to these injuries," he said.

"You've done enough here today," Bride said.

Relief said, "There's no one else can look after him, Bride. Mary Oram is dead and gone."

"Bring him up to the house," the Widow told them. "Mr. Clinch can deal with things there."

She looked to him with her half-smile which seemed the only expression she was capable of. A curt, self-satisfied dismissal of everything but her own way in the world, a willingness to follow that light into whatever darkness might come to meet it.

Abe Strapp was forced to spend days holed up at Strapp Manor with armed men on hand to guard against the anarchic anger he'd set loose on the shore.

The mutiny at the whipping post had been so general among the population it was impossible to single anyone out for punishment without risking a repeat of the uprising. Abe dictated rambling letters to the Beadle, describing his situation of being held hostage in his own house to the island's governor, how he was unable to walk abroad in daylight for fear of being set upon by barbarous ruffians who did not care a farthing for the King's laws. He suggested a naval presence might be necessary to restore order.

Quaker Hall at Looking Glass Pond was burnt to the ground the night of the riot. A week later someone set the Big House alight, the Abbess and her courtesans jumping from windows upstairs and down to avoid being burnt alive. A crowd gathered in the corona of astonishing heat to watch as the women retreated to Strapp Manor in their small clothes while everything they owned in the world was consumed. The onlookers offering up a cheer as the roof took flame and fell in on itself, throwing a glowing storm of flankers into the black night.

"I should travel to St. John's," Abe said. "To speak to the governor directly."

He was seated in the manor's dining room with the Beadle and the Abbess. "That would look like fear, Mr. Strapp," Clinch said. "Like weakness."

"The girls are all for leaving," the Abbess said. "I don't know if they can be talked from it."

The Justice convulsed suddenly and threw his plate of food against the wall. "I should burn the whole cursed place to the ground."

The Beadle pushed his chair back from the table. He'd nearly chewed through his tongue in the days since the riot. Hating the man-child he was bound to, the spiralling accretion of chaos that Abe Strapp wore like a starry crown. Before the packet boat arrived from St. John's that morning, burning the place to the ground had seemed a sensible course of action.

"He that is slow to anger is better than the mighty," the Beadle said, "and he that ruleth his spirit than he that taketh a city."

"Did you come up here to preach at me, Mr. Clinch?"

The Beadle shook his head. "I have had correspondence from Poole today. Concerning the Widow's properties and her interests on the shore."

Abe stared at his headman as if warning him against offering more bad news.

The Beadle glanced to the woman with them at the table. "It might be better discussed in private."

The Abbess was arrayed in a colourless, shapeless dress that fell to her ankles, something scavenged from materials belonging to a Strapp servant who'd died decades past. Her wig of curls had gone up in flames and her grey hair was so thin her scalp shone cadaverous through the wisp. She had the worn, loamy face of a woman who'd worked all her days in garden fields and in barns, shovelling shit. She said, "I can keep a secret, Mr. Clinch."

He looked to Abe Strapp and Abe turned to the Abbess. "We will have a minute."

It seemed she might argue the dismissal at first. But she pushed away from the table and left the room without a word.

"So?" Abe said.

"The court has appointed an assignee to oversee a dispersal of the Widow's assets to settle her outstanding debts."

"This is your news?"

"Do you remember Myles Taverner?"

Abe nodded uncertainly. "Elias Caines's cousin?"

"He was put forward for the role by Mr. Picco, given his knowledge of the shore and the assets in question."

Abe placed both hands flat on the table. "He left the Widow's service on poor terms, did he not?"

"I would say worse than we knew."

"Give me some good news, Mr. Clinch."

"Caines Mercantile requested dispersal at public auction, of course. But Mr. Taverner has approached our offices in Poole with an offer to sell by private contract. All of the Jerseyman's assets. And a portion of Caines's as well. The offices and warehouses in Nonsuch. Fishing posts in Powder Horn, Deadman, Lord and Lady Island, Scrape Cove, half a dozen others. With all buildings thereon, as well as the boats and sundry equipment. All at a very reasonable price."

"How reasonable?"

"Not a fifth of the value of the Widow's late possessions. I am sending word to make the purchase, of course. You will own most of the shore by Christmas, Mr. Strapp. And the rest of it within the year if that is your wish."

Abe was up from his seat, striding the length of the dining room and back. "Does the Widow know this?"

"To the best of my knowledge, Mr. Taverner made the offer without notice or consultation. It would be best, of course, if we don't speak of it until the ink is dry."

"As long as I get to tell that witch across the harbour when the time comes."

"I will leave it to you," the Beadle said, "to break the news as you see fit."

~

Lazarus was able to make his way to the Caines house from the whipping post with a hand to Solemn's shoulder, but he had no memory of the walk or being led into the kitchen. Coming to himself in the servants' room when the Beadle laid a length of muslin soaked in vinegar across the catastrophe of his naked back, the scald of it lifting him chest and legs off the bed. Lazarus calling for Bride out of that scourge, squeezing her hand as she whispered into his hair.

For the better part of three weeks Lazarus was forced to lie on his stomach as those injuries wept and bruised and scabbed over, the ugly welts constricting like lengths of wet leather drying in sunlight. Every shift in position was an agony in those first days and Bride made up a bed on the floor to avoid disturbing him.

Solemn arrived early to the house and stepped into the silence and the stale smell of sleep each morning. He stood to listen to them breathing, taking in that precarious raft of intimacy afloat on the world's dark ocean. Still half-choked with regret to have set them in each other's path. Trying all he could not to hate the girl for occupying that place on the floor beside Lazarus.

Sin lieth at the door, he thought, *and unto thee shall be his desire.*

He crouched down to touch Bride's shoulder and she put her hand to his to say she was awake. He went back to the kitchen to mend the fire while she dressed and came out to join him and they started their days as if the life they'd known wasn't fraying at the seams.

Aubrey and Relief were in the last stages of packing for the move to England and they visited every day, trying each time to convince Lazarus and Bride to leave with them.

"There's no telling what will happen here this fall," Relief said.

The Big House had just been torched and it was anyone's guess who Abe Strapp would blame or what he might do to balance the ledger. "There is violence before you if you stay," Aubrey said.

The youngster hefted himself up to sit on the edge of the bed, beads of sweat rising on his forehead from the effort. He lifted his head to the ceiling to take a breath against the raking flare of pain. "I am not afraid of it," he said.

Aubrey tapped his cane on the wooden floor. "It is not just the violence that might be done to you that concerns us," he said. "The enemy within is the real danger, Lazarus."

He said, "I am not afraid, Aubrey."

And they all sat in silence, parsing the ways his words might be taken.

The Widow's crow appeared in the doorway then. "Clever bird," it called out, the unexpected voice giving everyone in the room a start. Bride tried to shoo the crow into the kitchen but it hopped past her and closer to the bed, unconcerned.

"Get that Corinthian creature away from me," Aubrey said and Bride called for Solemn who was just coming into the kitchen through the servants' entrance. He scooped the bird under his arm like a hen before surveying the faces in the room. All watching him.

"Am I in trouble?" he asked.

"We are concerned for your safety here," Relief said. She looked up at the ceiling, toward the silence above them. "I know you don't want to hear anyone speak ill of her," she said.

"And yet you insist."

Aubrey said, "Listen to the voice in your heart, Solemn, if no other."

He turned away from them with the crow in his arms and Bride shut the door, leaning against it as if to prevent the bird sneaking in a second time.

"I won't leave my mother alone here," she said.

"Bring her with you, child."

"The woman won't so much as leave her house, Aubrey."

Relief said, "Wouldn't Solemn look out to her, Bride?"

"We won't leave Solemn besides," Lazarus insisted, trying not to show the anger that Aubrey had just cautioned him against.

Relief looked down into her lap. "I've got a dark brown feeling about it all," she said.

Solemn stopped by to see Lazarus later that afternoon, sitting close enough he could smell the faint vinegary whiff of corruption from his injuries. He said, "Is you two thinking of crossing the pond with Aubrey and Relief?"

"I am not running," Laz said. "Not from a dunghill the like of Abe Strapp."

Solemn reached to take his hand. "The Jerusalem above is free," he said.

"And she is our mother," Lazarus answered.

The first time he managed to put on a shirt was to see Aubrey and Relief off at the waterfront, the couple taking a packet boat as far as St. John's and sailing from there to Poole before the winter set in. The Abbess's girls had booked passage on the vessel as well, their business ruined by the fire and each of them terrified to stay longer within Abe Strapp's compass.

There was a press of people on the wharf and Aubrey seemed even frailer and more uncertain among the milling crowd. His eyes were rheumy and almost colourless, resting on the faces of the youngsters he loved as his own children and would not see again this side of Paradise. "Take heed of jars and strife," he said to them. "You must hang as a flag for others to take example by."

Relief reached her hands to hold Laz's face. "Wait in the light," she said.

His expression set with a grimace then, as if someone had shouldered into his back on the dock.

"We will always find each other there," she said, before the couple moved on to the dozens more waiting to say their goodbyes.

The only Quaker on the shore not present was the Widow Caines. She'd walked early to the empty offices of Caines Mercantile and sat in a chair at the window to watch them leave. And she took a perverse pleasure in seeing Relief guide frail old Aubrey up the gangway among a covey of pestilential whores. Assigned their proper company at last.

It was hours still before the ship set sail but the Widow kept her seat to watch the vessel out the harbour. Bereft and diminished and lighter than she'd ever felt.

THE SCARRED HAND. CHILDREN
OF THE LIGHT.

Everything slowed in the months that followed. As if the seriousness of the events they'd come through added weight to time on
the shore. As if their days were passing underwater.

Lazarus was able to amble stiffly about the Caines property
by the middle of the tenth month and he walked the Jerseyman's
horse and oiled its saddle and harness while Solemn raked over
the gardens and put the beds to rights for the winter. He and
Bride moved into the relative extravagance of the empty Picco
house and they both felt a sense of relief to be out from under the
Widow, away from her silence in the upstairs rooms which had
always felt like a crow watching from a treetop.

Solemn took to arriving earlier again at the Caines house after
the newlyweds moved out, boiling the kettle and carting the tray
upstairs himself. The Widow was usually awake and waiting in the
office. She seemed hardly to sleep at all anymore.

"Is Bride ill?" she asked the first morning.

"Bride is looking out to Laz."

"They seem a well-made match," the Widow said and his head dropped like a dowser's wand drawn by the gravity of an underground spring. She gave him a moment to collect himself before she said, "At least we have each other, Solemn."

He looked up to the woman who seemed to know him better than he knew himself.

"You are the only person who has never disappointed me," she said.

The woman was so rarely surprised by the world, he thought. She seemed completely without fear despite the losses at hand. Solemn wanted to immerse himself in that certainty, to drown himself in it.

"What do you think is going to happen?"

"With the firm? Or with Abe Strapp?"

"Both, I guess."

"Trouble, trouble, trouble," the crow said behind them.

It launched itself from the doorway to the back of the Widow's chair and she reached up to stroke under its chin before turning again to Solemn. "Nothing that can't be dealt with," she told him.

No one on the shore doubted there was a reckoning of some sort at hand, though as the winter settled in most began to feel it wouldn't be upon them before the spring. And that extended state of limbo was all people knew for calm.

At the beginning of November Abe dismissed the armed men from their duties. The Abbess had lost all her possessions and her considerable savings where she hid them in the floorboards of the Big House and she stayed on at Strapp Manor, cleaning and cooking for the master and his constables. She lived in her servants' clothes and spent the night in Strapp's bed though he was so often impotently drunk that she slept there largely unmolested.

The Justice himself seemed oddly at peace with the state of things, though he'd lost his father's home and the stable of doxies who'd worked there, though he was a figure of ridicule in every household on the coast. He was so unfailingly good-humoured, even during his occasional outbursts, that Matterface and Heater considered he might have lost his senses. He held his annual Christmas meal for his bachelor servants and lavished the handful who turned up with food and drink. He spoke of rebuilding the Big House and recruiting fresh cannon fodder to replace the whores who'd abandoned him in the fall.

"They was all of them worn to the nub anyway," he said. "It was like trying to swive a knothole in a piece of board. Present company excepted," he allowed, bowing his head to the Abbess.

The Widow spent most of the winter assessing the few properties that would remain in her possession and how best to leverage them to begin rebuilding the firm, meeting with servants she wanted to retain, assigning them the few positions still hers to distribute, all the time talking with the confidence of someone who had arranged these circumstances herself.

But everyone on the shore felt the ribs and rafters of the world shifting in anticipation of some coming breach. It was like watching a battalion of marauders crossing an empty plain miles off and feeling the ground shake beneath them as the horde approached.

By the new year Lazarus had healed enough to sleep on his back without pain and to move above his young wife at night. Bride feeling each time something opening at the root of herself when she reached down to guide him inside. Both of them shouting out so the darkness of the Picco house rang like a bell.

It seemed a miracle to the boy, to feel stripped and helpless and at the same time exalted, grateful. They lay in the quiet afterward as the fallen world leaked back into the immaculate space they'd briefly made their own.

By March month, Bride felt sure she was pregnant though she wasn't certain enough of her intuition to tell Lazarus. "Abe Strapp and his crowd idn't worth the trouble they wants," was what she said instead.

"This is," Lazarus told her. "You are."

That declaration made her feel like crying. Which she took as more evidence again she was carrying a child.

The first packet boat from St. John's was the end of their winter hibernation away from the outside world and it sailed into Mockbeggar at the beginning of April. Among the correspondence the vessel delivered was an official proclamation from the island's governor to the Beadle with instructions it be posted in a public space and read at holy services every Sunday for a month.

Clinch went directly from the firm's offices to Strapp Manor to present it to his employer. Abe glanced at the paper a few moments and handed it back.

"Read it to me."

The Beadle looked at the man's face, trying to decide if Abe was simply incapable of reading it or if he wanted to hear the words from Clinch's mouth, as some sort of confession.

"In light of repeated complaints of discreditable conduct, of unsound and prejudiced decisions, news of which has reached as far as the Privy Council in London," he read. "In light of the recent public unrest in Mockbeggar and Nonsuch in response to what is widely viewed as an abuse of the powers of his office. Abe Strapp is hereby removed from his role as Justice of the Peace, effective immediately."

"That sly witch," Abe said. He seemed too shocked to be angry.

"The Widow is a deep one. But your actions have done you no favours."

Abe leaned over his gut with his hands clasped at the back of his neck as if trying to stop himself vomiting. Coming back up in his seat suddenly, his blood-red face highlighting the white scar on his cheek. "Have they named a successor?"

The Beadle offered the proclamation again and Abe smacked it out of his hand.

"Just bloody tell me."

Clinch retrieved the paper from the floor. He said, "I am, Mr. Strapp."

"You are what?"

"I have been appointed to the position of Justice of the Peace."

Abe's expression slipped from smile to disbelief to smile a few times, as he tried to get to grips with what he was being told. "Well," he said, "I guess the Widow Caines is not the only deep one among us."

"Mr. Strapp."

"I suppose you and she have designs on my entire operation on the shore besides."

The Beadle could see the man working himself into a lather that refused all sense and he folded the proclamation and set it away under his cloak. "I beg of you," Clinch said. "Do not do something that would require me to stand in judgement of you."

"You are capable of nothing other," Abe said. "And I shall do as I bloody well please."

Clinch walked from Strapp Manor across the harbour to the Caines house. It was near suppertime, the day's light already duckish. Bride took him to the sitting room and he stood beside the fireplace as she went to call her mistress. The crow hopped into the doorway and paused before the unfamiliar figure. It cawed once and then again before making its ostentatious parade across the floor to take him in at closer range.

"Piss and corruption," it said.

"Yes," he answered.

When the Widow came into the room the crow flapped up to stand at the end of the chesterfield opposite her. She looked back and forth from the bird to the Beadle outfitted in his customary black cloak. "You two are near the spitting image," she said.

"I am hard pressed to say if it is the human or the animal company in this house I find most distasteful."

She shrugged. "I doubt this is a social call."

He took out the proclamation and handed it across the room, watching as the woman lifted it to the last light through the windows.

"I suppose congratulations are in order," he said.

"I thought to say the same to you, Mr. Clinch."

"I just came from speaking with Mr. Strapp. He is under the misapprehension we conspired in this undertaking."

The Widow laughed so suddenly she startled the crow and it flapped up to sit on the back of the chesterfield. She looked at the Beadle as if he'd just made a proposal of marriage. "Have you ever wondered," she said, "what we two might have accomplished had we been rowing in the same direction all these years?"

He smiled in a way she could not read. "Clearly not as much as your brother has," he said. "He went so far as to suggest we are plotting to cheat him of his business interests as well."

"If he dies without heirs," she said, "I have a claim. Otherwise, plotting is of no use to me."

"You have shown a remarkable gift for it, all the same. There is mention of the Privy Council," he said. "How did you arrange that?"

"You remember Captain Truss? He has some influence with that body I believe. My brother did not make a favourable impression on him and I sent him away with some pertinent correspondence. To be honest, I had no idea he was pursuing the matter."

The Beadle said, "Perhaps it would be best if you are not alone here for the time being."

"I am touched by your concern, Mr. Clinch."

"I would prefer not sending my employer to prison. Or the gallows."

"Don't tease me," she said. She stared at him a moment, seeming genuinely perplexed. "You see no life for yourself without him?" she said. "After all he has put you through? The state he's made of things?"

"God alone ordains the state of things," he said.

The Widow shook her head. "O fools learn sense," she said.

The Beadle flinched at those words, at the feculent gall of the woman to speak down to him with scripture. He said, "An adversary there shall be even round about the land. And he shall bring down thy strength from thee, and thy palaces shall be spoiled."

"The Book of Amos?" the Widow asked and he nodded. "Am I the adversary, Mr. Clinch? Or would that be you?"

"We shall have to wait and see," he said.

~

After she finished her supper, the Widow had Solemn bring her the rum kept in the kitchen and she presented the details of the Beadle's visit as she poured two fingers into a glass.

She said, "You will stay in the servants' room tonight."

"You think he'll come here looking for you?"

"The man won't be able to help himself."

"There's an old firelock of Father's down to the house I can bring up," he said. "In case he drags Heater and Old Soot along."

"Thank you, Solemn."

She sat two hours in lamplight then, drinking more than she was used to, sketching the crow's feet and its eye and the fan of its tail feathers as it posed about the room. She expected her brother to come careening through the door any moment and she tilted her head at each sound. Finding herself angrier, more anxious each minute her expectations were disappointed. There was a torment-ing calm about the Beadle that afternoon she couldn't decipher, a sense of something beyond her sight at work.

Before it had gone nine in the evening, the Widow went downstairs to put on her coat. She lit a storm lamp in the hall.

"Should I come with you?" Solemn asked.

"That would look to him like fear," she said. "Like weakness."

He couldn't see what good would come of the visit and was in a panic trying to talk her from it. She brought a hand to his face. It was the first time she'd ever touched the youngster and she could see it move through him. He looked like a child in a fairy tale being knighted by the queen.

A wet wind gusting off the water picked at her as she crossed the harbour. And a sense of unease picked at her the same, to have been wrong about Abe's response. It was as if something larger was at work in the shadows, something hidden he would trot out when he felt she needed to be taken down a peg.

The servant who answered the door was older and more matronly than any woman her brother would choose to have wait on him, the Widow thought.

"Mr. Strapp wagered you would show tonight," the servant said. And seeing the blank look on the Widow's face, she said, "It's Mrs. Valentine."

The Widow raised the lamp and still she could not see the curly-headed dam of the whorehouse in the figure before her.

The Abbess made a mocking little curtsey. "Forgive me," she said. "I am not dressed for company."

She backed away a step as the Widow douted her light and turned to lead her into the house. They passed a massive sitting room, Matterface and Heater and half a dozen hunting dogs turning their heads from the fireplace. The Abbess carried on to the dining room where Abe Strapp had stationed himself alone at the table, as if to receive her. He was half-seas over with drink and he clapped his hands when his sister appeared.

"I told this one you wouldn't be able to help yourself coming to gloat," he said. "She bet me a guinea you had more restraint than that."

She turned to look at the Abbess. "I'm sorry to have disappointed you," she said. Though it was herself she felt she'd let down. To have been no better than Abe Strapp's expectations of her.

"And she without two shillings to rub together. The old trumpery will have to work off the debt on her back."

"You see the bad loaf I've landed in," the Abbess said, "in a nugging dress and only tripes and trullibubs here for company."

"It's been my experience that people find themselves in the circumstances they deserve, Mrs. Valentine."

She looked at the Widow. "That is plainly not true for everyone, Mrs. Caines."

"Bring the Widow a glass," Abe called out. "We will drink to her little victory. Take off that coat," he said to her. "I never tire of admiring your rigging."

She draped the overcoat on a chair and sat kitty-corner to him. Feeling drunker than she had during the walk in the cold.

"You are a sly bitch, Sister, I will grant you that," he said.

"We all have our gifts."

He poured his glass half-full with rum and then shouted toward the door for the Widow's glass again. When the Abbess delivered it to the table he filled it halfway as well. "To our gifts," he said.

They stared at each other above their glasses, the Widow more certain than ever the man had something over her.

"You seem quite sanguine for someone who has just been stripped of his pet title," she said.

"Sanguine? Drunk, you mean?"

"Happy. Content."

"Well," he said. "I am not content. Nor happy. In truth, I would like to peel the skin from your grubshite face."

She watched him watching her and it struck her then—how they faced one another across a table like this as children, when she tried to beat the alphabet and the basics of grammar into his head as if knowledge was a club and he resisted her with a vicious, hateful helplessness. Neither she nor her brother had changed one jot in all the time since. Which in her case she counted a victory. She said, "I suppose I should consider your anger a compliment."

"Take it as you like. It matters not a damn in the end."

"Why do you say that, Brother? You've the look of a man who knows all his cards will turn up trumps."

He placed his hands flat on the table and turned his face to the ceiling. Unable to resist a moment longer. "You remember Myles Taverner?"

"Of course I remember him. I admit I am surprised that you do."

"You really have no idea?"

"About what, Brother?" She was in a blackened room and groping about with her hands before her face, furious to feel stupid in his company. As if it was the worst fate she could imagine.

"Honestly, I thought the Beadle had gone behind my back with you."

She got up from her chair and took her coat.

"Myles Taverner," he shouted after her, enjoying himself too much to let her leave.

"What about him?"

"Myles Taverner is the court assignee in the dispersal of your assets."

She felt all her blood sink into her feet. "That isn't so."

"Your Mr. Picco recommended him."

"Why would he do such a thing?"

"It makes perfect sense," he said, "if you look at the world as a good Quaker does. If you expect everyone will operate with the same sense of fairness as yourself. But you are not a good Quaker, are you, Sister? And neither, it turns out, is Myles Taverner."

She was drunk or ill or dying, the room spinning around her. "What has happened?"

"All the assets set aside to settle your debts and raise capital have come to me in a private sale. For a fraction of their worth."

She leaned her weight onto a chair back.

"Once I buy out the sliver you retain," he said, "I plan to rename the firm. Abe Strapp Company Limited. Do you like the ring of it?"

"It isn't so," she said.

"I will swallow you whole, Sister."

She rushed at him and they went over together in the chair, the crown of Abe's head striking the floor. She battered at his face as he tried to corral her arms, as he tried to collect his senses. He rolled onto her, grabbing a breast through her shirt and squeezing with all his strength. The Widow's body curling around his grip like a slug dropped into a fire.

"You dirty shag-bag," she said.

He hauled her up and bulled her back against the wall, her feet flailing clear of the ground when he pinned her there with his gut. She shoved her face into his neck and bit down, Abe twisting against the vise of her teeth until he managed to get a hand into her hair, pulling her head back against the wall. Their faces inches apart, both of them winded.

"Now my little blowsabella," Abe said.

"Don't," she said.

"You'll shortly be no different than Mrs. Valentine," he said. "The mill between your legs your only fortune." He leaned in slowly to lick her chin, rutting his hips into her.

She stared directly at him. "Brother," she whispered.

A look of uncertainty or anger or fear crossed his face and Abe stepped back just far enough she was able to slide down the wall to her feet. But she stared up at him still, a half-smile playing about her face. And she reached out to cup his crotch with her hand.

"Fuck off," he said, shoving her arm away.

The Widow broke into laughter. "So the rumours were true all along."

"Shut your mouth, Sister."

The Abbess appeared at the door to investigate the racket and the Widow walked past her brother, still laughing. "You are safe tonight, Mrs. Valentine. You will have to pay off your debt to Not-Able Strapp another time."

He lunged to take her by the hair and dragged her to the table, smacking her face against the wooden surface, punching at her head as the Abbess hung off his arm, screaming murder. Old Soot and Heater and the hunting dogs came running and the room was a churn of confusion as Abe was wrestled away from her and out the door, the dogs losing their minds until Heater herded them outside, locking them up in a goat pen behind the manor.

The Widow sat in a chair a long time after things went quiet. Her right eye swelling and closing up. There was blood in her mouth and she ran her tongue across her teeth, one of them so loose she could work it like a hinge.

"He'd have killed you dead if I wasn't here to stop him," the Abbess said. With something close to regret in her voice.

The Widow got to her feet and collected her coat. "I owe you a guinea," she said.

She went straight to her office at the Caines house, sitting without a fire or a light. Solemn came up the stairs minutes later with the crow scrabbling at his heels. He knocked at the door and spoke her name but she didn't answer. He knocked twice more before she heard him make his way back down, the crow following after him. She worried the loose tooth with her tongue as she sat in the iron dark, working it absently, obsessively, until she took it between a thumb and forefinger and levered it out by the root. She cupped the ivory shank in her hand as the blood pooled under her tongue.

Eventually she mended a fire and kept it high the rest of the night, setting the iron tip of the poker among the flames. When she heard Solemn moving about in the kitchen she lit the lamp, calling him in when he knocked. The crow hopped inside at his heels, flapping up to sit at her shoulder. He was about to set the tray on her desk but hesitated, freeing a hand to pick up the tooth from where she'd placed it. He stepped back, turning the object over in his palm, and he glanced toward the Widow. She let him take her in, her right eye closed over and bruised black, her top lip split and swollen twice its normal size. She smiled as best she could to show him the space the tooth once occupied.

"Jesus loves the little children," he said. "What happened?"

"My brother happened."

"Should I get the Beadle?"

She fixed him then. "The Beadle is Abe Strapp's godfather and headman," she said. "Do you think Mr. Clinch will hold him accountable?"

He gaped at her. "I don't know," he said.

"Abe Strapp tried to kill me, Solemn. The same as he killed your father. And the law will let him away with it." She held his eye, trying to judge if that might be enough to shoulder the goodness in Solemn Lambe. It was his goodness she'd been drawn to from the beginning, his incorruptible decency. His loneliness. Things she felt she might some day leverage to her own ends. She turned her head toward the fire. "He abused me besides," she said quietly.

"Abused how?"

"As he abused Imogen Purchase."

It was so far outside what Solemn imagined possible it took a moment to understand what she was saying. "He's your brother," he said.

She glanced back at him with her one open eye. "There is nothing he is not capable of."

He looked to be on the verge of tears. "What should we do?"

"Have you your father's rifle?"

He nodded uncertainly.

"He will kill me, Solemn. As sure as the sun will rise. And if he has his way, he will kill you and Lazarus and Bride besides."

He stood shaking his head before he turned to leave the room, still carrying her tooth. Heading downstairs at a clip, collecting the rifle and banging out the door into the morning's darkness. The Widow got up to close the door once the sound of his footsteps was out of range. She unlocked the desk's bottom drawer and took out the book of sketches, placing it on the flames, and she pushed the reddened tip of the poker deeper among the coals. She sat back in her chair and unbuttoned her shirt to retrieve the Pilgrim's ring, holding it in her fist. Watching the pages of her book curl and blacken at the edges, breathing in its contents as they turned to smoke.

The crow was agitated by the poisonous energy in the room and would not settle, flapping from chair to desk to windowsill and back. She whispered to it and whistled softly, trying to calm the creature. She was listening intently which made the time crawl and she'd begun to doubt herself, thinking she had misjudged Solemn's heart in the moment, until the sound of the rifle carried across the harbour. Another shot coming behind it like an echo.

The Widow placed the ring under her shirt and took off her green jacket, rolling her sleeves to her elbows. She knelt beside the fireplace, lifting the poker out of the coals, the tip a molten nib. The crow shifting about in a panic, spreading its wings wide and shaking them, launching itself helplessly at the window.

The Widow placed her right hand on the hearth and set the radiant iron to the skin, growling as that mark affixed itself, breathing in the miasma of burnt flesh. Her body suddenly awash in a cold sweat. She lay on the floor to take in the pulsing seethe of it, that dark star expanding with her heartbeat until it swallowed all other sensation and the entire room and the house itself disappeared inside it. Until it consumed C. Strapp & Son and the Beadle and the miserable little town and every soul on the shore. Until there was nothing in the world but that single blistering presence and herself breathing at its very centre.

"Trouble, trouble, trouble," she whispered.

Lazarus stirred to Bride's heat next him, the girl long awake and waiting patiently for her husband to join her in the early stillness. She turned and settled over his hips without speaking a word, his hands reaching up in the pitch to read the pleasure on her face as she moved above him.

Afterwards Bride mended a fire and they ate their breakfast in a slow, sated silence.

"Oughtn't you be getting over to the Caines house?" he said finally.

"Solemn is looking out to the Widow, don't you worry."

He laughed quietly. "He's hoping to be writ into her will, is it?"

"Whatever he's hoping for, I expect he'll be disappointed."

"She seems fond enough of him."

"That woman would eat her own children," Bride said.

It was such an incendiary claim that Lazarus thought to say something in the Widow's defence, but wasn't able to contradict the notion in the end. He thought she might say something more on the subject and he waited in silence awhile. But Bride was already gone. He watched her in the mantling firelight as she wiped molasses from her plate and licked the black sugar from her fingers. She'd taken to turning in on herself lately, disappearing into a brown study, as if she was guarding a secret or shielding some truth he wasn't yet prepared for. It was sobering and pro-vocative to think she would always be more than he could hope to comprehend. It made him greedy for her company.

Bride stood up and leaned into the fire with her back to him, as if she could sense Laz's scrutiny and wanted a little less of that glare in the moment. Like someone moving unhurried into shade on a bright morning.

"You don't regret it?" he asked. "Being married?"

She looked over her shoulder and smiled. "Not so far," she said.

It was nothing like he expected, being spliced to Bride. He seemed every day to know less about his wife. Or what he learned managed only to make the mystery of her deeper, more inscru-table. As it was with the world, with life.

The sun was brimming at the horizon and the stars dimming out when Bride left to make her way to the Caines house. Lazarus was breaking apart the embers of the breakfast fire when he heard her calling and seconds later she came through the door in a panic. She'd run into Solemn along the path, she said. He was upon her before she knew who it was and she followed after him with a hand gripping his arm, trying to slow her brother down. Abe Strapp had beaten the Widow or threatened to kill her or ravished her or something the like and she could not stop Solemn or turn him. He had their father's rifle, she said.

They went out into the silent morning together and they ran Solemn down just as he reached the charred remains of the Big House. The three of them rushing along the rim of that hollow, blackened ruin.

"There's Matterface and Heater up there too," Laz said.

"They're sound this hour of the morning."

"That pack of hunting dogs they got won't sleep through you waltzing in," Bride told him.

"I can do everything through Him who gives me strength," Solemn said.

"God have mercy," she whispered.

"You go on back to the Caines house," Lazarus told her.

But they all carried on toward Strapp Manor as if they were late for a formal engagement, drawn headlong like figures falling through empty space toward some extinguishing end. They were within sight of Abe's house when they heard the dogs start up in the goat pen where they'd been barred the night before. It seemed a sign to see that obstacle removed. It filled them with a sense of dread and deadly purpose.

"Bride," Laz said helplessly.

"You idn't going anywhere without me," she said. "Neither one of you."

Solemn used the butt of the rifle on the front-door latch and they pushed into the dark while the torrential barking behind the house ratcheted up another notch. They had never been inside

Strapp Manor and had no idea where they were going. They turned into the cavernous sitting room, all of them stopping in place when they heard Abe yelling for someone to deal with the bloody gnarlers.

They waited there as an argument went on through bedroom walls overhead, a door creaking open finally and footsteps coming down the stairs. A figure limped past in the hall's gloom and moments afterward they heard a voice outside the house cursing at the dogs.

"That's Heater," Lazarus whispered.

They headed in the direction he'd come from and found the staircase, making their way to the upper hallway. One bedroom door stood open and Lazarus touched their arms to have them wait. He stepped into the dim, picking through the clothes and belongings beside the bed until he closed his hand on Heater's pistol.

The barking had settled outside when Lazarus came back to them and they could hear a woman speaking behind a door, then Abe's voice growling something unintelligible. Solemn shouldered his way into the room, holding his father's rifle at his waist, Lazarus and Bride following behind. The sun just high enough to show two people sit upright in the bed, to show Abe Strapp duck behind the Abbess as the woman screamed murder for the second time that night.

The light started to leach from the room for Solemn, everything tunnelling to darkness in his peripheral vision, and he lurched along the bedside as he faltered, firing into Abe Strapp's chest from inches away before he blacked out, hitting the floor like all his bones had turned to water.

Matterface raced into the room, bringing up short when he saw the bedsheets rivering scarlet and Abe Strapp hemorrhaging behind the Abbess who had gone dead-eyed and silent where she sat. She nodded soberly to the man as if to say good morning.

He'd come into the room in his small clothes and unarmed and Lazarus levelled Heater's pistol towards him. "Old Soot," he called.

Matterface glanced frantic at the youngster before turning to run and Lazarus shot him between the shoulders, the ball knocking him to his hands and knees in the doorway. He swayed there, trying to remember how to crawl, before he set himself down gently like he was laying a sleeping infant in a crib.

The gunshots sent the dogs into an uproar again but everything in the room had gone still and airless. Bride stood against the wall with a hand to her mouth, Matterface stretched out at her feet. She moved past him toward Solemn next the bed and in spite of herself she looked into Abe Strapp's face. The plump infant's mouth hanging open, his eyes staring empty at the Abbess's naked back.

Bride crouched beside her brother and whispered his name. There was a tooth on the floor near his head, an object so bizarre that the room around her disappeared a moment as she tried to account for it. As if there was a story to its presence as unlikely and perplexing as her own.

Solemn came to himself and rolled onto his back, blinking at his sister. "Is he dead?" he asked.

"I think he's dead."

"What about the other ones?"

There was a sodden moan from the man lying in the doorway and Lazarus stepped over him to turn the miserable bastard belly up. Old Soot stared blankly awhile before he managed to focus on the youngster hovering above him. He was having trouble drawing breath.

"This one idn't long for the world," Laz said.

Matterface reached a hand uncertain. "You," he choked out. He fastened onto the youngster's wrist. "You is all a crowd of devil bastards."

"No sir," Laz said and he shook his head. "We are Children of the Light."

Bride stood and turned toward her husband. His face was gleaming wet, tears dropping onto the stricken man beneath him. "What happens now?" she asked.

He looked to the girl, wiping at his eyes to take her in through the glisten. Now we will hang as a flag for others to take example by, he thought.

"Lazarus?"

"You oughtn't to have come," he told her.

Her arms were folded severely like she was trying to stop the ropes of her intestines spilling from a wound in her stomach and for the first time he was struck by the unmistakable fact Bride was pregnant. That she was carrying a baby he would never live to see.

She hugged her arms tighter to herself, trying uselessly to shield their child from the world. "The Jerusalem above is free," she said.

ACKNOWLEDGEMENTS

Thanks to first readers Martha Kanya-Forstner, Martha Webb and Holly Hogan.

I'm particularly grateful and indebted to MKF for her encouragement, questions and suggestions, the latest in a decades-long thread of questions and suggestions and kindness.

Thanks to Lee Boudreau for joining that conversation.

Plenty of looting and pilfering went into the writing of this book. The most shameless pillaging was inflicted upon Francis Grose's *A Dictionary of the Vulgar Tongue* (Revised and Updated 1811 edition); Laura Thatcher Ulrich's *A Midwife's Tale: The Life of Martha Ballard, Based on her Diary, 1785–1812*; *Captain Cartwright and his Labrador Journal*; *The Life and Adventures of John Nichol, Mariner*; Bruce Whiffen's *Prime Berth: An Account of Bonavista's Early Years*; Melissa Mohr's *Holy Shit: A Brief History of Swearing*; and *The Dictionary of Newfoundland English*.

ACKNOWLEDGEMENTS

The Adversary was written with the financial support of the Canada Council for the Arts, can I get an amen? Martha Webb et al. at the CookeMcDermid Agency and Julie Barer at The Book Group found homes for this creature, can I get a hallelujah?

Holly Ann, Arielle and Robin, Mike, Benjamin. *Sin palabras. Ei sanoja.*

Helen Amelia Crummey 1940–2022
Stanley Louis Dragland 1942–2022